The author, who now enjoys time to pursue a passion for writing, draws inspiration from her life experiences as a mother of three daughters and grandmother of six, from her experiences as a social worker, and from memories of past adventures traveling the world with her husband. She lives in Western Canada.

The Rhapsody on a Theme by Paganini, a composition for a piano solo and symphony orchestra was written by Sergei Rachmaninov at his villa, the Villa Senar, in Switzerland from July 3rd to August 18th, 1934. He played the solo piano part when the piece premiered at the Lyric Opera House in Baltimore on November 7th, 1934. The piece is a set of twenty-four variations and the last of Niccolo Paganini's *Caprices for Violin*. Many composers have been inspired to use this theme, an example of classical harmony.

neeyom white

REMEMBERING RACHMANINOV

AUSTIN MACAULEY PUBLISHERS™

LONDON * CAMBRIDGE * NEW YORK * SHARJAH

Ordering Information:
Quantity sales: special discounts are available on quantity purchases by corporations, associations, and others. For details, contact the publisher at the address below.

Publisher's Cataloging-in-Publication data
white, neeyom
Remembering Rachmaninov

ISBN 9781643780177 (Paperback)
ISBN 9781643780184 (Hardback)
ISBN 9781645366652 (ePub e-book)

The main category of the book — Fiction / Romance / Contemporary

Library of Congress Control Number: 2019907825

www.austinmacauley.com/us

First Published (2019)
Austin Macauley Publishers LLC
40 Wall Street, 28th Floor
New York, NY 10005
USA

mail-usa@austinmacauley.com
+1 (646) 5125767

Ah, the sweet, sweet
music of love.

I cling to the wind as it stirs the scarlet leaves of autumn,
I dance on the waves as they kiss the rocky shores,
I am the staccato of raindrops,
I hide amid the stars.

I invoke the memory of lost loves,
I seal the bonds of friendship,
I transcend the strife of nations.

I am possessive and I am obsessive,
I am youth and I am ancient.
I cleanse the soul and fill the air with magic.

I am the spirit that haunts your dreams.

I AM MUSIC.

ANNA

I didn't come to know Grace until both of us were well along on the journey of our lives, but after our first meeting, it seemed we'd always been friends, perhaps even friends in another life. To some, that may sound quite outlandish. Many may scoff at such a notion, but Grace and I never made question of the circumstances of our meeting or the friendship we would come to share. And as I age, I've come to realize I may not understand the whys and wherefores of events transpiring in my life, but rather I've come to believe there is a power beyond that has a hand in orchestrating it all. I truly believe Grace and I were meant to meet when we did.

It was a fine spring day, a day that for me had begun much as any other. I'd risen at my usual time and said good morning to my cat, Friday. Friday had been so named because, as one might expect, he'd come into my life on a Friday. But there's much more to the story than that. I'd seen the cat's footprints in the snow on my veranda, just as Robinson Crusoe had seen the footprints of the man he'd later called Friday on the sandy shore of an island, an island where he'd thought himself the only inhabitant. But in the case of the feline Friday, when I opened the door that blustery January morning to further examine the prints, a puff of gray fur scuttled into the warmth of my living room, made itself completely at home and has been my faithful companion ever since. Friday is the first one with whom I speak each morning and the last one to hear my voice when I retire. And as much as I'd not anticipated the cat's arrival, I would now be lost without him.

But now I've run off on a tangent and must return to the story I want to tell you.

After breakfast on the day I would meet Grace, I dressed for church, happy that the weather had allowed for lighter clothing. For the past few years, I've mentally applauded winter's departure and almost swoon at the appearance of spring's first hardy buds of snowdrops. I cheer them on, watching as they thrust hopeful heads up through the remnants of snow clinging to the foundation and I urge the tulips and daffodils to follow with haste.

But I beg your indulgence; for once again I seem to have wandered from the story, a habit for which I've become quite known. I've somehow begun near the end and not the beginning. I recall the words of T.S. Eliot when he wrote, "What we call the beginning is often the end. And to make an end is to make a beginning. The end is where we start from."

But I will not start at the end but rather at the beginning to tell you the story of my dear friend Grace. Though she claimed no remarkable existence during her lifetime, we all know that everyone has a story. And though Grace and I did pledge to keep one another's secrets, I'm sure she will forgive this indiscretion. This is her story I now recall from conversations we shared over the years.

I hope she will approve.

1

"Summertime an' the livin' is easy," she sang, arms outstretched. She was standing stage right, under the branches of a plywood tree crafted by the school's art department.

She lowered her arms. *"Fish are jumpin', and the cotton is high."*

Turn, she heard a voice in her head say. *Walk towards stage left and stand behind the seat.* *"Oh, yo' daddy's rich, an' yo ma is good lookin', so hush, little baby, don' you cry."*

Walk around and sit on the stool, a voice said. *"One of these mornin's you goin' to rise up singin'."*

Spread arms. *"Then you'll spread yo' wings an' you'll take the sky."*

Stand, face the audience. *"But till that mornin' there's nothin' can harm you with Daddy an' Mammy standin' by."* *Walk to stage right.*

Grace sucked in a long breath and watched the other students come on stage to continue the show. She was never particularly nervous when singing in public, but always relieved when she was finished and satisfied her performance had gone well. This time, it had. And the girl was grateful she'd developed the ability to completely immerse herself in her music, especially when dressed in costume. Even donning a choir gown on Sunday mornings prompted that mind-set, allowing her to concentrate fully.

High school musical performances in the early 1960s were not, as a rule, very polished or sophisticated, but in this small school with limited resources, the evening's show had proven to be better than average. Grace had been blessed with a beautiful soprano voice and was always happy to lend her talent to any of the school's musical events. Performing helped set her apart from her peers and opened many doors for her. In days to come, some of her fondest memories would be of the times she'd been able to showcase her talent.

She smoothed out invisible creases on her peach-colored costume and moved to center stage to join the rest of the cast for the finale.

"Good thing the girl can sing up a storm," remarked a young man standing offstage. It was his job to pull the curtain at the conclusion of the show.

His companion nodded. "Yah, 'cause she sure can't dance for crap."

"Two left feet, that one. I tried to give her a few lessons before we went to a dance at the rec center the other night. But I'm afraid there's no hope for her."

"You're still going to ask her to Grad, though, aren't you?"

"Yah, probably."

The performers were taking their final bows and Rene pulled the curtain back and forth a few times to allow the applause to die down. Yes, it had been a very good show as amateur theater of the day went, and what the performers had lacked in polish, they'd surely made up for with enthusiasm.

"You sounded really good, Grace," remarked Rene as she left the stage.

"Thanks, Rene, but I'm glad it's over now. One more thing out of the way. With final exams just around the corner, at least there won't be any more rehearsals. I've got some cramming to do."

"Me too. Can I walk you home tonight?"

"Sure, I'd like that, Rene. But first, I need to go change and let my folks know. I'm sure they're expecting me to go home with them."

"No prob. I've got a couple of things to do here, too. Gotta put away some of the sets. I'll catch up with you in a bit."

Grace left the gym, walked down the hall, and pushed her way into the classroom that'd been repurposed for the evening as the ladies changing room. She removed her straw hat, thankful to pull out the hatpin that'd been clawing at her scalp for most of the evening. She tucked the pin back into the hat that she flipped onto a nearby desk. She'd purchased the boater-style at a small boutique in town and was fortunate to find matching fabric for the turn-of-the-century costume she required. Most of the young women in the room were modestly trying to change out of their costumes. Grace, who'd always found changing in front of others a bit uncomfortable, slipped off her long skirt and blouse and put on a white-and-mauve-striped shirtwaist dress. Expecting to ride home with her parents, she'd not thought to bring along a sweater and hoped the June evening would be mild enough for the long walk home from the school.

"Oh, Grace. Your solo was wonderful," called a fellow performer from across the room.

"Thanks, Marilyn," Grace answered over the chatter of the other young women in the room. She exchanged her stage shoes for a pair of flats and tucked her costume into a bag for her parents to take home.

"Well, I guess it all went pretty well," she heard someone say, "except when Bill got an elbow in the jaw and then nearly knocked Dan on his ass when he lurched." There was a series of giggles from those within earshot. Somehow, the self-absorbed Grace had missed that episode.

With a hasty brush of her long dark hair and a touch of lipstick, she was ready to join Rene, her on-again-off-again boyfriend. Grace tolerated his erratic attention to her for two reasons. In the first place, he was drop-dead gorgeous with dark wavy hair and deep-set, sexy brown eyes. And there was no doubt the slight gap between his two front teeth gave him a look of boyish innocence. But it was supremely evident to all bearing witness to his philandering that he possessed no such quality.

The second reason Grace allowed him the latitude she did was because he was a senior and due to graduate in a few days. In the fall of 1961, Rene would be off to university.

Grace would not graduate until the following year and in high school, there existed an unwritten dictum. Dating an upper-class man ultimately gave one much more status than dating a classmate. It was unclear what she'd do when it came to dating options once Rene graduated; though the university was nearby and she reasoned she'd see him from time to time at the community's rec center. But she decided to put that out of her mind for the time being for she was far more concerned that Rene would ask her to be his Grad date.

"Did you talk to your parents?" he asked as she joined him at the front door of the school.

"Yes, they told me not to be late – no later than eleven."

"Sure thing. I still have to be home at a decent time, too. Work tomorrow."

Grace always felt a little regret Rene had to walk all the way back to his home after dropping her off as he lived almost halfway back to the school. It was a good mile at least, and he'd often made the trip on bitterly cold winter nights. Rene was saving for the car he would need when university began in the fall.

He took her hand and they strolled in silence for a few moments.

"You really do have a lovely voice, Grace. Even Gina said she was blown away by your rendition of *Summertime* and you and she have never been that good of friends. You should think about a career in the theater or something."

"Thanks, but I don't know. I may want to go to university next year or maybe into nursing. I don't think I have enough drive to be performing all the time. Church choir, these school musicals, and singing at weddings and my dad's political events – we'll see. Who knows?"

The late-evening air was laden with an intoxicating scent, a heady smell drifting from the neighborhood's lilac bushes. The stillness of the air was broken by the night-scream of a distant freight train snaking its way along the hillside at the edge of the community. They walked slowly along dusty back roads, trying to stretch out their time together, chatting casually about some of their classmates, evenings at the rec center and their respective upcoming exams.

A block away from Grace's home, Rene let go of her hand and they stood for a few moments in the smoky glow sifting from the streetlight. He drew Grace to him and began to kiss her, his kisses lingering and exciting.

Grace felt breathless. Her heart began to beat furiously. Rene had kissed her before but this time it was more intense, begging.

She pulled away, almost faint, and heard him ask, "Are you coming to graduation with me?"

"Okay," she replied, still breathless.

They walked the rest of the way to her house in silence, and he kissed her once more before sending her inside.

Grace closed the front door and was glad her parents were not in the living room. She was glowing and warm and still trying to control her breathing. What an evening. Her performance had been flawless and Rene had invited her to Grad. Life could not have been more wonderful.

***

But teenage behavior is often both unpredictable and painful. The following day, Rene began taking an overwhelming interest in another classmate and completely ignored Grace until just two days before Grad. Such behavior Grace knew was typical of Rene, and yet something prevented her from taking him to task over it. She wanted to be seen with him at Grad, as shallow as that might seem, and hoped no one had noticed his recent lack of attention to her. But students, especially in a small school, rarely miss even the subtlest social nuance. The halls were abuzz ten minutes after Rene had thrown Sharon a beckoning glance.

Grace had gone to great lengths to make sure she looked fabulous when Rene came to pick her up for the event, choosing a shell-pink, sleeveless cotton dress with a skirt designed for twirling on the dance floor. In the end, she may well have thrown on a cast-off from someone's frumpy maiden aunt. When Rene wasn't tripping the light fantastic with his newly minted girlfriend, he was performing some gallant gesture for any other female vying for his attention. For most of the evening, Grace found herself sitting at a table with the sister of his chosen one. And when everything at the school wound down, Rene drove her home, gave her a hasty peck on her cheek, and dashed off. He'd finally taken the plunge and purchased a well-used green Volkswagen bug.

It was later reported to her that most of the graduates and their dates had gone out to the country for a wiener roast, chugged down large quantities of beer, and then made their way home the next day in various stages of inebriation and regret.

"Can't dance – don't drink," she moaned when she heard. What had happened? Just days before she was riding high; she'd had the world by the tail. But now here she was – a complete and epic social flop.

With the school year coming to an end, all looked forward to the high point, an inter-city school track meet. Grace, who was on the cheerleading squad, took out her Grad night frustrations by cheering herself hoarse, a move that brought stern admonishment from her singing teacher the following day. The squad had, however, won a first place trophy and that brought Grace a marginal measure of comfort.

And then summer was upon them.

The local recreation center, in conjunction with the community's outreach committee, sponsored a 'Celebration of Summer' and a 'Teen Queen Contest.' Grace had been selected as one of the candidates, something of a surprise to her, but also honor enough to buoy her spirits after the nightmare Grad caper.

During the days of Rene's waning interest in her, Grace casually dated another classmate, Dan. He was a jock and though also a senior, would return to school the following year and graduate at the same time as Grace. She knew neither Dan nor Rene would ever suit her in the long term but she found a certain charm in each of them. It was high school after all, and her plans didn't include facing the future as a pregnant teenage bride. She'd invested too much time and effort into academic and musical achievements.

Dan was blond, handsome, and he had a car. Before he'd begun to date Grace, he'd been 'going steady' with another classmate, a girl he would eventually marry right after graduation. But in the meantime, his attention offered Grace another dating option for the summer.

The celebrations began with a parade in which the queen candidates rode perched atop a white convertible, and the parade was followed by a variety of events on the main street and in the community's rec center. Grace and her family took in a few of the events then returned home until the grand finale, the crowning of the queen.

"Where the heck is Rene?" asked Grace's friend, Jo, as the two scanned the crowd in the hall at the rec center. "They're about to announce the winner of the Queen Contest."

"I don't know. He said he'd be here. Bad enough my dad had to drive us over here. The least Rene could have done was be here to offer a little encouragement before I have to go up on the stage for the announcement."

"Oh, there he is," cried Jo over the hubbub. She pointed to a table across the room. Rene was sitting huddled close to the latest of his conquests and engaging in what appeared to be a very intimate conversation.

The girls made their way through the crowd, Grace blinking in anger.

"Rene." She'd shouted his name.

"Oh, hi, Grace."

"I thought you said you'd pick me up tonight. I waited for you." She was trying not to tear up and smudge her carefully applied make-up.

"Hi, Grace," crooned Sharon. Big night, eh?"

Grace ignored that remark and gave Rene a look that would have been deadly if looks could, in fact, have the ability to kill.

"Oh, sorry. Did I?" asked Rene, loosening his grip on Sharon's hand.

"Yes. You did."

"Guess I got my wires crossed."

"You could be a little more supportive you know, Rene," put in Jo. "Tonight's kind of a big deal for Grace."

Rene was spared a response with the announcement from the MC that queen contestants were to make their way to the stage.

Grace shot Rene one last scathing look, flicked a curl away from her face, and walked with Jo to the steps leading to the stage.

"Good luck, Grace," said Jo, giving her friend a long, warm hug.

"Thanks, Jo. But the way the rest of my life is going right now, I'm not holding out a lot of hope." She took the steps slowly and went to join the other four contestants.

The crown and the glory were not to come to Grace that night, a confirmation that there was no need to stick around for another humiliating evening at a dance, hunched like some black-sheep relative at a table of 'we-had-to-invite-them' wedding guests.

Without a backward glance, Grace and Jo left the hall and shuffled along the dusty roadway home. Neither had much to say. There would be plenty of time for conversation about that evening in days to come. Summer had just begun.

**

Grace began her senior year in the fall of 1961 and, for the next few months, followed her old pattern, alternating between Rene and the jock, enduring the dry spells between the two, accepting the odd date from others. But the very worst event of the year came when she was not given the lead in the school musical and had to live up to her name watching another girl perform the role she'd thought she had in the bag.

But by June of 1962, high school was all but a memory and Grace looked forward to graduation and the beginning of a new phase of her life. The high school finale began with Grace and Jo going to the hairdresser, where Grace's medium-length hair was teased into a style of the day referred to as 'baby-doll.' Over the past few months when Grace and Jo endured some 'lean' Saturday nights without dates, they'd turned to bleaching their hair in slow stages. Grace's hair had transitioned into a golden auburn.

On her way home from the hair salon, she picked up a corsage of white sweetheart roses and cursed Rene whom she'd invited to be her date that evening. When he showed up later without a corsage, she knew she'd been right assuming he'd ignore such social protocol. He'd not so much as asked the color of her dress.

The gown was a knee-length, frothy aqua chiffon that Grace wore with white satin pumps and a pearl necklace that'd belonged to her deceased Aunt Irene. She knew Irene would have approved of how she looked and was sorry she was not there to witness first-hand how splendid her niece looked. Grace had idolized the woman, considering her to be a fashion icon.

The banquet, with the standard fare of turkey and predictable trimmings, was held at the rec center with graduation exercises taking place later at the high school. Each student nervously accepted a diploma and tiny green school pin. After seemingly endless words of congratulations from everyone, the gym floor was cleared of most of the chairs. That move signaled an end to any enjoyment Grace would have until much later in the evening.

Oh yes! The dance, wherein Sir-Dance-a-lot flitted from partner to partner leaving Grace to make small talk with her math teacher's hard-of-hearing wife. But at least Rene made some concession and said he'd accompany her to the after-party, the traditional wiener roast to be held on an acreage west of the city.

"I'll pick you and Jo up in about forty minutes," he said dropping her off after the dance, an event Grace considered unworthy of the name since she'd spent the entire evening glued to the seat of a metal stacking chair. Apparently, everyone in her class was unwilling to challenge rumors about her lack of prowess on the dance floor.

"We'll be ready," she assured him and went inside to change into casual clothing.

"Are you really going out again?" queried her mother. It's already after eleven."

"I know, but it's Grad, Mom. The only night in my whole life I'll be able to do this."

"Be careful, Grace. We all know there's going to be a lot of drinking out there. I'm not really comfortable letting you go off all night to heaven knows where."

"I know. I know. We've been over this a thousand times already. It's not that far. I'll drive home if I have to. You know I won't be drinking."

As if, Grace, said a voice in her head. *You don't have the first clue how to operate the stick shift in Rene's bug.*

"I gotta change," she said, ignoring the voice. "Rene will be here shortly and anxious to get going. Oh, there's Jo at the door. Can you let her in? Don't worry so much, Mom. We'll be fine."

Grace ran down the hall to her room and changed into her fourth outfit of the day.

***

"Beer, Grace?" asked Grant coming to stand beside her. He was tilting a bottle of the local brew towards her.

Grace was sitting alone on the improvised seating near the campfire. Smoke from the fire was wafting in her direction and everyone else had moved to the other side to avoid the billows and sparks drifting there.

"No thanks. I'll have a Coke if there's some."

Grant went to the cooler and returned with a Cream Soda. "This all there is." He popped off the bottle cap, handed her the drink, and took a seat next to her.

"Thanks. That'll do."

"Where's Rene?" he asked.

"Good question. Who else is missing? Of the female persuasion, I mean."

"Hard to tell in the dark. Though I think there're a few couples in their cars and some, well…out there somewhere." He gestured towards a small gully in the distance. There was just enough moonlight for folks to have found their way to a patch of scrub in the hollow.

"Why do you let Rene treat you the way he does, Grace?" asked Grant after taking a long drink of his beer. "You deserve better."

Grace liked Grant. She'd never dated him, but they'd been pals for most of their years in high school.

"I don't know. We do have *some* good times. Like the other evening at your place – the first time any of us ever had Chinese food. He was fun that night, making a big thing of trying to teach me how to use chopsticks. But he didn't have a clue either." She chuckled at the remembrance.

Grace turned and looked at her friend, noting the way the fire lit up his features. He had a boyish face and would probably always look younger than his years.

"Maybe I'm…afraid to be without him."

"That's crazy, Grace. It's not right – the way he treats you. You need someone steady and reliable."

"Someone like you?"

"Well, yah. Someone like me. We should get married, Grace."

"I think you've had a bit too much beer, Grant."

"No. Not really. We get along okay, don't we? You and me. It could work."

"Well, I'm certainly not ready to get married right now anyway, and especially to someone that I just 'get along' with. But thanks for the offer." She smiled at her companion and took a sip of her soda.

"Well, it's on the table if you ever want to reconsider. Don't expect Rene to ever ask you."

Grace reflected on Grant's words for a moment and then said, "I wonder where we'll all be in five years."

"I wonder," he said with a shrug. "But drink up. Time to form a posse and go in search of your missing date. Besides, I'm choking on all this smoke."

They took a few more sips and placed their bottles on the growing pile of empties. Grant took her hand and they moved away from the fire, out into the moonlit field. Rene was nowhere to be found.

By early morning, however, he did surface and helped Dan, Grant, Grace, and a few others to clean up the campsite. Jo had gone home with friends before dawn.

The group piled into their vehicles and the convoy made its way through the field and out onto a rutted country road. After a few miles, the car driven by Dan suddenly came to an abrupt stop causing those behind to slide to a stop as well. The roadway spewed up a cloud of dust.

"What the hell, Dan," yelled Grant from his car. "What're you stopping for?"

But after a few moments, it became clear and the boys all began to bolt from their vehicles and run towards a fenced area secured by a wooden gate. Someone slipped away the rope holding the gate shut and the group bounded through. Grace was not sure whether to follow, but then finally realized what it was all about. They'd happened upon a country graveyard and for some reason known only to boys who've spent a night ingesting copious amounts of beer, the idea of a romp between gravestones seemed a fitting finale to it all.

Grace pulled herself from the bug and followed the others, immediately regretting her decision as she found herself knee deep in tall dew-laden grass. In seconds, her pants were wet to the knees and her runners sodden.

While the boys stumbled and whooped like a pack of wild animals, Grace took a moment to look at a few of the stones. It troubled her that some of the graves held infants and children, and she felt a deep pang of sympathy for the parents of those tiny souls.

"Who's ready for breakfast?" shouted Dan eventually running towards the gate. A chorus of 'I am' erupted.

"Meet you at the Esso by the bridge," he called and was off before anyone had a chance to object.

After a breakfast of toast and coffee, Rene dropped Grace off and she found her suitcase, a graduation gift from her folks, sitting on the front porch.

"Nice touch, Dad," she chuckled and went inside.

"Well, good morning, Grace," greeted her mother. "I'm very glad to see you home in one piece. Breakfast?"

"Nope. I had some toast at the Esso. I just wanna crash."

"How was your night? Did you have fun?"

"It was a blast. Best time ever. Lots of kissing and hugging. I guess beer does that. And no! I just had Cream Soda. Jo got sick and had to go home, but then she does that sometimes. She plays out quickly."

"Was she drinking?"

"Not much. Just a sip of beer or two. Not enough to make her heave like she did."

"Oh. You'd better call her and make sure she's okay. "

"Yah, I'll call her later."

"What about Rene. Was he drinking much?"

"Don't know. I hardly saw him. He disappeared right after we got out to the acreage. I didn't see him until this morning. But then that's typical Rene, isn't it? He didn't even dance one dance with me." Grace yawned and rubbed her eyes.

"There are other fish in the sea, Grace," said her mother.

Grace had no comment. In her present state, she didn't feel like getting into a debate with her mother about Rene's character flaws. She was well aware of them.

Grace's mother looked at her daughter and shook her head. She knew the girl wanted nothing more than to go to bed. Dark circles were beginning to form beneath her eyes and her lids were droopy, but she said, "You can't go to bed, Grace. You have to serve tea at Dad's reception this afternoon. He's counting on you."

"Oh crap, Mom. Do I have to? I can barely hold up my head."

"You promised your dad you'd do it. Go take a shower and wash the smoke out of your hair. You smell like you just wandered away from a forest fire."

"Ohhh, no. I hate politics. I hate teas and receptions. I hate that whole scene," she moaned. "Any other day… Why today?"

No sympathy came from the girl's mother who merely chuckled to herself at Grace's dramatic protest.

"What time?" Grace continued with a sigh.

"We have to be there at 1:00 o'clock to set up. The reception starts at two."

Grace trudged down the hall, went into the bathroom, and stripped off her smoke-infused clothing. She threw it all down the laundry chute and turned on the shower. Her head was fuzzy despite the two cups of coffee she'd had for breakfast and she was feeling slightly nauseous. The only thing that was keeping her from falling asleep in the shower was the remembrance of what a terrific time she'd had the past few hours. She lathered her hair, rinsed it, and scrubbed the pungent smell of smoke from her skin. She allowed the water to run cold. That did help perk her up.

She wrapped herself in a towel, wandered into her room, and threw on some Saturday clothes.

She tidied up her space and picked up her Grad gown from the chair where she'd tossed it the evening before.

"Yah, I do wonder where we'll all be in five years," she said to the dress before hanging it in her closet. "Rene, Grant, Jo, Dan. Me."

After hanging up the gown, she searched the closet for an appropriate outfit for the afternoon and chose a beige Coco Chanel-styled suit that she paired with a darker beige blouse. She laid the garments on her bed and sat at her dressing table to drag the tangles from her hair.

"Boy, you look a wreck," she said to the image in the mirror. "But it was super great, wasn't it? A night to remember."

***

By the time Grace arrived at the gathering, her energy level had dropped to a serious low but she was well aware she'd be in deep trouble if she did anything to embarrass her family. And she did have a bit of an image to maintain with the organization as well. She'd often been asked to perform at events such as this and would likely have further opportunities in the future. And there was that cash incentive.

After she'd delivered a few cups of tea, she began to wish she'd worn flats. She figured that trying to balance overfilled china cups, negotiate the narrow pathways between crowded tables, and teeter on a pair of high heels was enough to tax the ability of even someone in full control of her faculties. The expression *she can barely walk and chew gum* flashed through her mind.

But she soldiered on, finding some amusement studying those around her.

That purple floral is not a good look on Mrs. Norman and that ill-perched pill-box has seen better days, said a voice in her head each time she had to accept a sloshing cup of steaming tea from the matron. *And where'd she get that hideous color of lipstick?*

Stop it, she told the voice. *The poor woman has just recently lost her husband, a man who'd been a long-time friend of her parents.*

Grace was sooo tired.

Four o'clock came and marked a merciful end to the affair. Grace could not have been more grateful. It'd been a long, long day but she'd made it. She declined supper and at 6:00 PM fell into bed where she immediately lost consciousness. She awoke fifteen hours later.

Grad! Yeah!

2

For the most part, Grace had loved her high school years, thankful that the good times had outweighed the crappy ones. She'd been involved in a number of school activities while still managing to date some of the cooler guys. She'd also achieved a credible scholastic average. But she was ready to move on. Her girlfriend, Jo, was off to nursing school, and though Grace's father had encouraged her to do the same, or at the very least think about a secretarial course, Grace had decided to go to university and enrolled in a General Arts program. In truth, she'd no idea what she wanted to do with the rest of her life.

It was a small campus, but having come from a very small high school, that suited Grace just fine. The university was located about fifteen minutes from her home and knowing that a few other friends would be attending as well, Grace couldn't wait for her freshman year to begin.

Frosh Week was everything the newbies could have asked for. Course selection became easier once students learned how to negotiate the line-ups. The opening ceremony and speeches were inspiring, the teas bearable, and initiation into the only sorority allowed on campus was both spiritual and memorable. Of course, these and other activities were interspersed with the dreaded dance evenings. Rene did not even pretend an interest in taking her to those.

But he did make an appearance the morning after the first dance with an offer of a ride to the campus. When she answered the door, Grace was still in her pajamas and had a bowl of cereal in her hand. She declined the offer, however, since she'd nothing scheduled and silently pledged to discontinue the old 'now you see me, now you don't' cycle with Rene. Her biggest regret was he'd found her disheveled and groggy while he was dressed in his usual impeccable style, flashing one of his super-sexy smiles.

Grace would later rethink her decision to spurn Rene's attention, reasoning that a regular ride to the university was preferable to waiting for the city transit, especially with winter on the horizon. She even relented and accompanied Rene on a shopping trip to the College Shop where he'd planned to purchase new dress pants. His enticement had been a patronizing remark about her excellent taste.

The following day, Grace could barely get a word from Rene and when she saw him flirting shamelessly with one of her girlfriends, she knew that was it. There'd never been any stated arrangement between them. They'd never been 'going steady' and she'd long since realized Rene's behavior would never be anything but cavalier, but it bothered her. At first, she wasn't sure why it bothered her so much, but then it hit her. She was really angry with herself for allowing him to treat her the way he did. It was infuriating that Rene expected her to respond the minute he called her '*mon chere*' but within minutes transferred his interest to the nearest thing in a skirt. No, actually, it was beyond infuriating. It was demoralizing. It'd been the same with her other high school beau, the one who kept alternating between Grace and the girl he would eventually go on to marry. What was wrong with her? Had she made herself so available to these two young men, a date of convenience between their other relationships? Why hadn't she just run screaming off 'stage-left' when she saw the pattern repeated over and over again? Grant had been right, she did deserve better. Grace finally decided to throw herself into her studies, leave Rene to his harem, and forget about dating for the foreseeable future.

But fate would intervene with a plan Grace could never have foreseen.

She had, for many months, been the soprano soloist in her church. The past June had seen the retirement of the elderly organist/choir director after many years of faithful service, and there'd been no word of a successor.

"When does choir start up again, Grace?" her mother asked one Sunday afternoon.

Mother and daughter were relaxing on the front porch, enjoying one of the last super-warm days of fall. Crinkly, golden leaves littered the lawn, and Grace could already hear the howls of protest coming from younger brothers expected to pitch in with the raking.

"Next Thursday, I think. It won't be the same without Mr. Jackson, though. He was so terrific – brought out the very best in all of us. Haven't heard who's replacing him, have you?"

"Can't say I have. Maybe Dad knows."

"I guess we'll just have to wait and see. How bad can the new guy be?"

"Yes, I guess we'll see. Oh, look at the time. I'd better go put the roast in the oven. Grandma's coming for supper."

"I'll be in to give you a hand with the table in a while. I'd like to stay out here a little longer." Grace took a deep breath and watched the poplar shed a few more leaves. They trickled slowly and silently to the ground. "The fall air is so…" She didn't finish but took in another long invigorating breath.

In months to come, Grace's mother would have cause to ponder parts of that conversation.

***

Grace had a late class at the university and with no time to go home before choir practice, made her way straight to the church. She knew she was early but thought she'd just sit in the hall and catch up on the reading for her history assignment.

She threw off her coat and hung it on a peg in the foyer but before she could sit down, she heard music coming from the sanctuary. Curious, she approached the door that was slightly ajar, and pushed it open. She listened a moment to the dramatic chords leaping from the piano, chastising herself slightly for intruding on what was surely a private moment for the young pianist. Never before had she heard such extraordinary music coaxed from the tired old upright. She stood in the dim evening light, enraptured by the sound. With a final flourish, the performance came to an end, but Grace, uneasy about moving forward into the hallowed space, stood in silence, framed in the doorway. The young man gathered up his music and sensing her presence turned towards the door as she was about to leave.

"Oh, hi there," he called. "There was no one here earlier so I thought I'd get in a little practice. Are you in the choir?"

"Hi. Yes I am. I'm Grace. That music you were just playing…absolutely wonderful."

"Thanks, I'm Lee. The new 'organist slash choir director.'"

Grace allowed herself to move forward into the sanctuary and smiled at Lee. He was certainly not what she'd expected. He was very young, probably about the same age as she, had blond, curly hair and dark-rimmed glasses. He didn't appear to be very tall. He wore a casual shirt and unflattering brown pants that brought attention to a rather dumpy physique. She studied him for a moment. He was certainly no Rene and those pants had not come from the College Shop.

"I-I'm a soprano soloist," she said, mentally crossing Lee off her list as future dating material.

"Oh, that's great."

"I loved what you were playing just now. I've never heard music like that before here, especially from that old piano."

"It is a bit of an old clunker, isn't it?" He gave a little chuckle. "I'm practicing for a concert I'll be performing in soon."

"I don't think you need to practice anymore. It sounded perfect to me."

"Thanks, but you know what they say."

"Yes, I know. Practice makes perfect. My singing teacher says that all the time."

Lee reached for the hymnbook on top of the piano and opened it.

"Do you know this one?"

She came closer and peered at the pages. "Oh, yes. My Glee Club performed it with a mass choir a couple of years ago."

Lee played the intro and Grace began.

And did those feet in ancient time walk upon England's mountains green?
And was the Holy Lamb of God on England's pleasant pastures seen?
And did the countenance divine shine forth upon our clouded hills?
And was Jerusalem builded here among these dark satanic mills?
Bring me my bow of burning gold: bring me my arrows of desire:
Bring me my spears: O clouds unfold! Bring me my chariot of fire.
I will not cease from mental fight nor shall my sword sleep in my hand,
Till we have built Jerusalem in England's green and pleasant land.

"Lovely," he said turning towards her. "You have a nice clear voice. I think we're going to get along pretty well here."

"I think so," she agreed and smiled.

He smiled back.

***

Grace was surprised a few days later to see Lee emerging from a classroom at the university. She didn't speak to him, but realized that given his age, it was logical he would be attending classes there as well. There were a scant number of buildings on the campus at the time, so her chances of running into him regularly were optimum.

Campus life was exciting, but the early sixties were a time of unrest in the world. The Cold War was commanding much of the world's attention. In October of 1962, an event took place that could have changed the course of world history and Grace found herself witness in small part, to the happening. Women on the campus had been given a small lounge in the basement of one of the buildings, a part of their sorority membership. The men on the campus were barred from entry. On Friday, October 23, Grace and a few other classmates were sitting in the lounge when a group of male students came to the door with looks of grave concern on their faces. They asked to enter and listen to the radio, one of just a few on the campus. Judging by their faces, the girls knew something very serious was afoot and when the group tuned in, the reason became obvious. The report was that the invasion of Cuba by the United States was imminent, the Cold War situation having escalated since September when nuclear weapons had been found installed in Cuba, in collaboration between the Cuban and Soviet governments. This was something the US had thought unlikely, but then upon discovery of the missiles, invasion seemed the only solution, the distance between Cuba and the US a short 90 miles. The US had tried other tactics such as quarantines and blockades as well as negotiations between the US president, John Kennedy, and the Soviet premier, Nikita Khrushchev, with no luck. Cuba's president had even called for a pre-emptive strike on the US. According to the broadcast, the American fleet was on its way to a full-blown invasion. Things were very tense indeed.

Fortunately, cooler heads prevailed, President Kennedy pushing for an agreement through the UN to have the Soviets dismantle the missiles as long as the Americans promised not to invade Cuba. There was even a rumor the agreement would include removal of US missiles from Italy and Turkey.

Though the whole event was fascinating to Grace who'd enrolled in a couple of Political Science courses, it was nonetheless extremely unsettling, and she was always thankful that her world had not been toppled by events having nothing to do with her. Those huddled around the radio that day had been born during the last major conflict seen by the world and hoped for a much better adulthood than their parents had seen.

Grace and Rene would continue to travel to school together, and he'd taken to transporting a couple of others as well. No mean feat in a Volkswagen, especially when everyone traveled well-bundled for winter's frigid temperatures. Books, lab reports, and lunch bags crammed every available space, but the group made it every day, grateful to miss the challenge of public transit. And before the term was over, Grace's parents would make the move to a home closer to the university.

3

"If you wait for a bit while I run over some of the music for Sunday, I can give you a lift home," he offered after choir practice.

"Oh. Sure, thanks," she replied, taken off guard. She laid her coat aside instead of shrugging into it as she'd planned and went to sit on a pew near the choir loft. She fiddled absently with the woolen scarf hugging her neck. A ride home in the wintertime was, after all, a ride home.

Lee sat at the console and set out his music. The magnificent old organ was the pride and joy of the congregation and held an enviable position as one of a few such instruments in the city. It'd cost a fortune to maintain but in response had produced exceptional music at the hands of top musicians.

Lee adjusted the stops and began to play. Stirring strains of Handel's *Water Music* filled the sanctuary, and Grace found herself transfixed. Her musical training had given her a good ear and she was extremely grateful for the money her parents had invested in her singing lessons. The lessons had given her enormous respect for the discipline. Listening to the young man play that evening, she'd little doubt he was also taking his musical education seriously. Immersed completely in Lee's flawless performance, Grace found her eyes misting. The power of the music filled every cell of her body. It was hypnotic. She wondered what supernatural force had possessed Handel, inspiring him to compose that piece of music. And what magic prevailed in that centuries later Lee could sit in a church and recall every single note Handel had intended the world to hear? It was truly mystical.

She drew in a breath and looked around, her breast swelling with emotion. This place had always been her home away from home. Years earlier, her parents had met while attending the church's young adult's group and for Grace and her family, regular Sunday attendance in the sanctuary was a given. The parents were on several boards and committees and Grace couldn't imagine her life without being part of the church community.

Lee finished the selection and turned to look at her. She was sitting lost in a moment of reflection, combing her fingers through the tassels of her scarf.

"Grace. Where are you? I was asking you how it sounded."

"Hmm? Oh. Oh, it sounded great, Lee," she mumbled. "Sorry, I guess I was on a little trip inside my head."

He chuckled at her response. "Well, we should call it a night I guess."

"Can you play something else for me? The piece you were playing that first night we met before choir practice? What was it?"

"It was a little Rachmaninov. A little Paganini," he said, discounting the need to explain Rachmaninov had used Paganini's theme when composing his Rhapsody in 1934.

"It's got a haunting melody, don't you think?"

"Yes, it does," he agreed, looking through his case for the sheet music. "I'll need to come down to the piano, though. The old clunker." He shut down all the mechanics of the organ, stepped out of the choir loft and took his place at the upright near her. He placed the music on the sloped support and began. And even though the piano was in no way adequate for the music expected of it, the sound took her breath away. With each note, she became more enchanted and was sorry when Lee played the last chord and put his hands in his lap.

"Oh, Lee. That was just unbelievable. Thank you. I think I could sit here all night listening to that piece."

"Well, I've got homework. You too, I bet."

"How do you know I'm a student?"

"It's not a very big university, Grace. I've seen you in the halls a few times."

"Oh," she giggled, not daring to admit that she'd seen him too.

She snuggled into her coat and after Lee turned off all the lights and locked the doors of the church, they headed to his car. It was a Volkswagen bug.

She thought of Rene.

Grace and Lee made small talk – talked about their university courses. He was, of course, a music major and driven by his profound love of his craft. Grace too was committed to her music, grateful for the talent God had bestowed upon her, but she was also aware just how much effort she needed to apply without compromising other interests in her life. It was fortunate she was a quick study when it came to memorizing lyrics and she felt that for the most part, she was able to give a credible performance.

"Just turn here," she said as they approached the end of her block. "I hope I haven't taken you too far out of your way." She had, in fact, done just that.

"Thanks, Lee. I appreciate the ride," she said as she crawled from the confines of the bug. *One would think I'd be better at this*, she thought to herself, remembering the awkward exits required after riding in Rene's bug. "See you at church on Sunday, and I'll have a run through my solo once more at my singing lesson on Saturday."

"Sure. But you sounded fine tonight. See you then."

"Thanks again." And she closed the door of the car.

That became the pattern for the next few weeks.

***

"Thanks, Lee."

"No problem. See you on Sunday."

***

"It's awfully nice of you to bring me home all the time."

"See you at church."

***

"Thanks again."

"No problem. Maybe see you in the hall at the U tomorrow."

***

"So great of you to run me home tonight."

"My pleasure."

***

And then one night "Would you like a root beer?"

"Root beer?"

"Uh huh, a root beer. We could stop at the A&W."

She thought for a moment. Was he actually making an effort at social interaction with her? Up until that point, she'd merely considered him a musical partner and nothing else, for they were perfectly matched as soloist and accompanist. Sure, they were compatible in age and both enjoying their freshman year at university. But he was just, Lee, the church organist. In her mind, she hadn't even moved him to 'friend' status. For the most part, she hadn't given him much thought at all.

But what the heck, she considered. It was just a mug of root beer. No need to read anything into that.

"Sure, I guess," she replied then. "Sounds good."

The A&W drive-in was just a few minutes away from the church and Lee pulled the bug into a vacant spot, rolled down the window, and ordered two mugs of root beer from the carhop. He looked over at her and smiled.

He is sort of sweet I guess, she thought. *Did he have anyone in his life? A steady girlfriend? It would be impertinent to ask.*

"How's school going?" he queried.

"Pretty good, I guess. You?"

"Good. Good."

They sat in silence.

"It's almost Christmas. I can't believe the year's gone so fast."

"Yah. Me too."

She'd never had this much trouble making light conversation with Rene. Except, of course, when he was distracted by a potential conquest across the room.

"I think the music for the Christmas service is sounding pretty good, don't you?"

"Oh yeah. Sounds…really…really…good. Uh huh."

Thankfully, the carhop arrived with the mugs of root beer on a tray that she attached to the open window of the car. Lee gave her a few coins, took the glasses, and rolled up the window as far as it would go, shutting out the blast of winter air.

They sipped at their root beer, probably not the best choice of beverage at a drive-in in December.

"Uh," Lee began, gripping his mug between his hands. "Reverend Lester is thinking about starting up a young adults group and wants to have a get together on Saturday."

"Really? That sounds…sort of neat."

"Just wondered if, well… Do you want to go?"

"With you?" she blurted, turning to look at him. *Good grief, Grace, that sounded horrible,* said a voice in her head. She sucked in a breath and said, "I mean, are you…going?"

"Yah, I thought I would. I could pick you up."

"Saturday?"

"Yah, about seven."

"Seven?"

"Yah seven. It starts at seven thirty."

Come on girl, said the voice. *Give the guy a break.* "Well, okay, Lee," she said at last. "That's sounds like…it might be kinda fun." She turned to look out her side window and rolled her eyes.

Lee took a gulp of his root beer, and Grace turned back to look at him. She wondered what on earth she was doing. But then, what else did she have going on. She'd had it with Rene, finished hitting her head against that brick wall. In fact, she'd sworn off dating anyone from high school ever again. The last date she'd been on with a former classmate had been a suicidal road trip where they'd woven in and out of traffic so furiously, she was sure she was doomed to an early death in a roadside ditch. But it'd been just slightly better than the date with another high school chum who took her on a fascinating surveillance of all the laundromats his father owned in the city. How bad could an evening with Lee at the minister's home be by comparison?

She wasn't sure how to dress for Saturday evening and opted to wear a cute navy jumper, a white turtleneck, and navy pumps. She'd never owned a pair of jeans in her life until she entered university. That night, jeans didn't seem appropriate and though she'd occasionally worn them to class, she was finding most of the women on campus preferred wearing dresses. Grace was always conscious of putting her best foot forward and had always been fastidious about her appearance. She was after all still on the hunt for Mr. Right.

Seven o'clock on the dot Lee's Volkswagen chugged into the driveway of Grace's home and because her parents were somewhat acquainted with him, there was no painful hovering and third degree session as to his intentions towards their daughter. In fact, Grace would overhear her mother in conversation with her grandmother, flatly admitting she was never worried when Grace was with the young organist. "He seems pretty tame," was her comment.

Lee and Grace were welcomed by the minister's wife and after introductions to some of the others who'd shown up to join the fledgling group they retreated to the rumpus room in the basement of the manse. There followed a few silly 'get-acquainted parlor games' after which a couple of fellows pushed aside the overstuffed chairs. The furniture in the room was typical of that found in many homes occupied by clergy. The kind that'd been well used over the years by parishioners, then deemed a practical option for service in the church manse, donors considering the accumulation of lumps and stains on the pieces merely an enhancement of their character. Besides, what was wrong with a couple of slipcovers?

Someone went to the phonograph and put on dance music.

Oh, just great, thought Grace. There was nowhere to go. No oddball tablemates to engage with idle chitchat. No chance of disappearing under the radar. No distraction to occupy her while her date jostled and cavorted with others endowed with the grace her name suggested she should have, but sorely lacked.

"Do you want to dance?" Lee asked, ignoring the look of pain on her face.

"Sure. I guess."

Well, he asked for it, said a voice in her head.

He took her hand. It was a jive. She jiggled and twisted, and came close to losing her balance. She kicked off her shoes to make it easier. She continued to twirl and heave her body hoping no one noticed she was a world-class klutz. But then she looked at Lee. He was stumbling along in the same awkward fashion as she. She burst out laughing. She'd finally met her match. The Lord had a given Lee two left feet as well. *Perhaps*, thought Grace in a flash of insight, *it was why the two of them had been endowed with other talents.*

"Having a good time?" he asked, twirling her towards an armchair.

"A good time?" she gasped, avoiding a collision with the furniture. "I sure am. I'm having the best time ever." And she laughed again, waddling back and forth. "This is just great!"

A week later, on a Sunday afternoon, Lee and Grace went to the opera. It was the first time she'd ever seen a professional production, though she'd seen and been involved in many amateur theater experiences. It was fabulous, and Lee seemed so totally entranced by the event, as he didn't speak during the entire performance. She glanced at him once or twice noticing the rapture on his face and tried to follow the story line as best she could. But she dared not look at her program for clarification lest she disturb his mood. At intermission, they wandered out to the lobby. Lee met a couple of his friends and while they were engaged in conversation, Grace settled on a sofa to people-watch. It was mid-afternoon, but many of the patrons were dressed in furs and jewelry, attire she'd thought more appropriate for evening. She felt a little under-dressed in her afternoon frock, a simple tailored little number with a white top and slim black skirt. But it fit like it was designed for her, and she hadn't sewn it up as she had with most of her wardrobe.

After the opera, Lee dropped her off and went on his way with a cheery 'see you.'

Grace went inside, slipped off her shoes and teal-blue car coat, and joined her mother in the kitchen. The woman had just finished crimping the crust on an apple pie.

"How was the opera?" her mother asked picking up the pie and placing it in the oven.

"Pretty good. I didn't understand most of it, but Lee seemed really absorbed."

"Rene called."

"He did? What did he want?" asked Grace, picking up a piece of crisp celery from the drain board. "Has he exhausted every other female option on the campus?"

"I don't know. He wouldn't say. I told him you were out with Lee. I made it sound like it was a big deal between the two of you. You know. Maybe remind Casanova you're not sitting home day and night waiting for him to call." She went to the sink, ran her hands under the tap, and flapped them dry on her apron.

Grace took a bite of the celery stick and gave her mother one of those looks.

"Rene and I are over, Mom."

"Well, you never know," remarked her mother.

"Yes, I do know. It was never going to work out between the two of us. Everyone else could see what he was like. I don't know what was wrong with me. I feel like such a big dope now. Wasting all that time on him. And you know the worst part of it all? He didn't seem to care if he hurt me. He knew I'd put up with all his antics. But no more. I'm done."

"Well then… Lee?"

Grace gave a toss of her head. "Well, you more than stretched the truth on that one, telling Rene that Lee and I are a 'big deal.' We've known each other for a few weeks now. He brings me home from choir all the time and we've gone out on a couple of…I guess they're dates. But there hasn't even been a handshake. At least I never had that problem with Rene. I don't know. What's wrong with me now?"

"There's nothing wrong with you, Grace. Lee's probably just a little shy."

Grace failed to observe the look of glee on her mother's face. And the gesture of relief. The woman had found Rene a likeable enough fellow, charming and clever, but she knew he had the potential to be a gigantic boatload of trouble. There was a silent rejoicing within the mother's heart that Grace was spending time in the company of the quiet and reticent young musician.

***

It was a 10-cent root beer and occasionally a 35-cent Mama Burger every night after choir practice. Grace usually picked nervously at her burger and in truth was not much for eating after supper or doing so anywhere other than at a table.

Every evening the pattern was the same. After a stop for root beer, Lee would turn towards her home and drop her off with a few parting words. One evening, however, he headed the Volkswagen in the same direction but then made a right-hand turn and headed to a hilly area in the city's northwest quadrant. Grace said nothing and when they pulled into a secluded area at the top of the hill, she was dumbfounded. He turned off the engine and sat for a moment looking straight ahead, then turned slowly, and reached for her hand. She froze.

"Are you alright with this?" he asked.

She turned to him with a look of wonder. "Lee? I-I…"

The Volkswagen offered little space between them and he slid his arm around her. His lips were warm and soft and his kisses short. They had nothing of the passion of Rene's probing advances. But she responded to him, sliding her arms around his neck, holding him close as her heart began to pound furiously. It had taken him ages.

They released each other and she felt him looking at her.

She tried to focus on his face, as well, but saw only the glint of starlight reflected in his glasses.

"Lee, I-I didn't think…"

"You didn't think what?"

"I thought we were maybe just…well maybe just…friends," she stammered.

"Is this okay? There's no one else, is there?"

"No, there's no one else…in particular," she chuckled. Her mind projected a fleeting image of Rene and then just as quickly the image disappeared. "I just didn't know… Yes, it's okay," she murmured circling her arms about his neck once more.

For Grace, that night on the hill was the beginning of a whole new world, a world in which she'd fall unexpectedly, hopelessly, and helplessly in love. And no one, especially the girl herself, could ever have imagined it happening the way it did.

So there it was. Grace and Lee. They did seem perfectly matched.

The young adults group began to grow and thrive, and that together with a few other youth activities in the city gave the couple most of their social life. Young folks of subsequent generations would cringe at the thought that hootenannies, bible studies, and Sundays at the philharmonic could provide such enjoyment. But it did. Grace was deliriously happy and that was reflected in her grades. Singing, quiet moments with Lee, the touch of his gentle kisses on her neck, and sharing the seductive music of Rachmaninov's piano concerto, those were the moments Grace lived for. Each time Lee finished playing and laid his hands in his lap she would say, "Thank you, Lee. That was wonderful. I never get tired of Rachmaninov."

The girl was sure she'd lost her mind falling in love with a young man who had the fashion sense of Harpo Marx, a man who could pass her by in the hallway of the Arts Building without noticing her, a man who'd never take her hand in public. But it was so. The bond they shared was music; music that at times took Grace to such emotional highs she could barely breathe. She was convinced she and Lee had it all, the golden trio – music, love, and God.

They would go to their special place on the hill and talk about their lives – school, faith, their music. To Grace it was all they needed. And after a few months, there was no question in the minds of those closest to them that Lee and Grace would share a future.

Before the world knew it summer had settled in, and Grace was offered a clerical job at her father's company. She would make enough to pay for the following year's tuition and books and still have enough left over to add to her wardrobe.

Grace hadn't seen Rene in ages. In fact, she'd all but forgotten the cad ever meant anything to her. Night and day, her life now revolved around the young musician. He was the center of her universe.

***

"Dad and I and the boys are going camping in a couple of weeks," her mother announced in early August.

"Yah?" Grace answered absently. She was applying the top coat of nail polish to newly manicured nails.

"Well, you have to work."

"Yah, I'll be okay here for a few days. I can take the bus to work."

"Well, that's not really what I'm getting at."

Grace screwed the cap onto the bottle of clear polish and looked at her mother with curiosity.

"What then?"

"It's Lee."

"Lee? What about him?"

"Well…you and Lee. Dad and I don't want you in the house together while we're away."

"What!"

"Well, you know what I mean."

"I know what you mean, Mother. Give me a gigantic break."

"We've talked about it, Dad and I, and I've made arrangements for you to stay with my friend Barbara while we're gone."

"You did what? Mo-o-m!"

"Don't argue. It's all arranged."

"Oh, for Pete's sake, Mother. Lee and I aren't *doing anything* and even if we were, it wouldn't matter if I was staying at home or not. And anyway, you once told Grandma you never worried about me when I was with Lee."

"Well, that was before you started seeing…so much of him."

"Seriously? Seriously, Mom?" Grace gave a long dramatic sigh. "Do you know how long it's going to take me to get to work every day? Barbara lives on the other side of town. Arghh!"

"Well, it's done. And I'm not changing my mind."

"Mom! Please, not Barbara! Her house smells funny. What if I smell like that every day when I go out? And I seem to remember that you left home and traveled halfway across the continent to be with Dad when you were my age. Arghh. Arghh!"

Grace gave her mother a pleading look. It was returned with a slight shrug.

"You can still see Lee while we're away, though for the life of me I don't know what the attraction is. After Rene."

"You wouldn't understand, Mother. And you do remember what Rene was like, don't you? I could see your concern if I was still with him. He's always been…well he's always been…Rene. But…don't get me wrong. He and I never… That was just a high school thing. In fact, I think Rene spent most of time we were together looking for his next date. But Lee? You know he's…"

You'd better put this right, Grace, said a voice in her head. *You know you've fallen in love with Lee, but your mother's not stupid. She knows what inevitably happens when you're young and in love.*

"Lee and I," she began. "We have a lot of the same interests. I love to listen to him play and I think we may…well, we make a good couple. He's so talented. And…Mother, he's always been a perfect gentleman." She glanced at the woman to make sure there was an understanding. Grace mentally chastised herself for overusing the word 'Mother' in her protest.

She was silent for a moment, waiting for a voice in her head. When she heard nothing, she took it as approval and summoned the courage to continue. "Lee, he could become…a…bigger part of my life one day. Maybe."

But the words she'd heard earlier from the voice did echo once more. Grace's mother was no fool and fully aware Grace was falling for Lee in a big way. All the telltale signs were there.

"Grace. I told you. It's done. Barbara's looking forward to your company for a few days. She's been very lonely since…well, you know."

Grace picked up the nail polish and the rest of her manicure items and went to her room.

"Arghh. Barbara," she grumbled on the way. "Talk about a solution looking for a problem! And why does it have to be Barbara? She has a moustache!"

***

Despite the inconvenience of staying with the unattractive and malodorous Barbara, Grace survived but never left her inhospitable accommodation without applying a generous amount of cologne. The Saturday her parents left for holidays, she and Lee decided to go to the mountains. He picked her up mid-morning and they stopped at a roadside diner, purchased some sandwiches and lemonade, and made their way west. It promised to be a wonderful day for the two away from the city in a peaceful setting where they could forge new memories.

"I love the mountains, don't you, Lee? They're right here on our doorstep and we just take them for granted," she said as they approached the towering peaks.

"I've never really thought about them that much. You're right I guess. They've always just been here."

"But that's exactly what I mean. Shouldn't we think of them as something special? Folks come from all over the world to see them."

"Well I guess…now you mention it, it is kind of unique having these old rocks so close."

"These *old rocks*," she giggled. "That's not very romantic."

"I'm not really a very romantic fellow, Grace."

"You'll do," she answered. And she meant it. "But you have such a musical soul, Lee."

He took his eyes off the road for a moment, looked over at her, and smiled.

She loved that his smile lit up his whole face.

"You say the funniest things sometimes, Grace."

"Do I?"

"You do."

They pulled off the road to secluded spot with a solitary picnic table. Nearby, a glacial stream tumbled over jagged gray boulders and overhead a cocky jay flapped and cursed the human intrusion. Grace spread a picnic cloth over the nature-stained table and put down their lunch bag.

"Hungry?" Lee asked.

"A little," she answered, opening the bag of sandwiches.

"Oh, I forgot the drinks," he announced heading back to the car.

Grace took a swipe at the picnic bench, decided it was clean enough, and sat down.

When Lee returned he put the bottles of lemonade on the table and gave her a peculiar look. "I just had the strangest feeling," he said. "A déjà vu. Like I've been here before and done this exact same thing. But I know I haven't. What a weird feeling."

"It is weird. Wonder what it means?"

"Who knows?"

"Maybe it's the mountains' way of reminding us of our spiritual past. We are a pretty minute part of the universe you know, and you realize it when you see the magnitude of the mountains. And the way nature's wonders are all spread out before us here in the shadow of your *old rocks*." She gestured and gave him a playful smile, but continued in a more serious vein. "Our ancient ancestors believed every place has a Spirit looking after it just like we have a soul. Everything – the trees, animals, the water, even the mountains."

"Why Grace, I hadn't thought of you as being so…"

"So…spiritual?"

"Yah, I suppose. You believe in God and go to church every Sunday. Me too. I guess I'd really never thought much beyond that. But I kind of like your idea – that everything has a spirit. I sometimes find church services kind of mechanical. I forget about how connected I should feel, concentrating my thoughts on the next hymn I have to play or something. You know. I bet it's the same for you when you're singing. Sometimes during the sermon, my mind drifts off to some assignment I have to finish for school. I have a lot of things to think about."

"I do too. And you're right. I'm so concerned with making sure every note is right, I sometimes forget I'm singing a hymn of praise. That's why we should come to the mountains more often, Lee. To renew our spirits. Just take some time to draw in the heady fragrance of the forest. Rejoice in the squawk of that blue jay up there. Of course, God *is* there in the church, especially in our music, but He's here, too. All around us. Can you feel Him?"

Lee didn't answer but threw his leg over the bench and sat down beside her. He took her hand and laced his fingers through hers. His fingers were not long and tapered as one might expect of a pianist, but were nonetheless skilled, able to dance readily across a keyboard and showcase with ease, the music of the masters.

"Grace, I…"

"What is it Lee?"

"You and I, well… It is nice to get out of the city for a few hours, isn't it?"

"Of course," she replied giving him a curious look. Was that really what he'd meant to say?

"I'm glad we came up here today."

"Me too, Lee."

He took off his glasses and kissed her sweetly. She liked it when he remembered to kiss her that way, with nothing between them. Nothing could ever come between them.

4

They made love one night there on the hill. It was unplanned, surprising both of them. It was her first time and as she judged by his fumbling, his as well. They'd begun as always, kissing one another sweetly, she laying in his arms stroking his hair, he looking fondly into her eyes.

"Your eyes, Grace... I wish I was a poet so I could tell you how beautiful they are."

"I think you just did."

He kissed her more intensely and slipped his hand down, cupping her breast. She didn't stop him. His hand continued to wander and Grace felt an exhilaration she'd never before experienced. It was over before either of them could process what'd happened.

"I love you, Lee," she'd whispered.

He did not reply.

When they sat up, they hastily restored order to their clothing and he took her home, parting without a word. But even though Lee had not professed his love for her, Grace thought of their lovemaking as a pivotal moment, a moment confirming everything was evolving in her life as it should. They'd sealed their love and the vision of an incredible future with Lee was all Grace thought about for the next few days. It'd been Thursday evening after choir practice. He picked her up as usual on Sunday evening and they spent a pleasant time with their friends in the youth group. But after the meeting, they didn't go to the hill. Grace didn't read too much into it, thinking perhaps Lee still had homework to finish.

University sessions were well under way, and both Lee and Grace had heavy loads of music to practice for the church's Christmas events.

Lee parked in front of her house and sat for a moment, his hands on the steering wheel. He stared straight ahead at the snow pellets hitting the windshield.

"Grace."

She looked over at him and in the glow of the streetlight could detect a strange look on his face.

"Grace, I don't think…I mean… you and I… I need to break up with you."

Lee's words hit her like a thunderbolt. Had she heard him correctly? What was he saying? He wanted to…break up with her?

"You what," she gasped. The words he'd spoken began to swirl around in her head and she felt as though she was in free-fall. "You need to…break up with me. I-I… What?" she stammered.

"I'm sorry, Grace. I think it's for the best. I-I don't want you to rue the day you ever met me."

"Rue the day? What? What on earth does that mean? I don't understand. You can't mean it," she choked. "You, I mean, we…"

"I'm sorry Grace. It's just that…"

"Lee. No. I…I thought we…we…" Words failed her, her stomach lurched, and she feared throwing up right there in Lee's bug. She grabbed for the handle, threw open the door and narrowly missing pitching out onto the sidewalk. When she regained her equilibrium, she slammed the door and ran up the concrete steps of her home, batting wildly at snowflakes mingling with her tears. With trembling hands, she fumbled open the bungalow's front door.

No one saw her come in and she went straight to her room, shut the door, and threw herself on the bed, winter coat and all. What had just happened to her well-ordered life? It was incomprehensible. The first time she met Lee she'd completely discounted him as any kind of romantic partner. He'd been nothing like her other boyfriends. And it'd taken him so long to show any kind of romantic interest in her. They'd made love for the first time just days earlier. She'd willingly surrendered her virginity to him in an age when young women were expected to take their purity to their marriage bed. In her wildest dreams, she could never have predicted she'd fall so hard for this young man. She couldn't even say how or why, but she'd fallen so totally in love with Lee it made her ache.

Between retching sobs, muffled so no one in the house could hear, she probed her mind for answers. Were they too young to make long-term commitments? Was Lee afraid their lovemaking might take that wrong turn and they would 'have to get married' as folks were wont to whisper of such scandal in the quaint vernacular of the day. She and Lee had a few more years of school to complete and, of course, he did have a reputation to maintain at the church. What would folks think if they knew the choir director had crossed the line with the soprano soloist, was having sex with her in his father's car (had he planned it after all, borrowing the car for the occasion?), risking losing the job he relied on to pay for his education? It was the mid-1960s and the beginning of the age of free love, but in the mainstream, it was presumed such activity was confined to those hanging out on Haight Ashbury

Street, not clean-cut young musicians attending a family-centered church. Grace and Lee always appeared squeaky clean, sitting piously in the choir loft Sunday upon Sunday, sharing their music, exhibiting not a hint of any impropriety.

Grace searched for answers and none came.

After an hour, she rose red-faced and tear-stained and took a shower. She was glad she'd finished her reading for the next day knowing fully well she'd be unable to concentrate on a single word. Her life was over. She'd had it all planned. She and Lee would finish school. They would travel. Teach. Perform. And now what? Would she even finish school? That was the last thing on her mind at that moment.

The next morning Grace's mother, not unaware of the young woman's mood, glanced at her from time to time from across the room. Grace rarely ate much for breakfast but this day she could stomach nothing and was sitting silently at the table, flicking the toast on her plate from side to side.

"What's up?" the mother asked casually, coming to sit at the table.

"Nothin'."

"Eat up. You're going to be late."

"I don't care. I hate my life."

Of course, it didn't take an abundant brain activity to determine what was wrong with Grace, so her mother let it drop. She'd been young once. She knew. And she knew better than to mention to Grace that apocalyptic heartbreak was not exclusive to the current generation.

"Gotta go," said Grace finally pushing aside the plate of toast altogether. "Model Parliament meeting first thing this morning."

The woman looked at her. Grace appeared as though she'd been up all night. She had dark circles under her eyes and her hair didn't seem right somehow. Yep. Things were definitely off kilter in the romance department. She felt sorry for the girl. She'd never seen her that way before. With the fellows in high school, there'd been peaks and valleys, with Rene in particular, of course, but Grace had always rebounded and though she'd liked the boys, her mother was sure Grace was not really looking for a long-term commitment with any of them. They were just high school kids having fun. But now, with Lee, well, something was definitely different, though she'd no idea of the intensity of Grace's feelings for him. She wanted to say, "You're young, move on. I don't know what you see in him anyway," but she knew Grace would hate that.

Lee called later in the day before Grace came home from school, and her mother couldn't help querying him about the situation between the two of them. Lee did confess to the breakup and was surprised by the response he received. Grace's mother alternated between berating him for breaking her daughter's heart and congratulating him for setting Grace free to find someone more worthy of her daughter's affection.

Grace never forgave her mother for that breach of sensibility, the whole episode bringing about many awkward moments thereafter when Lee had to interact with her family at church events. The hardest part for Grace, however, was during rehearsals and musical performances. On the occasions she'd had to stand in the choir loft and look at Lee directing her, she was forced to choke down a large lump in her throat. Grace had lost entirely, the ability to feel detachment, something she'd come to rely heavily on in the past when she was performing. It was one of the hardest things she'd ever had to do. And the fact she didn't seem entirely herself did not go unnoticed.

But her girlfriends were still asking about the possibility of an engagement and she foolishly blew them off saying she and Lee were keeping it low key because they still had to finish school.

But then, seemingly in a change of heart after Christmas, Lee began to take her home from choir practice and the young adult's meetings. They parked in front of her home for a few quiet moments each evening. But they never talked about their relationship or the reason for his wanting to break it off earlier. Or why, once again, he wanted to be with her. He would kiss her sweetly and look affectionately into her eyes. She was confused. It was crazy after what he'd put her through the past few weeks, but because she loved him so desperately she dared not ask and complied with his advances. He appeared to be the same sweet and gentle young man. He still stroked her cheek and playfully smoothed away the stray locks of hair that fell upon her brow. But that was all there ever was. Nothing more came of it. He never took on a date anywhere. He never took her to their special place on the hill. Grace never allowed herself to give up hope that one day things would return to the way they'd been.

The young adults group continued to meet Sunday evenings and many of the members dated one another, swapping partners until in some cases, permanent mates were settled upon. Even though Grace and Lee would attend the meetings, forever wondering about the end-game, she began to date Jim, a young man who'd recently joined the group. It was not a serious relationship, Grace comparing it to the dates she'd been on when Rene found flirting with others more fascinating than being with her. But during those social evenings, Lee and Grace would often glance at one another, glances giving others serious speculation it was not really over between them.

January gave way to February and Grace's new dating partner faithfully came to fetch her for a meeting one Sunday evening. And there sitting in the back seat of Jim's old Chev was Keir, one of his workmates. She hopped into the front seat beside Jim.

"Oh, Grace, that's Keir back there. We work together," announced Jim.

"Hi," she said turning to look at the young man.

"Hi, Grace. Nice to meet you."

"You too."

"Keir was looking to meet some young people, so I invited him to come out to the group tonight," Jim explained.

"Oh, that's great."

"Yah, I just got into town awhile back, after a couple of years away. Jim mentioned the church group, so I thought I'd give it a shot," said Keir continuing the explanation.

"Oh good. I think you'll like it. There's about fifteen of us who come out regularly," she said still twisted around in her seat looking at Keir.

"I know I will," he replied, giving Grace a long serious look. Even seeing Grace's face by the streetlight's subtle glow, he'd seen enough to know he was indeed going to like it just fine.

Dating Jim satisfied that part of Grace's life that required an escort for social activities. He was not a bad looking guy, quiet and unassuming and he seemed smitten enough with her, but as far as having any flair, he was about as far off the other end of the scale from Rene as one could possibly be without toppling off completely. In fact, Jim barely rose to the standard of boring. But that didn't matter to Grace because she was still hopelessly in love with Lee. Grace felt safe dating Jim because she knew nothing would ever come of it.

As Keir found a footing in the group, he began to date one of the other young women, but Grace would often notice him looking at her. It was disconcerting. She and Lee continued their non-relationship, he taking her home occasionally and offering nothing more than a sweet goodnight kiss. He didn't engage her in any conversation at school, often passing her by with a bundle of music clutched precariously under one arm. By March however, the relationship between Keir and the girl he'd been seeing had fallen apart and one night he showed up to take Grace to the young adult's meeting. He'd been able to purchase a vehicle – a black Ford of some questionable serviceability.

"Where's Jim?" she queried when he came to the door.

"Couldn't make it tonight. I thought I'd fill in."

"Oh, that's nice of you. New car?"

"You could call it that," he laughed.

They moved down the steps to the sidewalk and she hopped into the passenger side.

Keir did not live up to the meaning of his Gaelic name – dusky and dark-haired. He was tall, over six feet, had gorgeous blue eyes and straight blond hair worn slicked back in the style of the day, or rather the style preferred by those not emulating the shag sported by the famous Brit-band.

The Ford performed surprisingly well, though Keir would discover when spring thaw finally came, most of the vehicle had been held together by frost and providence. The less-than-roadworthy black buggy required constant attention and no small amount of cash to keep it running.

"I enjoyed your solo on Sunday."

"Oh, thanks. Do you sing? Play? Any musical interests?"

"No, I don't play anything but I love classical music. I have a pretty good collection of LP's."

"Really, that's great. I love the old masters too. It's hard to imagine how they were able to write such complicated pieces. It's as if some hand beyond this earth moved to inspire those compositions."

Keir glanced over at her as they drove. He'd expected lighter conversation from this girl, someone he barely knew.

"How's school going?"

"Pretty good. What about you...your apprenticeship?"

When Keir wasn't on a construction site with Jim, he was attending a technical school working towards a journeyman's ticket in carpentry. He was the third generation carpenter in his family.

"Good. Good. It'll be nice to finish so I can make a little better money. Even then, construction doesn't pay that well. What do you plan to do after graduation?"

"I wasn't really sure where I was headed when I started university, but now after taking a few Poli Sci courses, I've been thinking it would be fun to work in an embassy somewhere. I've spent my whole life here in this town. I'd like to see a bit of the world before I settle down."

"With Jim?"

"What? Jim?" she said explosively. She hadn't meant to blurt it out that way. "No," she continued more calmly. "Jim and I...well, he's just a pal. There's nothing serious going on between us."

"Is that so?"

"Yes. It is so." She turned and stared at the young man beside her. What'd Jim told him?

"You and Jim. You say you're not serious about him but I get the impression he'd be okay if something developed between the two of you."

"Really? I never wanted to give him that impression… He knows how I feel about…about Lee."

"Yah, and what's that all about anyway? I see the way you two look at each other all the time. Are you getting back together, or what? "

"I don't know. It's complicated."

They rode in silence the rest of the way, the subject of the *complicated* relationship between Lee and Grace hovering like threatening rain.

When after what seemed like hours of awkward silence, they pulled up in front of the church and stepped out into the crisp evening air. Keir reached out to touch her arm, and then threw caution to the wind.

"How complicated is it, Grace?" He looked into her eyes but what was reflected back told him nothing. They walked in silence to the side door of the church and joined the others.

After the meeting, Lee approached Grace and asked if she needed a ride home.

"Oh gosh, Lee. I-I…came with Keir tonight."

"Okay. See you then…on Thursday?" Grace studied his face and felt a pang of sympathy. Lee looked tired. His full load of music and university studies appeared to be taking a toll on him.

"Oh, Lee, wait," she reconsidered. "I guess I can…go home with you."

Keir sat and watched Grace and Lee leave the hall then glanced around the room to see if anyone else had witnessed the departure. But the rest of the gang were gathering their things, leaving Keir rooted to his chair.

"Thanks, Grace," he mumbled to himself. But what did he expect after all? Jim had told him all about Lee and Grace, how everyone had thought their match so perfect, their relationship solid. "Complicated. Complicated." He tossed the word back and forth, imagining a string ball unraveling. He hated that word complicated.

Grace regretted her decision the moment she and Lee had settled into his car for the drive to her home. She thought of Keir and how rude and thoughtless she'd been accepting a ride home with Lee after the other young man had picked her up for the meeting. The words of an old mantra she'd heard chanted by her grandmother echoed in her head, 'go home with the one who brung you.'

Too late now.

By the time Lee pulled the Volkswagen to the curb in front of Grace's house, she was almost in tears. He laid one hand in hers and slid his other arm around her, unaware of her mood.

"Lee, don't. I can't do this," she cried snatching her hand from his grasp.

He looked at her.

"I'm sorry. I just thought…"

"No. it's my fault, Lee. I've given you more than enough reason to think this is okay. Bringing me home, kissing me goodnight but offering me nothing else. I don't understand this charade. What happened to us? I thought we had something real."

"Grace, I'm…I'm sorry. I know this isn't right. I'm such a fool."

"No, I'm the fool, Lee. I did the same thing in high school. Always available Grace. Just come back to her when it suits you. Grace will still be there hugging the back wall of the gym, waiting to be retrieved when convenient like some pathetic odd running shoe waiting for its mate to turn up."

"What are you talking about, Grace? You're much more than that, I can assure you," he said, giving a slight sympathetic laugh at her analogy.

"I don't understand you. Lee. I lo…" She stopped short of saying she loved him. What was the point? She reached for the handle on the car door and said, "Until you can give me some kind of answer for all this, then I'm simply not going to do it anymore."

She lunged out of the door, nearly toppling onto the sidewalk. It was a most undignified and 'ungraceful' exit. *The hell with dignity and grace*, she thought, righting herself. She ran sobbing up the front steps and into the house. *That was it. The end. Goodbye. Goodbye to Rene. Goodbye to the jock. Goodbye to Lee. Yes, the hell with them all.*

Her parents and brothers were all in the living room and witnessed her dramatic entry.

"Grace?" called her mother. "What's wrong? Is it Keir? Did he do something?"

"I'm done," Grace sobbed. "I'm just done." And she tore into her room slamming the door behind her.

"Should I go see what's wrong?" asked Grace's mother of her husband. "I've never seen her so upset."

"Leave her be. I don't think you're going to get much out of her tonight anyway. She probably just needs a good cry."

"I hate to see her like that. She hasn't been the same since…well, since she and Lee broke up. I guess I didn't realize how much she cares for him. I don't really know what happened. It was over and then it wasn't. And now, I don't know what on earth is going on with her." She threw her hands in the air for dramatic emphasis.

"I do. It was never going to be Lee," chimed in Grace's younger brother. "He's all wrong for her."

"What? Why would you say that," asked the mother, turning to stare at the boy.

"He just is. Just wait and see. She'll figure it out one of these days."

"When did you become such an expert on the subject?" laughed the mother.

The boy shrugged and headed for his room but threw one last remark over his shoulder as he retreated. "You know what I think? It's Keir. He's definitely the one for Grace. Haven't you seen the way he looks at her when he's here with that bunch of goody goodies she hangs around with?"

Grace's parents looked at one another. The shared look asked, "What's he talking about?"

***

The next day when Grace returned from class, there was a bouquet of pink sweetheart roses sitting on the coffee table.

"Someone sent you flowers," announced her mother.

Grace flipped off her coat and threw it on the living room sofa. A tiny white envelope was tucked in amongst the blossoms. From the tone of her mother's voice, Grace knew she'd already opened and resealed it. The girl plucked out the envelope and peeled it open expecting to find a passionate message of remorse from Lee – a plea to be forgiven and a longing to return to their relationship. But it said: 'Thanks Grace, Keir.'

She threw the card at the wall and burst into tears. The flowers lasted an unprecedented two weeks and when the petals began to fall silently onto the table's hard wooden surface, Grace matched each one with a tear.

She stayed away from any involvement at the church – choir practice, the young adults club, even Sunday services – and threw herself into her studies. Unfortunately, by the time final exams rolled around Grace was recovering from a bout of German measles and she struggled each day, to make it to the exam hall. And even though still not fully recovered from the virus and wallowing in the more debilitating disease, a full-blown case of lovesickness, she managed to complete her second year of university. But her marks were less than stellar.

Summer brought some relief from the pressure of school. Grace was once again able to work and make enough for her next year's school expenses. Summer was also a time to enjoy trips to the mountains with groups of friends from the church. It was casual – no pressure there either, just friends hiking and finding peace and companionship surrounded by nature's most spectacular scenery. Lee never went on any of the excursions.

Keir was an avid hiker and explorer and knew all the back roads and country pathways. Evenings brought them all together at campfires or back in the city in basement rumpus rooms where those who'd paired, snuggled and indulged in some handholding and fond glances. Others in the group would be content to enjoy the camaraderie. And because they all traveled from place to place as a pack, they did so in whatever sized group would fit in a given vehicle. Those who were 'single' just tagged along in any car or truck that had space.

Grace took pains to avoid riding with either Jim or Keir, feeling a measure of guilt for having dated Jim on the rebound and conscious of throwing up a barrier to discourage advances from Keir. He was a nice guy, smart, articulate, slight of build, and extremely handsome. And when he looked at her with those dark blue eyes, she did feel the slightest flutter in her breast. No, she told herself. No! I'm a soloist. No duet for me right now.

***

The summer of casual fun and youthful escapades came to an end and fall marked the beginning of a new school year, the last year of Grace's undergraduate studies.

***

Keir stopped by her place one evening a few days into the new term. One of Grace's younger brothers answered the door and just to annoy her yelled down the hall in the loudest voice he could muster, "Grace put on some clothes. There's a guy here."

She peeked out the door of her room and when she saw Keir standing in the hall, she nearly retreated. Conscience got the better of her however, and she took a few steps towards him.

"Hi there," he said as she approached. "Just in the neighborhood and thought I'd stop by." Then a big 'gotcha' grin.

"Hi, Keir. Uh, just in the neighborhood, eh?"

"Yah. Interested in going out for pizza? I know a great place down on 5th."

"Oh, I don't know, Keir… I…"

"Can't think of an excuse can you?"

"Nope," she laughed. "You got me. I'll get my jacket."

Surprisingly, the old black Ford was still running and the two settled in onto the well-worn upholstery. They headed downtown and easily found a place to park on the street.

Inside the restaurant, they were greeted with tables dressed in red-and-white checkered tablecloths. In the middle of each table was an empty Chianti bottle topped with a candle, the taper alight and melting onto a wicker wrapping. It was the most romantic place Grace had ever seen outside of a movie.

They were seated at a small table in the corner. *Finally*, Grace thought, *she'd been seated at a back table with someone who'd chosen to be with her.* The music was Italian, an opera she didn't recognize and was playing low enough to allow for polite conversation. And, she reflected, Lee had never taken her anywhere but A&W the whole time they'd been together.

"This is really nice, Keir. Certainly a cut above the neighborhood pizza joint where everyone ends up sitting at those picnic-style tables."

"Yah, I've been here a couple of times."

She didn't ask with whom.

"So you're back in school."

"Yes, last year. I'm going to miss it. I love the atmosphere at the U. Everyone is so keen and excited about life. There's a kind of magic there."

"I envy you that. No real magic at the technical school. But I'm only there a few weeks at a time. The rest of the year, it's heavy construction. And winter's coming. I hate working in the cold. I'm sorry now that I left Hawaii. But it was too hot. Crazy, eh?"

"Wow, you lived in Hawaii. I envy you that. I want to travel a bit when I'm done school."

"Yah, I remember you'd said that."

"Hawaii, eh? That's where you were before you came back here? I remember you'd mentioned being away from town the first time we met."

"I started my apprenticeship there. I was the only white person in my class."

"Why on earth were you there?"

"Long story. I'll tell you sometime. I want to keep you in suspense so you'll go out with me again."

Grace smiled at him. *No*, said a voice in her head. *No! No! No!*

The waitress came by with a menu and a couple of glasses of water.

"What do you like?" he asked.

"Nothing too spicy."

"Okay, let's see what we can find."

They debated for a few moments and when the waitress returned Keir ordered a Hawaiian pizza. Grace thought that was kind of funny.

It was a mild evening and after leaving the restaurant, they walked along the avenue for a time, looking into the windows of all the shops. Keir had taken her hand and she'd not resisted. She thought of Lee and how he would never hold her hand in public when there were other people around.

Back in the car, they drove around the city for a few minutes and Keir pointed out some of the building projects he'd taken a hand in over the past few months.

"How neat," she said, "that you'll be able to see your handiwork in the city for years to come. I wonder if I'll ever be able to leave my mark on the world."

He looked over at her. "You already have, Grace," he said.

They pulled up in front of Grace's bungalow. She'd had a wonderful evening. A romantic restaurant, delicious pizza, and charming company. She didn't resist when Keir reached over, cupped her chin, and kissed her softly.

She skipped from the car with a quick "thanks, Keir. I had fun."

As she stood on the porch and watched Keir pull away into the night, a voice in her head said, *You'd better be careful. Seriously, you're looking to have your heart broken. Again! He's just too good to be true.*

***

Keir charmed his way into the hearts of Grace's family. They all loved him. It seemed Grace's brother had been right after all. And Keir's family had embraced her as well. The girl was taking her time though, determined to improve her grades, that she might follow her dream of seeing a bit of the world. She and Keir continued to spend time with the group, Grace still trying to avoid any contact with Lee. He did not appear to be dating anyone else.

When had her friendship with Keir turned to love? Grace could not put her finger on just when it'd happened, but one day she found her mind pivoted immediately to thoughts of Keir the moment she awoke. She'd grown into the relationship with him in a way she'd never been able to with the other young men she dated. With Keir, Grace's world expanded to include so much more and she began to see just how one-dimensional her relationship with Lee had been.

Keir was an avid reader and self-taught in so many areas Grace was truly amazed by his knowledge and insight. His love of the mountains he explored was profound and she discovered he was also a bit of an amateur geologist. He had a collection of rocks and fossils to rival a small museum. Weekend trips would take them all over the countryside to places Grace had never known existed.

After a mere four months of courtship, the couple became engaged on Christmas Eve, 1964, before Grace had even completed her last year of university. There'd been no fanfare. No romantic dinner, flowers, or music. They'd been traveling through the city and while stopped at a red light, Keir reached over, opened the glove compartment of the old black Ford, pulled out a small velvet box, and dropped in it her lap. Then he proceeded through the green.

So much for keeping love at bay, said a voice in her head. But the sparkling solitaire she took from the box and placed on her finger argued with the voice in her head. She hated to think what Keir had sacrificed to pay for it.

He would write to her when he was forced to take jobs away from the city, "Years ago, I would never have thought that I would find a girl I would be capable of loving even half as much as I love you. From the first time I saw you, I knew that it would be possible but that I would be loved again by you was even beyond my fondest expectations. The rose I picked was not a rose at all but an orchid. I love you to the point where I don't know what I would do if I ever had to stop loving you."

Grace had finally found the happiness she'd so longed for and often reflected on how much her life had changed in so short a time. She pondered the future with Keir, wondering what the world had in store for them. And from time to time, she thought of Lee too, wondering where his life would take him.

***

It is well we as mortal souls cannot look into the future. At best, we can but face it with hopeful expectation.

5

A few weeks before graduation, Grace sat for an exam; the results of which she hoped might secure her a position in one of Canada's foreign embassies. Though the job would likely be entry level clerical in nature and with minimal pay, it would afford her the chance to see another part of the world. Any part – she was not that selective. But she was not unaware that if she was offered the position, it meant leaving Keir. She hoped their relationship could withstand a separation for a few months at least.

Grace had managed to bring up her average significantly and received a Bachelor of Arts degree, her major Political Science. The irony of it all was that her father was unable to attend the event as he'd already committed to attending one of his own political affairs. But Keir and her mother sat quietly cheering as she climbed the stage to receive the diploma. Despite all the moments Grace had spent in the spotlight, this was her very proudest. She'd been the first in her family to obtain a university degree.

Grace and Keir spent a lot of time in the mountains that summer, exploring for fossils, wading in the shallows of turquoise streams, and enjoying another of Keir's passions – mountain climbing. That one almost did her in. Hiking – okay. Stumbling across a log bridge risking a fractured tailbone – well, all right. But climbing – that was quite a different matter, though, at the top of one of the climbs was a treasure, a cave in which the two were able to pick their way through a maze of ice crystals. And the trip down wasn't bad either. Keir showed her how to take a run and slide down the scree a few feet at a time. It was a little scary at first but once she got the hang of it, it really was a rush. They sipped water from clear-running streams and made love in the quiet grasses of deserted meadows, listening to the song of mountain birds. If there was a heaven on earth, Grace had found it and for the first time in her life, she felt she was not a placeholder. Keir was truly and completely in love with her. And she was just as much in love with him.

In one small way she hoped she wouldn't make the cut for a foreign job as it would separate her from the man she'd come to love, but she knew she'd always regret it if she didn't take the opportunity if it was offered. And it was.

"There's a letter there from the government," announced her mother one afternoon in late August. Had her mother already opened it?

Grace felt her palms begin to sweat as she tore at the large brown envelope.

She read the covering letter slowly, so as not to miss a word, then screamed at her mother, "I made it! I made it! Oh my god. I did it."

"Where are you going?"

"I don't know yet. There's a bunch of stuff I still have to fill out... I guess preferences. Wow! I even have a choice," she cried waving the enclosures.

"Oh, Grace, I'm so happy for you. It's such a wonderful opportunity, but we're all going to miss you. Especially Keir."

"I know. We talked about it. He wasn't happy about the possibility of me leaving, but he understands that I've worked hard and he says he doesn't want me to miss the opportunity if it comes up. I guess it will be a true test for us."

Grace's mother looked at her daughter. She was extremely proud of the girl for all she'd achieved during her short life. She smiled fondly at her and sent up a silent prayer that all of Grace's dreams would come true. So far, so good.

***

Grace chose Paris for no other reason than – well – it was Paris! She read everything she could get her hands on about the romantic city because she didn't want to miss a moment of any enchantment it offered. She figured the work at the embassy would be mundane but she planned to spend as much of her free time as possible, soaking up French culture.

The night before her departure, she and Keir sat silently contemplating their separation.

"I'll write every day, Keir. I promise."

"Me too. I don't know what I'm going to do without you, Grace. I know it'll be much easier for you though, being away in such an exciting city. Maybe someday I'll get there too."

"I know, Keir. I'm leaving you here in this dull old place. But I've only signed on for a year. The time will pass quickly. You'll see."

"You think? Every day will be a lifetime for me."

"You still have school, Keir. That should help a bit."

"Yah. Last year, thank goodness. And the first thing I'm going to do when I'm done is buy a new car. The old girl doesn't have much life left in her."

Grace chuckled. How many times had they been stranded on one of their excursions when the old heap of metal had given up? Their friends were slowly running out of patience at having to spring to their rescue time after time.

"When you get back let's get married right away, Grace. We'll buy a house – hell, I'll build us a house in the country. We'll have a passel of kids…"

"How much is a passel?"

"Oh, I don't know. Ten, twelve."

"Keir, I don't love you that much."

"How much do you love me?"

She looked deeply into his eyes and brushed her hand across his cheek and down his neck. She felt the day's growth of beard and realized it was one of the things she'd miss most about him. It gave him a maturity she'd never seen in any of the other young men she'd been with. He put his hand on hers and smiled.

"I don't know how I can ever measure it. You've made me so happy. I never thought I'd be as happy as this. You know how I once felt about Lee. I really thought he was the one but when I look back at it all, I can't even imagine what my life would have been like with him. If I'd never met you."

"It was ordained, Grace. God put us on the same trajectory at just the right time. I was meant to go to the church with Jim that night I first I saw you. It was not God's plan for you to spend your life with Lee."

Her eyes misted at his words. For all the times she'd sat in church listening to messages of inspiration, the words Keir had spoken at that moment transcended them all.

"Oh, Keir. Keep talking like that and I'll never be able to leave."

"Okay," he said and kissed the tip of her nose.

***

Goodbyes at the airport were tearful for Grace, her family and especially Keir, who tried and failed at macho bravery. The young man and Grace's parents stayed in the terminal and watched as the plane taxied down the runway and out of sight.

"I give him a month before he's on the first plane off to Paris," said Grace's mother to her husband as they shed their coats at home.

"Three weeks," said the father.

He was right.

6

As Grace would write to her parents, the first few days at the embassy had been a blur. The place was a maze of hallways, offices, and conference areas, and when she was not shadowing one of the slightly higher-up underlings fetching coffee or sorting mail, she was trying to memorize a list of the personnel she was required to know by name. The first real task given her was just as she'd expected. Menial. Several boxes of files were dropped beside her table – she didn't even rate a desk, and she was instructed to go through each one to make sure the proper documents were in each, each page identified with an individual file number. That job made her head ache, but she knew she was on the very bottom rung of the ladder, and threw herself into the task as though she was researching for a thesis. She refused to allow herself to make a mistake. Not that anyone was ever likely to know, for as she noted, most of the files were many years old. When she did find something misfiled, she removed it from the Acco fastener and placed it in a basket. The basket was emptied periodically by some other lowly staff member who had to search the tombs for the correct file. She was thankful that at least she didn't have that job.

She'd taken over the apartment of the young woman whose job she'd also inherited. One could not really call it an 'apartment,' at least not by Canadian standards. It was just a room on the fourth floor of a walk-up. The room housed a bed, a small round café-style table with two chairs, a lumpy lounge, and two puce-colored side chairs that'd seen many a better day. These 'splendid' furnishings were rounded out with a couple of side tables and a tiny kitchen, strung as an afterthought along the back wall. A single overhead light provided most of the illumination in the room.

But Grace thought it was wonderful, imagining it akin to the garret rooms reportedly inhabited by starving French artists and poets. Of course she was far from starving, but her take-home pay wasn't that great either. She did try on her limited budget, to dress up the place a bit, but the room would never lose its cachet of shabbiness.

Grace loved the idea of coming home at the end of the day with a satchel of fresh vegetables, a French loaf or pastry, and stalks of field flowers purchased from the markets nearby. This was the Paris she wanted to soak in and was grateful that even her basic French was serving her well, allowing her to get by while she integrated more fully into the language. Almost everyone at the embassy was bilingual.

The young woman had not set out on her own on too many trips around the city, but had, of course, accompanied other work-mates on a few tours. But there was still plenty of time. One of the things she'd done was attend a few theatrical presentations. She'd made her meager income stretch to include those, and found some of the French productions different than she was used to – most quite quirky in fact.

***

He watched her as she made her way down the street towards him. She was juggling her handbag, satchel of groceries and a pot of blue violets, conscious of the calling cards left by the French curs roaming the Parisian streets. He was sitting on the stoop marking entry to her building, a duffel bag at his feet. He didn't call out to her but let her approach. He hadn't written that he was coming.

Grace shifted her bundles and looked up, wondering why someone would choose to be sitting on her steps. The weather was cooling. Winter was on the horizon and she knew anyone clad as he was in a light jacket, would be feeling the chill.

Suddenly, her face lit up and her eyes sparkled as she recognized him.

"Keir. Oh, Keir. What are you doing here?" she cried.

"I heard things were pretty good in Paris this time of year." His face broke into a broad grin, showing off his perfect white teeth.

She laughcried and put down her things to fall into his arms.

"You crazy guy," was all she could think to say.

"Crazy about you," he said and kissed her long and hard.

Those passing by barely noticed. Paris is known after all, as the city of lovers.

***

"Nice place," he commented. "Great feng shui. Where's the rest of it?"

"The bathroom's down the hall," she said.

They shed their outerwear and he came to stand beside her, helping to take the food from the shopping bag. He picked up the potted plant and set it on the windowsill, noting that the view from the window was a garbage-filled alleyway. He thought he saw movement amongst the debris. A rat. He was aware that beyond the obvious charms of the city, it was regarded as quite dirty and now he was seeing for himself that it was.

"The bathroom is shared with everyone else on this side of the hall. A bit of a scramble in the morning sometimes."

"Super great! This place just oozes luxury."

She laughed and put her arms around him.

"I can't believe you came all this way over here and didn't even let me know. What about work? And school? And the airfare?"

"Sold the old black beast. She wouldn't have seen another season, anyway."

"Poor old Betsy. Guess she headed straight for the wrecking yard, eh."

"Yep. But she served us well when we needed her." He held her close and stroked her hair. "God, I missed you. I couldn't sleep at night. All I could think of was coming over here to be with you. I started planning the moment I got home from the airport the day you left."

"How long can you stay?"

"My visa's for three months, but I know someone who works at the embassy. Maybe she can pull a few strings," he laughed.

"Not likely," she replied moving away from him and going to sit on the bed.

"The only strings I pull are the ones tying piles of old files together."

"Well, let's make the most of our time together," he said, sitting beside her. He slipped his hand beneath her blouse. "Starting right now."

Grace was grateful she'd not seen much of the city to that point, for she was now able to explore and enjoy every new experience with Keir. True to his adventurous spirit, he was able to take her to see things many would never have thought to seek out. They did all the touristy things – the galleries and museums, the Champs Elysees, Notre Dame – and despite some inclement weather, they also managed a few trips to the French countryside, joining others aboard wheezing tour buses.

One Sunday afternoon, they left the small apartment (though most Sundays they didn't want to venture much further than their rumpled bed) and spent the day exploring the area near the Eiffel Tower. They took with them a picnic lunch to share and sat on a metal bench near the famous landmark.

After they'd eaten, Grace pulled the guidebook from her handbag and began to read from it. "The Eiffel Tower was named after the engineer Gustave Eiffel, whose company designed and built the tower. It stands 984 feet high, the tallest in the world and was the entrance to the 1889 World's Fair…"

Keir took the book from her hand and closed it up.

"Everyone reads the same thing when they come to see the Eiffel Tower. Did you know that it was nearly taken down after the fair? The people of Paris regarded it as nothing more than an eyesore. They thought it looked like a big ugly gangly giraffe."

"Really?"

"Really! It's true."

"How do you know that?"

"I read a lot, but I don't believe everything I read so I do a lot of research."

"That's what I admire about you, Keir. You always have a different take on things."

"It's not the only thing you admire about me, I hope."

She giggled. "You know that. So what happened? The tower is still here attracting thousands of visitors every year. It's what most people think of when they think of Paris."

"Well, Gustave Eiffel was not about to give up so easily after all the engineering and building that'd gone into the tower so when it was threatened with demolition he tried to encourage people to climb the stairs to the top with the incentive of receiving a commemorative coin for their effort."

"Wait a minute. You mean he expected folks to climb all the way up there just for a coin?"

"Well, I guess it wasn't incentive enough 'cause that didn't seem to work."

"What then? It's still here."

"Well, then Eiffel thought the tower could be used to study aerodynamics so he started tossing all manner of stuff from the top to demonstrate the differences in air resistance – things like feathers and heavier stuff, things with different weights. Still no dice."

"People must have thought he was a little nuts."

"Probably, especially the French government. They didn't buy any of it. The big hunk of steel seemed doomed to end its life in a wrecking yard, just like our old black Betsy."

"So, then what happened?"

"Well, in 1898, almost a decade after it was erected, Eiffel had one last shot at salvaging his masterpiece. And it came about because of a new development."

"What was that?"

"It was radio. At that time, radio signals were often obstructed by high objects like mountains, but the tower was higher than anything around and the perfect place for a radio transmitter. The first broadcast transmitted from the Eiffel Tower was to England and that event made the French military suddenly sit up and take notice. And so, because the military began to see the value of such an innovation, the French government decided to allow the tower to remain. In the end, the French military used it during WWI to listen into German radio transmissions and that greatly helped the French war effort.

"That's really fascinating. I had no idea."

Keir took her hand and looked fondly into Grace's eyes and said, " so now we sit here today at the foot of this impressive monument, two adventurous lovers from thousands of miles away, supremely grateful for the advent of radio, for without it where would we be?"

"Probably back at the loft making love," said Grace.

Okay. The heck with the Eiffel Tower. Let's go."

***

Predictably, Grace's mother inquired as to where Keir was staying during his impromptu trip abroad, well knowing he didn't have sufficient funds for any kind of decent hotel. Grace would reply that there were a number of reasonably priced youth hostels available. She knew that her mother was not buying that line for a moment. But it was Paris. And they were in love. What did her mother expect for heaven's sake?

Keir was able to make a few francs '*sous la table*' washing dishes at the small café around the corner from their love nest. Sometimes he was even able to take home some 'leftovers.' The café had a great chef, and he'd taken a shine to Keir, though perhaps not in the most proprietary of ways. Keir danced a fine line between feigning encouragement in order to keep the supply of awesome food coming and juggling the distance between himself and the chef when things became too uncomfortable. Besides, he knew he would never see the man again when his visa ran out and he had to return home. Regrettably, there was no thought of staying in Paris at the end of three months. He had to get back to finish his apprenticeship and make some money. And first things first when he got there, he needed to buy a new vehicle.

"I'm sorry your time here in Paris had to be during the worst weather, Keir," she remarked as they ventured out on a Saturday afternoon. It was December, and they'd bundled up to take a stroll wearing heavy jackets, rubber boots and knit

61

hats. Keir had written and asked his mother to send him some warmer clothing. But even though the weather was cool and wet, Paris is not known to have much snow and the couple went out most Saturdays to explore the wonderful small shops and curiosities so prevalent on the street of Paris.

"Well, it's certainly not as bad as the weather they're having at home right now," he answered. "And as long as I have you to keep me warm every night, I don't mind a bit."

"Don't let my mother hear you say that," she giggled and took his hand. "I implied you were staying at a youth hostel while you're here."

"And I'm sure she believed every word," he laughed.

Grace gave a nervous giggle as well. "I'm so happy you're here, Keir. I don't think I could have lasted a whole year by myself. Paris is such an exciting and interesting city it should be shared with someone you love. Rain or shine."

"Yup, rain or shine. And here comes that rain – again."

They ducked into a small café, sat at a wooden table with a wobbly leg, and ordered two cups of '*chocolat chaud.*'

"It has been pretty wonderful though, hasn't it?" he said, picking up the thread of the conversation. "Waking up together every morning, coming home and making dinner together, just like a couple of old married folks. We should make this a permanent arrangement."

"I thought that was the idea." She waved her left hand at him with a dramatic flair.

"Oh right." He laughed.

"I love it all, even the rain. And I love you, you nut," she said reaching across the table, letting her hand linger on top of his.

"I love you too, Grace. And I always will," he said. She squeezed his hand and felt him respond. She did love him and she especially loved the way he always said he loved her whenever she said the words. Had Lee ever been in love with her but could never say the words? And why did it still bother her that he may have loved her and couldn't say so? Why did it still matter to her? She had no answer for that.

They finished their warm drinks and ventured out again. The rain had let up, and Keir and Grace continued their walk, making a circuit around the block and along a path winding through the green space near their building. The sun was making an effort to shine and had brought warmth and some marginal dryness to a bench at the edge of the park. Keir made a big thing of sweeping away any remaining raindrops and the couple sat down, happy to enjoy the brief spell of sunlight struggling from behind the rain clouds.

"Aren't the buildings here just grand? Those ones there for instance," she said pointing to a row of classically designed four story buildings across the street. The colorful detail on them was stunning. "I have no idea what style they may be. I should probably make a study of some of the architecture here while I have the chance. What do you think?"

"I guess," Keir said. "I wonder if any of the buildings I work on at home will still be standing as long as these have been here. And I wonder how old they are, anyway? Built with a lot less technology than we have now, too. Just look at all that elaborate trim around the windows and doors. And even the building we live in has to be at least a hundred years old. It was probably someone's very fine home before it was turned into apartments."

She knew she could always get a conversation going with Keir when it came to buildings and architecture, recalling he usually studied places at home with a very critical eye. Anything out of plumb or square seemed to drive him crazy.

"Do you think we'll ever come back to Paris one day?" she asked.

"We should. In a few years, when we can afford to come in style. But only in the summer, okay? I'm freezing out here. The sun's disappeared again. Let's go home."

They rose from the bench and headed through the park towards their room, two young lovers on the brink of life, lovers looking forward to sharing all the adventures yet to come.

Grace turned and threw a backward glance at the bench. "We'll come back and sit on that same bench someday, Keir," she waved. "And we'll remember today…the rain, the hot chocolate, and how happy we are right now."

He drew her close to him as they walked the rest of the way, out of the park, across the avenue and through the front doors of their building. He pecked a kiss on the end of her cold nose, and they climbed the three flights of narrow stairs, happy and content as only young lovers can be.

***

"I don't know if I can do this, Grace," he sighed. They were lying together in the bed they'd shared for the past few weeks. Moonlight was streaming through the single window throwing a shadow on her lovely face. There were tears in her eyes.

"This has been the happiest time of my life, being here with you in Paris. Not a care in the world. If everything suddenly disappeared tonight, I'd die a deliriously happy guy."

He propped himself up on an elbow and gazed at her with so much love she knew she'd do the same.

"Will we always be this happy, Keir? I mean, once I get home and we have to face reality. Married life. Kids. A mortgage. Scrapping the frost off the windshield five months of the year."

"I'll build us a garage. But first we need to get the car."

"You have an answer for everything," she sighed.

"I hope so, Grace. I'm completely committed to you. I want us to grow old together. It's all I want."

"You once asked me how much I love you and I said I couldn't measure it. But now I realize there isn't a measure for it because it just keeps growing."

Keir slid down and cradled her in his arms.

"How did you get to be so wise?"

"I had a good teacher," she replied and held him close. He was leaving the next day, and she could not bear to let him go.

7

Grace was eventually given more stimulating tasks at the embassy but without Keir in Paris, time away from her job had lost some of its charm. Occasionally, she went out with some of the other young folks from work, but every time she saw a pair of young lovers on the street, her heart did a flip-flop. She and Keir wrote faithfully but she didn't have a lot to report. Surprisingly, his news was more interesting. He had managed to finish his technical courses and had secured a job but was often forced to stay home when temperatures dipped too low to allow for outside construction work. He spent time with Grace's family and reported that he was teaching one of her younger brothers some carpentry skills as they worked on building a room in her parents' basement. He hadn't been to the church in ages – not the same without her and would she please hurry up and come home, for goodness sake! He was losing his mind without her.

And then April came to Paris. Yes, the magic of April in Paris was all around. Bright-colored blossoms erupted everywhere – in every window box, in flowerpots near the small bistro tables and in well-tended flowerbeds on the boulevards and avenues. The outdoor cafés enjoyed a resurgence of traffic and the air was electric with renewed life.

She saw him before he saw her. He was sitting at a table in front of the café near her flat, his hand absently toying with the coffee cup in front of him. Her heart gave a lurch at seeing him there and she felt almost faint, a myriad of thoughts racing through her mind. This could not be happening. She tossed her head and drew in a long breath trying to compose herself, then considered taking a circuit around the block so he wouldn't see her.

He still looked the same, though he was better dressed, his style of casual shirt and unshapely pants gone, replaced with a suit she could call almost stylish. His hair had been cut shorter.

Grace could not will herself to move.

What on earth was he doing in Paris and just a stone's throw away from her place? She combed her hand through her hair.

He looked up and saw her standing there, staring at him. He returned her stare. Neither spoke. Time stood still. At last, she moved forward and came to stand beside the table.

"Hello, Lee."

"Hi, Grace. What a surprise."

"Really? You hadn't heard I was in Paris?" There was a touch of frost in her voice. "What are *you* doing here?"

"I got a chance to study here with a great teacher. And yes, I did know you were here. But Paris is a big place. I didn't expect to run into you like this."

"How long have you been here?"

"Just a few days. How are things going with you?"

"Pretty good. Well, the work at the embassy's not that challenging but there's been a few interesting days and I've met some interesting people. And I do love Paris. I live just down the street."

Wrong thing to say, said a voice in her head.

"What a coincidence," he said. "The maestro's studio is right over there." He pointed to a group of buildings across the green space.

"Oh really? What are the chances?"

Yes, what are the chances, said the voice.

The green space across from her building. The park she glanced at everyday as she came and went from her flat. The green space she and Keir had so often strolled into. And now here was Lee telling her one of the buildings across the way, one of beautiful structures she and Keir had admired that rainy day was home to his teacher. Hmm. What were the chances?

"Why don't you sit down? Do you want anything? Café au lait?"

"No, I'm fine thanks," she said, sliding out a chair and putting her handbag on the table. She sat down and tried to control her breathing.

Breathe from your diaphragm, said a voice in her head. *Like when you're singing.*

She breathed in and sighed. "Everything okay at home? Your folks?" She'd liked them. They'd always been kind to her.

"They're good. Dad's about to retire."

"So, you're finished at the church?"

"Yep. Had to give it up to come here."

"You graduated?"

"Yes. Bachelor of Music."

"Congratulations."

A pause. Awkward silence.

He studied her face. "Look Grace," he said. "This is a little…"

"It's okay, Lee. Really. Keir and I are engaged. Oh, but you know that." She laid her hand on the table, displaying the ring. It drew the light and sparkled in the late afternoon sun.

"Nice rock. And Keir? He's…?"

"He's back home. He was here for a few months until his travel visa ran out. I guess he hasn't been spending any time at the church."

Lee shrugged and took a sip of his coffee. "So, how long are you here for?"

"Just till the first of October when my contract runs out. I could renew it but I don't think I will. Keir and I want to…get married when I get back."

She saw a strange look on Lee's face but failed to read its meaning.

"Lee… Lee, look, it's good to see you. Why don't you…come over for supper on Saturday?" She reached into her bag for a pencil and piece of paper. She wrote down the address, figuring since he'd almost landed on her doorstep anyway, he'd have no trouble finding it.

"The place isn't much," she said handing him the paper. "And I don't have a phone, so if you don't show up, it's no big deal."

He took the paper and saw that her hand was trembling.

"Oh, I'll be there. I'll bring some wine."

"Sounds good. About six? Spaghetti, okay? It's the one meal I'm pretty good at." She rose to leave.

"Grace."

She looked at him and felt her face flush.

"Yes?"

"I'm glad I ran into you."

Grace didn't reply because she was listening to the voice in her head screaming, *What in the name of all that's holy are you doing?*

***

He was a little breathless when she answered his knock. The climb up three flights had winded him and she chuckled a little remembering how Keir, the slim-built young mountaineer had flown up the steps, often taking two at a time. *Lee needs to lose a couple of pounds*, she thought.

He handed her a bottle of medium-priced Pinot Noir.

"Thanks. Come on in. I'll show you around," she said facetiously. "This is the living room." She pointed to the sofa and two lumpy side chairs. Backing up she said, "And this is the kitchen and the bedroom is on the left. The '*salle de bains*' is down the hall to the right."

He laughed at all her nervous gesturing.

"Smells delicious. You entertain a lot?"

"Oh, sure. The ambassador and his consort were just here for a reception last week," she answered mockingly. "Actually the only people who've been here, besides Keir, of course, are a couple of friends from work. This is hardly a place for gracious entertaining. Half the time there's not even any hot water. It brings the term 'cold water flat' to a whole new level, and it sure gives one an appreciation for North American housing. But you can't beat the charm of Paris." She was rambling.

"I haven't seen much of the city yet. Maybe you could show me around a bit." He heard her quick intake of breath. "Oops, sorry. I didn't mean to presume…"

She saw his lips moving. Heard his words. There was no question it would be a bad idea to begin socializing with Lee again. It'd taken a lot, but she felt she had him out of her system. Didn't she? And what right did he have to insinuate himself back into her life and try to pick up where they'd left off. Especially now that she and Keir were so happy and on the brink of a wonderful life together. But in fairness, it was her own fault really, wasn't it, for inviting him to dinner?

She turned to attend to the pot of spaghetti sauce burbling on the hotplate. She broke some pasta into the boiling water on the other burner.

"Grace. I'm sorry about the way it went for us."

"Don't Lee. Please. Let's just leave it all back there in the past where it belongs. It's over. We can be friends here for a few months. I don't mind getting together once in a while. It'll actually be kind of nice to have someone here from home. Even after all the months I've been in Paris, I'm still really homesick."

If only it wasn't Lee, said a voice in her head.

"Do you have a corkscrew?" Lee asked trying to lighten the mood.

She did. It'd been one of the first things Keir had purchased when he moved in.

She handed him the bottle of wine and the corkscrew and turned to take a couple of cheap wine glasses from the clumsy old cabinet that served as kitchen storage.

He poured the wine and handed her a glass.

"Cheers. Here's to Paris…and…friendship."

"Cheers," she said and took a tiny sip. "I'm not much of a drinker."

"We can save some for another time," he said.

She looked at him, cursing the cheek of that remark. She wanted to change the subject.

"How's your music coming?"

"Very well. It's hard work but I love it."

She took some plates, cutlery, and napkins out of the cabinet and laid them on the table. Earlier, she'd spread it with a small blue and yellow Provençale-patterned cloth purchased from a street vendor. In the center of the table was the pot of violets and a white candle in a glass holder. She liked the look of a well-set table.

She put down her glass of wine and said, "Sit down, Lee. I'll get the salad." She moved toward the small fridge in the corner and took out two plates heaped with fresh greens.

Lee ignored her request and waited until she put the plates on the table, then held her chair before sitting down.

They ate in silence, their forks clinking against the stoneware, neither sure in which direction to take the conversation. Grace cleared the plates and put them on the sideboard near the small, once-white porcelain sink. She stirred the sauce.

"Will you pour out the pasta while I cut the bread?" she asked. "There's a colander in the sink."

He complied and the rest of the meal was finally on the table. After dinner, they piled the dishes in the sink and made their way the three feet to the 'living room.'

You're like a couple of middle-aged empty nesters, said a voice in her head. *Just sitting about trying to think of something brilliant to talk about. You do know this is all wrong.*

The small amount of wine Grace had drunk was making her dizzy and Lee could see it was time to leave. He thanked her, gave her a friendly peck on her cheek, went out the door, and made his way down the stairway into the April night. He came for dinner the following Saturday. And the next.

And even though Grace knew it was a bad idea to see so much of Lee, he managed to talk her into taking a few sightseeing trips with him.

She went to see him perform one evening and felt herself slipping back into those old feelings, hypnotized by the magic he was urging from the concert grand. He came for her one Sunday afternoon, to take her across the green to the maestro's studio. They climbed three flights of stairs, Grace chuckling to herself as they did so. *If Lee stayed in Paris long enough, he might actually get into shape,* she thought.

"Maestro, I'd like you to meet Grace. Grace, this is the man I've been telling you about. It's such an honor to be studying with him."

The man stepped forward and took her hand. He was ancient, with shaggy white hair, but his grip was firm and his hands smooth as a child's.

"My pleasure, mademoiselle," he said.

"It's a privilege to meet you," she replied.

Grace glanced around the studio. The ceilings hovered at a height of at least twenty-five feet and a narrow winding staircase led to a mezzanine level. At the top of the stairway sat a grand piano surrounded by a myriad of shelving housing everything from old books and manuscripts to small musical instruments and randomly piled sheet music toppling over in disarray. The main floor was a cornucopia of small chairs, dusty tables, and more instruments and boxes of musical scores spilling out onto the parquet flooring. An old yellow dog of questionable breed dozed in the corner near a huge copper fireplace. A suit of armor, also in danger of toppling over, stood in the corner next to a desk heaped with yet more paper. The rooms smelled like old wood and dirty socks. Grace thought it the most fascinating place she'd ever seen.

"Your young man here shows great promise," the maestro said nodding in Lee's direction. "But he must practice, practice, practice."

She glanced over at Lee to see if he understood the maestro's assumption, they were a couple. His face was expressionless, but he said, "Grace knows all about practice. She's a musician as well. A singer. A very fine soprano."

"How lovely. You must sing something for me then," said the maestro.

"Oh, no," she replied blushing at the request. "I haven't done any singing in quite a while – not since I've been here in fact. I'm so out of practice."

"I insist. Come, Lee. You must play for her."

Grace and Lee shared a look of reticence then followed the old elf up the stairway to the mezzanine where Lee took a seat at the piano. It was the only thing in the apartment that wasn't covered with a layer of dust.

"Gesu Bambino?" Lee asked. "You sang it a couple of years ago at the Christmas Eve service."

How on earth did he remember that? she wondered. The only thing she remembered about the service was how hard it'd been to get through it. She and Lee had just broken up a few days earlier and she'd been a wreck.

Lee played the intro and she struggled to put aside the memory of that time. But the music and words came back easily to her and she gave a credible performance. Lee swiveled around on the piano bench, stood up and gave Grace a strange look, a look the older gentleman seemed to miss.

"Bravo," cried the maestro clapping his hands. "Well done. I can hear you two are used to performing together. You make a fine couple. Now we must have a glass of wine. I have some very nice Bordeaux – somewhere here," he gestured.

"Uh, thank you," she said, eyeing Lee for approval. "Just a little. Wine makes me woozy, I'm afraid." Lee didn't reply and turned from her gaze.

They moved down the stairway and their host went to search a small cabinet for the decanter of wine and three glasses. The crystal was delicately crafted and etched in an intricate pattern. Czechoslovakian she was later informed.

They sat for a time on the maestro's deteriorating old furniture, sipped their wine, and talked a little about Grace and Lee's time in Canada. Grace was hoping that the teacher's questions would not be too probing. She glanced at Lee once or twice to gauge his comfort level with the conversation and he gave her a slight eye-rolling nod.

"Well, I think we must be off, maestro," she said finally, leaving a half-full glass. "I have to get home and prepare for work tomorrow."

"Lee tells me you're at the Canadian embassy."

"Yes, that's right. For a few more months anyway. Then I don't know."

She was certainly not going to say she could hardly wait to get home to marry Keir. She was sure the man had seen the engagement ring on her finger and that had prompted his comments about Lee being her 'young man.'

"I'll see you first thing in the morning, sir," Lee said as they approached the door. It was a magnificent piece of work, carved in an intricate pattern and at least two feet taller than Lee. It swung open on three massive tooled iron hinges.

"It was so nice to meet you," said Grace, offering her hand.

"And I am charmed, mademoiselle. You are most welcome anytime. Come and hear your young man practice sometime. And sing for me again."

"I may," she said, and knew she would not. There was no way she wanted to encourage the man's mistaken assumptions about her relationship with Lee.

***

Lee brought dinner the next Saturday night, for it was now 'understood' he'd turn up like clockwork for the weekend meal. He brought more wine.

It's just dinner, she said, to satisfy the voice in her head she knew would soon be screaming at her.

Grace heard Lee's polite tap at the door and stood up to smooth out the pleats of her dress, a cool white frock of simple design. She'd cinched it with a narrow red belt then matched it with red sandals. She chuckled to herself each time she chose to wear those shoes as once Keir had told her only prostitutes in Europe wore red shoes.

"Come in, Lee," she called. After all these weeks of a regular routine, she thought he might just have come in unannounced.

"Hi," he said offering two small sacks of food and yet more wine.

"Hi." She took the food, placed it on the table, and watched as Lee went to the cabinet to get the corkscrew. He opened the bottle to let it breathe. It was all too cozy.

He'd stopped at one of the bistros nearby to pick up the meal.

"What did you bring?" she asked opening the bags. "Smells delicious."

"I'm not sure. It was the chef's special. And there's salad, too."

"Shall we have the salad first or wait till after the main course. Apparently that's a French custom someone told me about."

"Let's just stick to the Canadian way."

She went to the kitchen area, divided the salad onto two plates, and set them on the table.

They sat and munched on the salad, a mixture of tiny greens, carrot curls, and a type of crumbled cheese neither could identify. The main course turned out to be a tasty concoction of meats, vegetables, and gravy wrapped in a flaky pastry.

"Wow, what was that," asked Grace. "I've never had anything like it before."

"Not sure. But it was really good, wasn't it?"

"Yes. I guess I'm going to have to learn how to cook something besides spaghetti one of these days. Maybe a Cordon Bleu course while I'm here."

"Ah, an aspiring Julia Child."

She laughed.

Now that they'd been seeing so much of each other they were becoming more comfortable but had never acknowledged the elephant in the room. They sat quietly sipping their wine, watching the small candle on the table wither in the glass until it flickered out completely.

Lee stood up and cleared the plates from the table. He came back and took a sip from his wine glass. He looked at Grace and then went to turn off the overhead light, leaving the room awash in the stream of moonlight filtering through the grimy kitchen window. He moved to the edge of the bed, took off his glasses, and laid them on the bedside table. He held out his hand for her to join him.

She looked at him standing there in the dimness of the room. The wine was making her dizzy. Slowly, she rose and went to him. She took his hand and he kissed her softly. All she could think about was the taste of the wine on his breath as he guided her onto the bed, pushing aside the toss cushions. Her heart pounded when his fingers began to caress her breast. His kisses became more insistent and she was suddenly transported back to those early days when it was all so new for them, the youthful yearning, the mystery of it all, the love she'd felt for him. She began to close her eyes, to shut out all but the moment, for hadn't it all been leading to this? The closeness rekindled. Sharing once again their love of music. And the new magic of a being alone together on a moonlit Paris night. But it was the moonlight that shattered it all. As Grace reached out to circle her arms around Lee's neck, it happened. As she looked over his shoulder, she saw a sliver of light dance off the diamond in her engagement ring. She would have missed it if she'd closed her eyes and given in to Lee, allowed him to make love to her. With a gasp, she moved from beneath him and lay breathless on the edge of the bed. The room ached with silence.

They lay on the bed, time suspended, the moonlight spilling over them, mocking them.

"You have to go now, Lee," she whispered at last.

He rose, fumbled for his glasses, and moved to the door where he stood for a moment on the threshold. She heard the door open, then close behind him.

And then, there it was…the voice in her head. *You are such a fool, Grace. You almost made the biggest mistake of your life.*

She didn't even get up to change into her nightgown but kicked off her red shoes, shoes she'd never wear again, and crawled into bed fully clothed. A torrent of tears gushed down her face and she cried long and hard. It all came back to her. Everything. The night Lee had said he wanted to break up with her. And the night she'd gone home with Lee instead of Keir, the night she'd finally told Lee it was over between them. She'd cried endless bitter tears those nights. Lee had been the only one in her life who'd ever given her reason to cry like that.

When sleep finally came to her near dawn, she dreamed that she was with Rene. They were dancing, Fred and Ginger style, all around the base of the Eiffel Tower.

She didn't see Lee for the rest of her time in Paris.

8

It was a small affair – a few close friends and relatives, church folk and a few business and political associates of Grace's father.

Grace stood nervously with her dad at the back of the church. She was clutching the little white Bible her parents had given her. It was topped with a single white orchid nestled in a spray of stephanotis, and tied with a trail of white ribbons. Her dress was a two-piece white lace with a slim skirt and velvet trimmed sleeves. Jo, clad in a simple mauve dress, was her maid of honor and Jim, Keir's workmate, the one who'd initially introduced the couple, was the best man.

Grace slipped her arm through that of her father and they proceeded down the aisle of the church they both knew so well. Grace nodded nervously to those who stood in attendance. She was beyond grateful the organist was an elderly spinster who could barely turn the pages of the sheet music in front of her.

Keir had tears in his eyes when she joined him. She handed Jo the bible and took her groom's proffered hand. They stood in silence, gazing at one another.

The congregation took their seats and Grace's music teacher, a man well known for his exceptional singing voice, sang *The Wedding Prayer*, a request she'd made of him upon returning from Paris.

After the musical presentation, the congregation stood once more as Rev. Lester turned to the first page in the *Our Marriage Book*. It would later be presented to the couple as a certificate of their troth.

"Our help is in the name of the Lord."
"Except the Lord build the house, they labor in vain that build it."

"Dearly beloved: We are met together in the sight of God and in the presence of these witnesses to join together Keir and Grace in the bonds of holy matrimony according to the ordinance of God, the custom of the Christian Church, and the laws of this province, and to implore on their behalf the blessing of God.

"Marriage is an honorable and holy estate instituted by God, sanctioned and honored by Christ's presence at the marriage in Cana of Galilee, and likened by St. Paul to the mystical union which exists between Christ and His Church. It was ordained of God as the foundation and bond of family life, for the mutual help and comfort of husband and wife, and for the welfare of the state. Marriage is therefore not to be entered upon by any lightly or thoughtlessly, but thoughtfully, reverently, and in the fear of God.

"Into this holy estate these two persons now desire to enter; therefore, if any man can show any just cause why they may not lawfully be joined together, let him now declare it, or forever hold his peace."

Grace held her breath and waited for Lee to materialize at the console in the choir loft. All was still. *Give it up, Grace,* said a voice in her head. *This is the real thing.*

"Moreover, I charge you both, before God, the Searcher of all hearts, that if either of you know of any impediment why you may not lawfully be united in marriage, you do now confess it. For be assured that so many as are joined together otherwise than God's Word doth allow are not united by the Lord; Neither is their marriage blessed by Him."

Grace looked into Keir's eyes and knew this was right. *Go for it,* said the voice. And she did.

The couple retreated from the church to the thunderous chords of *Mendelssohn's Wedding March* and Grace barely noticed the organist did a complete hatchet job on the piece. They stepped out into the gentle rain that'd begun to fall. Some say rain on a wedding day bodes well for a long and happy marriage. Time would tell.

They rented a small house and Grace went back to work with her father's firm using her minimal clerical experience in the accounting department. More boring files to plunder and little stimulation adding up columns of figures for annual reports. She reckoned her father had been right about her chosen career path.

Keir continued to work heavy construction, and though there were many lean days for the couple, they could not have been happier. Their days became even leaner when a third mouth to feed arrived in the form of their first child, a daughter they would name Jane after Grace's grandmother. A son, Benjamin, followed four years later.

They took their two little blond babies to the mountains they so loved, ferrying them up and down slopes, watching them splash and cavort in glacial streams, and at nightfall, tucking them into bed between them in their tiny two-man tent.

Often at home they would just stand at the end of the children's beds watching them sleep, feeling blessed by the two small miracles they'd created by their love.

Keir and Grace returned to their church, celebrating the births of Jane and Benjamin at the baptismal font. They even took on a few church duties, though Grace refused to take part in the choir under the direction of the less-than-skilled organist. Membership in the choir under her hand had dwindled, nearly casting the group into oblivion.

It seemed that life for Grace and Keir was all that they'd hoped it would be. Keir even started his own construction business, a move that spared him much of the outside winter work he so disliked. Money was still tight, but at least he was working for himself and for that reason he put in long, hard hours.

***

Keir's brother, Ian, was two years younger and he'd taken a very different path in life. He'd been a brilliant student and had enrolled in the university where he'd been granted Bachelors and Masters of Science degrees, majoring in Archaeology.

Though the brothers had been very close in their early days, the eventual direction taken by each of them could not have been more disparate. Keir had enjoyed some travel, especially loving the few months he'd spent in Paris with Grace, but that couldn't begin to compare with the adventures Ian was enjoying. He wrote long letters back home reporting the many archaeological digs in which he'd taken part. From Colombia, he wrote:

Hope all is well at home. We have reached the furthest ends of civilization yet they have Time magazine here. I fear that I am a temperate climate guy and not well suited for the tropics. Living in an armpit is difficult. However, if for no other reason, the beauty that can normally only be found in a greenhouse at home makes the place worthwhile. We go out in the day, pick up shards and are tired in the night. The weather here has been sort of strange. It is now legally summer – or at least it is supposed to be. This means that it should not rain. However, it has rained 3 days in the past week. People are very happy about it because it will help the coffee.

We have been digging tombs lately and have been successful in finding something the last couple of times. Yesterday, we were at a tomb that was 3 ½ meters deep. There was considerable carbon in it – at least enough for a date. There were about ten ceramic pieces in the tomb – some of them very pretty. The Quindio seem to have tombs, (here they are called guacos) on nearly every flat piece of land. Everywhere we go, there they are. People have been digging tombs *here for 500 years since the Spanish came. The ones left are not the richest – to find gold, especially something very nice is rare. Some man tried to sell us 3 gold figures (very small and flat) for 20,000 pesos (about $1,000.00). That was really funny. We have a girl from the gold museum working with us. She said they would pay about 5,000 pesos. The Gold Museum here buys from people who find it for about 130 pesos a gram. That way it does not get out of the country. However, people also know that foreigners will usually pay more than the Museum and they will offer it to people from the outside first.*

Last week, I went to a place where tombs are carved into the rock (or hard clay as the case may be) with much painting and faces. They were really fantastic. We had to ride horses to some of them – finally a spirited animal in Colombia. We are leaving for Peru in about a week.

Ian's next adventure took him to Sudan, but not before seeing a bit more of the world. It seemed getting there was half the fun.

London is pretty interesting, but quite expensive, even the youth hostel there costs $1.50 a night. However, it is a lot of fun wandering around the place and generally getting mental indigestion. Copenhagen was beautiful and then I boarded a train to Munich. Thank goodness for 12th grade German. From Munich the train went straight thru Yugoslavia which is a very heavy place and then on to Athens. However, there the problems started as my visa was not there. Nor was the Sudanese Embassy which was supposed to grant the visa. On the day (one week later) that I was going to buy a ticket back to Copenhagen, I got hold of my visa. So to save time, I flew rather than taking a boat to Cairo. Cairo is not a nice place. I had to spend four days there to catch the train which correlated with the boat from Aswan. While in Cairo, I visited the pyramids at Giza and the sphinx (by taxi) and various other goodies which have been vastly overrated by tourists for several centuries. I took a train from Aswan where I waited the next day for the train to High Dam. From the High Dam you have to take a boat which sounds okay since this has 1st, 2nd and 3rd class decks. However, democracy has struck this part of the world and the boats are no longer large affairs with servants in cummerbunds. The scow that we sailed on had smelly closets for first and second (not me). Third class was out on the nice open, airy deck – with huge numbers of Nubian camel herders. Two and a half days later, I arrived at Wadi Halfi, which sounds okay but is actually a very small collection of mud-brick buildings and a train station. I took 4th class to Kabushiya. This consisted of a converted cattle car with wooden slats for windows and wooden slat seats in church pew style. One and a half days later, I arrived very dusty at my station. For the whole trip, so much dust and sand poured through the slats that I had to breathe through my clothing.

But Ian's next letter reflected a side of him that was unexpected by those at home.

Here I do some archaeology, some palynology, and a hell of a lot of carpentry. This seems to be my primary function and I don't mind it at all. Maybe what I need is a trade, rather than a profession. Hope you have your own construction company by the time I get back so you can hire an itinerant laborer with a PhD.

Ian, just like Keir, had never been a fan of extreme heat such as he experienced in Sudan, much preferring the cooler temperatures in Canada. But his complaints fell on deaf ears, especially during the winter months when his family was suffering sub-zero temperatures.

This country has a great lot of possibilities if the world ever runs out of sand and gravel, since this is the major harvest of over 50% of the country. I have been busily doing everything except what I came for since I arrived. Third world bureaucracy is up to its usual high standards of excellence and finally after one month of letters and telegrams it looks like I will get permission to dig a lousy hole in the ground in the middle of a barren, non-cultural part of the desert.

The archaeology here is quite different from North America. You mark out an 8 x 8 meter square, hire yourself 23 desert nomads, hand them some picks, shovels, baskets, and wheelbarrows and stand back. When the dust settles, you leap into the pit and try to keep the camel herders from digging through walls and busting up too many pots.

Any hopes of my learning much Arabic have been dashed. I've learned a few nouns but the verbs are impossible.

The food here is quite reasonable – mutton and bread mostly, but since we have a cook and other domestic staff, it gets served on plates with boiled potatoes or vegetable marrow. The trouble is the people here have some weird ideas about dishwashing and the camp is periodically swept with the 'green apple trots.' Which brings me to the subject of plumbing here. Build one square maze of mud brick (7 feet high), dig a hole in the middle of the maze, lay two boards over the hole and voila, you have one Arab world crapper over which you squat and perform your role in assisting the local nitrogen content. Though there are no scales here, I am sure I have lost quite a bit of weight.

One of the old locals – a wily WWII smuggler, rents camels to us upon which we bound with graceful spasticness across the desert like epileptic Lawrences of Arabia.

"Ian sounds like he's having a pretty interesting time," remarked Grace as she put one of Ian's letters aside. Keir was sitting at the table working on a quote for a small renovation. She put her hands on his shoulders and propped her chin on the top of his head.

"Have you ever been sorry that you're stuck here, hobbled with a wife and two kids, struggling to make ends meet, while Ian's out there in the world digging up old ruins, discovering tribes that've never seen white people, and heaven knows what all else?"

Keir put down his pen and put a hand over one of Grace's on his shoulder.

"Never," he said. "And I never will."

"Good," she said. "It's your turn to bathe Benjamin."

***

When Ian undertook to study for his PhD, he did so in Australia. The day he left Canada was the last time the family would ever see him.

***

Well, I've arrived. With my usual luck in having lots of time to do everything, the permission to complete my project in Sudan came through 3 days before I was due to leave there. So I made like a slave driver and worked with a morning and afternoon shift of Arabs until I was done. My route to Canberra got pretty involved. Instead of going straight east, I had to go north to Beirut. For some strange reason the airline put me up in a hotel there for 6 hours and fed me and drove me to and from the airport. This however gave me time to wash my shirt and catch some sleep, both of which were needed. From there I flew to New Delhi. I didn't have much money. However, I managed to trade my tape recorder, two shirts, and an alarm clock for two 50-year-old Persian rugs worth $ 150.00 in India. He would have given me a good deal on my underwear as well (honest) but I felt I had to draw the line somewhere. From there, I flew to Hong Kong (busy and industrialized), Sydney, and finally Canberra. Go to India. What a fantastic place, even New Delhi was okay. And it is supposed to be the crummy part.

"What a world traveler," exclaimed Grace when Keir had finished reading the letter to her. "Do you think we'll ever get to any of those exotic places?"

"Sure. Why not? We just have to make sure we take spare underwear. Just in case. You know?"

"Keir. You goof. But seriously. That short time in Paris just made me want to see more of the world."

"Me too. And we will do it one day, Grace. Just wait and see."

Much of Ian's research took him to dig sites in New Guinea. He wrote of excavating bones of possums, rats, wallabies and kangaroos, tools, axes and some plant life, but after he'd been there for a few weeks, he was desperate for a break and a return to civilization in Australia.

The native women who looked truly ugly when I first arrived are beginning to look awfully nice, but the amount of material that I have found is just about enough to suggest that there is quite a lot here that needs doing. We have just come down to the valley bottom again after our second week of digging here. Mist and drizzle most mornings and rain in the afternoon. My house is a little hut with a roof made of leaves and an internal fireplace. The trouble with the internal fireplace is that it dries all the leaves on the roof and leaves huge gaps which you don't need in a rainy area. So we had to supplement the local technology with plastic sheeting. One goes quietly mad working with the people here. As a white man you represent the source from which all good things flow and people are constantly trying to gain some advantage over you which will make you psychologically and morally obligated to them so they can tap you for the good things that you represent. They don't realize that you probably have less than them and that your priorities are different. When they come and look into my house here their eyes just light up at the sight of all the goodies. Whereas, if I go into their houses all I see is a sleeping platform, a good shirt, pair of shorts, a machete, an axe, a spear and a set of bows and arrows. A central hearth is used for cooking, warmth and light and the pigs share one end of the house. Still, it's lovely country and I'm trying to see as much of it as possible.

Later he wrote:

I am living in a Catholic Mission. My writing is a little stranger than usual because my thumb picked up some kind of exotic infection in Port Moresby. For the first week, I have been recording oral histories of the tribes living in the valley. This gives me some idea of the time depth of the various tribes and lets them know where I am and what I am doing here. Because of the rapid rate of change here, the old men are pleased that I am writing these things down for their children to learn about later on. Things happen fast and furious around here when they happen. The day before yesterday I drove a child with pneumonia to the hospital. I had barely gotten back when a woman was brought in. She had twins but only one of them had been born. Luckily, I was able to give that little problem to the Catholic priest. There is a native medical orderly here, but since no one wants to die quickly, they don't go to him.

Right now, the local councilmen are trying to avert a tribal war. A driver of a passenger truck hit another car yesterday killing several people. He ran off as soon as the truck stopped because he knew what would happen. Sure enough, all the rest of the tribes want to kill him. Failing that, they would settle for a member of his clan. Do try to reassure Mom and Dad that I won't get myself killed in the local wars here.

I am solid flea bites from my wrists to my ankles. I understand you get used to it.

By the way, I came within a hare's breath of being arrested when I got off the boat here last time. I was carrying something in my pockets that I shouldn't have been. While they were singling me out for a body search, I managed to slip it into a car which was waiting to carry me to where I was staying. The dangers of long hair. Let me tell you – I may be searched again but I will never be that close again.

Work here is proceeding fairly slowly. I'm doing a lot of running around from one place to another. And, until I dropped my camera in the river, I was doing a lot of filming. Still hope to continue the filming. Started digging again last week and it was alright until yesterday when I fired everyone. I don't really think I'm a tin god. This society needs very different measures than reasonable suggestions. I know I've tried the latter sometimes. Anyways, we're all conferring again with no hard feelings and should be starting work again.

This time we are at 7300 feet and facing east on a promontory of an eastern running ridge. During the night, the valley bottom fills to about 6000 feet with cloud and in the morning, you can watch the red sunrise above the cloud which has peaks of mountains breaking through here and there. Definitely worthwhile and since I have no mattress and sleep on the ground, I sleep so lightly that the first glow of dawn wakes me up at 5:00 AM. By 7:00, I've walked half an hour to work and already digging. So far, we haven't found anything exciting but hope to have better news before I go back to Australia this time.

Later on during a break from excavating when Ian had returned to Australia, he stayed at a country house near Melbourne. The letter he sent from there reflected a sentimental side of him that Keir had rarely seen.

I took a stab at some carpentry while here, gluing chairs and picture frames back together. I really do think that my innate talents are wasted on Archaeology. I should have followed the family tradition.

Keir chuckled a little at that. For the most part, he'd tried to suppress the mild resentment he felt about the freedom Ian had had in choosing a career. Keir was, after all, the eldest son and had dutifully taken up the family trade. It'd been expected of him. But it wasn't until one of Ian's last letters from New Guinea that Keir was truly overwhelmed with emotion. There was something about that letter – something unexpected.

Let's not let the time grow so long before we communicate again. After all, I'm the only little brother you have even if I am over-educated and unemployable. I envy the hell out of you.

Tomorrow if the weather is clear, I'm going to fly near the sites that we've dug and hang out the window taking pictures. So tonight I've sent nine men off to the bush. Tomorrow they have to make small fires all day until they hear the plane coming, then they throw leaves and moss on the fires to make smoke and hopefully these will mark the spots where we've dug before. Small rock shellies in the forest are not too easy to see amongst the trees.

Why don't you come to New Guinea? You could start your own vocational school and teach carpentry to the locals at the high schools. There will be openings for Europeans for the next five years.

Keir thought about the idea and was even mildly tempted. He'd not seen Ian for years, but was certain Grace would not be in favor of the idea. And he was dead sure that his parents and Grace's family would not be happy about the idea either. As much as he wanted to experience even a fraction of the adventure Ian was having, his reality was Grace and the children, and that was enough for him.

Ian and the young woman he'd chosen as a companion during his time 'down under' were what many referred to in the day as 'hippies.' They were back-to-the-landers and had purchased a small plot of land – a couple of acres with a creek and a small pond. They'd repaired the dilapidated cottage on the property and planted fruit trees. They were unbelievably happy. After a day in the city, they'd make the trip home in a battered old Volkswagen bus, never needing anyone except one another. By the light of the moon, they'd wander around the garden, plucking up vegetables and fruit for dinner, sometimes just eating the peas and carrots fresh out of hand in the quiet of the evening, close to one another, listening to the sounds of nature around them. And they would say to one another, "I am so happy."

With Ian turning his research in New Guinea into a thesis, he and his girlfriend drove the van forty miles into the university every day. But then one tragic morning in December, it would all change. Traveling along what was for them a very familiar road, they took a hill on a narrow stretch and were hit head-on by another vehicle traveling in the opposite direction. Ian was killed instantly and his companion injured, though not seriously.

The news for the family was unbelievable. Ian had been in the prime of his life and on the way to a very promising career. His girlfriend was beyond devastated. They'd been planning to marry once Ian had finished his studies. They'd also planned for Ian's family to come to Australia for the wedding, to see for themselves what life was like on that small rural acreage.

Keir's grief was immeasurable. He and Ian had shared so much growing up. They'd spent untold hours in the mountains, hiking, climbing, and exploring. And though Keir had told Grace he had no regrets about the life path he'd embarked upon with her and the children, she couldn't help but think Keir might have been just a little jealous of some of Ian's pursuits. And now, here it was. For all the education, adventure, and promise, Ian's life had been cut short without warning. And in such a commonplace way.

It was hard to understand.

Many evenings, Keir would sit on the end of the children's beds, listening to them breathe. He would hold Grace close to him in their bed wanting nothing more than to just be near to her. They grieved together.

Letters would arrive from Australia, letters in which Ian's girlfriend would express her own grief.

I am at my parents' house and furiously busy doing things so I don't have too much time to think. The hardest thing is not allowing happy memories to make me sad. Because it was so happy, sometimes neither of us could believe it. We'd just look at each other in amazement – and after three years, neither of us took the other for granted.

I believe that Ian is aware of me, that he is still alive in me. He has to be. Everything I do or say or dream reminds me of Ian. We used to think things at each other when he was alive and here, so why not now? I have to believe that otherwise I would wish myself dead too – and Ian would have hated that to happen. So now, I'm thinking that he would want me to go on.

I will go back to our little farm – Ian will be everywhere. But I think it's something I have to face, otherwise it will all be a dream, and I'll be running away. It wasn't a dream. It's probably the most real and perfect thing that's ever happened to me. A little bit of me has died with Ian but a lot of him is still alive in me.

I will tell you about the accident. It was really a perfect way to die – the sort of death everyone hopes for – absolutely instantaneous. It's just that I became conscious again and Ian didn't – not here anyway. And it was a lovely morning. We'd been for a walk early and came back to find there were enough strawberries ripe for breakfast. We were so happy that morning.

The longest I had ever been away from him was three days. I miss him so much, but he made me strong enough to go on without him.

Grace would read that letter and weep. She could not imagine her life without Keir.

***

Keir and his father took Ian's ashes to the mountains, to the small green lake Ian had always regarded as his own sacred place. He'd written often to Keir and Grace and expressed hope that one day he'd be able to bring his young lover to that place, to allow her to see first-hand the mountains he so loved, just as she had shown him her fascinating country.

Father and son took the short hike along the pathway through the forest of spruce and down the slope to the lake. It was late June, the season to witness the blooming of wild Lady-slipper orchids. They walked slowly, Keir's father not as robust as his son. Along the way, they searched the underbrush for signs of the hardy yellow-lipped little flowers.

Sitting on a log at the edge of the lake, they watched gray ducks bob, dive, and snap at any small particles of food the water would yield.

"Ian and I used to sit here a lot," Keir told his dad. "We talked about our life, our plans for the future. You know he was the essence of an outdoor warrior – always eager for adventure, even more so than me. And he said he always wanted to be an archaeologist – and yet – in his last letters he said he envied the life I was leading as a carpenter. Crazy, eh?"

"I know you two always shared a love of the outdoors." Keir's father hesitated for a moment and then asked, "Do you ever wish you could have done something different with your life?"

Keir turned to look at his father, a man with whom he'd not always seen eye to eye.

"I used to think I'd drawn the short straw. Being the oldest son and expected to follow you and my grandfather into the trade. But now, with Grace and the kids – I wouldn't change a thing. The business is finally taking off. We may even look for a piece of land in the country and build a new house."

"Who could ever have foreseen that Ian's life would've turned out the way it did. He worked so hard in school – and for what?"

The man's son couldn't think of a response and the two sat in silence for a few moments. Keir turned and watched as his usually dispassionate father wiped away the tear finding a pathway through the wrinkles on his cheek. He'd never before heard his father speak in such a way. Nor had he ever seen the man cry.

Keir rose, picked up the urn containing his brother's ashes, and stepped over a few twigs beside the log. He opened the urn and released the ashes over the water, careful to avoid the nibbling ducks. The ashes floated on the water's surface, then mingled with a patch of reeds.

Ian was home.

"Goodbye, Ian. What an adventure you'll be on now," whispered Keir. "I'll come and climb some new mountains with you one day."

"Goodbye, son," choked the father. "It's not right that a father has to say goodbye to his son like this. I should have been the first one to go."

Keir's father was dead within the year.

***

It was several months later that Keir received a letter from Ian's girlfriend.

You'll know that I've been wanting to write to you for a long time now. I'm very sorry I've not done so. It's not because I haven't thought of you. I'm sitting in the bush away from the house, on top of the hill and looking at the mountains – the Snowy Mountains. They are the highest in Australia, and the closest things to the Rockies. That is something I am very grateful to you for – taking Ian's ashes back to the mountains. It is just what I knew he'd want and I'm glad you knew it too. Just another thing that I have to tell you – you and Ian didn't write much so I don't know you very well from your end, but he talked about you a lot so I do know a fair bit from his end, if you can understand that. I still can't really believe that Ian isn't actually here anymore. In a sense, he's always going to be because he left so much of himself with me, if I can only use it usefully. I try to let his memory and memories of the past three years make me happy. They do very much so, but they can also make me sad if I'm not careful. I hope you are very busy at the moment because I find that doing things – especially things that are active – need concentration. So, I've tried my hand at carpentry. You, Ian, and your father, I'm sure, would be horrified, but at least I can only get better.

That letter was the last the family would receive from Australia, and Keir knew by all the correspondence they'd received that Ian had chosen well in this young woman. She'd loved him with her whole heart and soul and because of such a profound love, he also knew she would find the strength and courage to move forward with her life.

9

Grace loved being a mother, loved presenting her children to the world well-dressed, and for the most part, well-behaved. Each Sunday, Grace, Keir, and their children went to the church and enjoyed a time of worship with friends and other family members. Mid-week groups for Keir and Grace were also important as long as they didn't interfere too greatly with the children's activities.

If the family wasn't off in their camper on one of Keir's adventure tours, it was entertaining family and friends, undertaking craft projects or just enjoying quiet evenings at home. They did in fact consider themselves to be a perfectly normal, well-adjusted family.

The bottom dropped out of this 'normal' life for Grace and Keir the day their young son, Benjamin, was diagnosed with leukemia. They could not believe it – their perfect little boy, a robust child who'd barely had more than a cold during his first four years. It was a devastating blow and would spell the beginning of a long and arduous journey for the family.

The diagnosis came when after minor surgery on a small gland on the boy's neck, it was confirmed there was in fact a malignancy. The child, who'd actually not been feeling ill, was told he was sick and needed treatment.

He was hospitalized for three months during which time he did indeed become ill. It was difficult to explain that scenario to a small child. He was told he was ill and sure enough when he went to the hospital, he became sicker than he'd ever imagined.

Between the intensive chemotherapy and radiation, Ben suffered the usual results – hair loss, pain, psychological issues, and confusion. It was no easier for Keir and Grace, for they felt every injection, blood test, and lumbar puncture just as intensely as did their small child. They hovered by his bedside day and night praying earnestly for the recovery of their son. They'd never known anyone else who'd ever been faced with such an ordeal. It seemed beyond comprehension, though they did meet other families along the way that were just as anxious and perplexed as they were. Many of the couples were unable to survive the crisis, the diagnosis catalyst enough to propel an already tenuous relationship into the ditch.

During their days at Ben's bedside, they heard many tragic stories, and even though they grieved for the suffering Ben endured, they were still grateful they had tremendous family and community support. And doctors had reassured them Ben's chances were very good. He'd been placed in a low-risk category with an eighty-five percent chance of complete recovery. Of course, as Grace would say to others some months later, there is that fifteen percent. Right?

Ben's first relapse came the summer after one of Grace's brothers was married. The family had attended the wedding and a few days later reported to the hospital for Ben's routine check-up. He'd gone just twenty-two months before the relapse.

They began again. More blood tests. More intensive chemotherapy. More radiation. More hospital stays for infections and minor surgeries.

The child was amazing. Some power beyond seemed to be giving him the strength to endure what many adults could not have dealt with. Keir and Grace would never forget the courage of their little son and the way he rebounded time after time.

They would come to find the one thing that sustained Ben and the other children with whom he shared the dubious distinction of being a 'cancer kid,' was a camp designed exclusively for them. It was a salvation no one could have foreseen.

The first year when Ben was just eight years old was the worst for Keir and Grace. They'd spent the week he was away in absolute hand-wringing torture. But when camp was over and they went to pick him up, he barely acknowledged them.

"Oh hi, you're here," he'd said and then returned to playing a game of pool with a new friend.

When the camp was announced, they'd agonized over sending him, fearing at the tender age of eight he'd be overcome with homesickness, the medical staff would be unable to administer his drugs properly and he'd be unable to make friends with any of the other campers.

Whatever happened at that camp, they would never know, for Ben spoke little of his time there. It soon became blatantly obvious to parents of those 'special' children that inexplicable bonds had been forged between campers, medical staff, and counselors. In those few short days together, they'd become soul mates and would forever remain so.

And parents would also come to find that children lived long beyond their expected time of survival in order to return to camp that one last time.

With Ben's ongoing needs, Keir and Grace decided to forgo any plans for a new house in the country and decided to approach the owner of their rental home to see if he would sell it to them. When the owner agreed, it gave them the freedom to renovate and make the home more their own. It seemed a satisfactory solution at a time when there were other more pressing priorities. And working on the house gave the family something to concentrate on besides the obvious.

The home was given a complete makeover. A second story addition gave Keir and Grace a large bedroom suite with a walk-in closet and private bath featuring a sunken tub. Part of the space became an office area with display cabinets for Keir's collections of rocks and artifacts. Upstairs and down the sloped walls were clad in cedar planking, a move that gave the rooms both a warmth and feeling of homey comfort.

Keir had already observed Benjamin had inherited a talent for using his hands, though at times, he seemed better at taking things apart than putting them together. But the renovations proved to be a wonderful time for Keir and Ben to be together, the boy learning quickly the skills of his father's trade.

Ben, like his father, had a mind for detail, and though he didn't often apply that skill to his formal schooling, like Keir he found independent learning more enjoyable. His favorite reading material was the *Radio Shack* catalogue, and the boy would often hang around that store in the mall, chumming with the staff and soaking up any electronic information available. He was often the recipient of 'spare parts' from shelves behind the display area. His room was a maze of wires and gadgets. Opening the door would often set off a stereophonic chain reaction of alarms and buzzers, a warning to all who entered to respect his privacy.

Jane was not without her own needs. She was a sweet and sensitive child and hated the turmoil in the house, not only during the renovations, but just life in general. She loved her younger brother, but did exhibit all the classic signs of a child that struggled for attention in the face of a family crisis.

As every parent knows, it is absolutely impossible to divide his or her attention equally between all children in a family. It is especially difficult when there is a special-needs kid in the mix.

***

After the children had gone to bed in the evening, Keir and Grace would often sit in front of the fireplace, glass of wine in hand, and talk about their life together.

"This is not the way I thought our life would go, Ben's illness and all. It's a parent's worst nightmare. I still can't believe it's happened, even after all these months – years. It's been what nine years already? And how many relapses. Three? Four? I've lost count. It just seems to go from one crisis to another," moaned Keir.

Grace glanced at her husband. He looked tired. In fact, they were both exhausted from the years of stress.

"You're right. And yet he's taken it all in his stride, hasn't he? He was just four. He's turning thirteen next month. He'll be a teenager soon. And Jane. She's going to graduate from high school in a few months. It hardly seems possible, but when life is so busy with everything like this, time just gets away on you. I can still remember my graduation like it was yesterday. All the excitement, the dress, the date, the after-party."

"Yah. Whatever happened to what's-his-name? The guy who'd never dance with you when he took you out?"

"Rene? Oh, I heard he's on wife number three. Not a big surprise, somehow."

For Grace, the mention of Rene's name somehow brought thoughts of Lee to her mind. Keir had never asked if she'd heard from Lee over the years. She hadn't told him about her time with the young pianist in Paris, though she suspected he knew Lee had been there. Someone in the church would surely have mentioned it to Keir. Namely, someone in the 'stitch-and-bitch quilting group,' the unofficial board that always had an ear to the ground for such information.

Grace sipped at her wine and stared into the flames playing leapfrog in the cavern of the fireplace. When her mind had traveled to thoughts of Rene and Lee, she'd lost the thread of the conversation.

"I just can't understand how a beautiful innocent child has to live like this," Keir was saying. "Being poked and prodded at every clinic appointment, feeling like crap a lot of the time."

Grace, still lost in thought remained silent.

"Grace?"

She turned to look at her husband and realized how much he'd aged without her realizing it until then. The dancing flames were bringing accent to the lines forming around his eyes. She loved him so much. She loved the way he worked so hard for his family and she loved that he was so wonderful with his children. And she loved that he never mentioned Lee.

"I was just saying I can't understand why Ben and all the other kids like him have to live the way they do."

She sighed and took another sip of wine.

"I ask God about that all the time, Keir. Why? Why Ben?"

"Does God answer you?"

She continued to gaze at the man she'd pledged her love to those many years ago. Yes, the years had flown by, those twenty-plus years. Life – the good times and the bad. She and Keir had bobbed along on the current of life like two logs on a river, never knowing where it would take them next.

She sighed and said at last, "If he does, I can't hear him."

How did those years become such a blur? Grace would ask herself. It was more than just the daily grind of attending to Ben's medical needs. He'd relapsed a second and third time, and with each relapse, it was hammered home that unless there was a miracle, Ben would never reach adulthood.

And yet, he soldiered on. No one knew how. The fortitude he exhibited astounded all in his acquaintance. He rebounded repeatedly from infections, low blood counts, and just life in general.

He'd entered junior high with a full head of hair and a determined attitude. Though he'd never been much of a scholar, getting by mostly on charm and a smile, he did excel in courses such as shop and art, courses that allowed him to use his incredible dexterity.

In addition to those bonds of friendship existing between Ben and his fellow campers he did have ties to a few good friends, but really felt most comfortable with those much younger or much older than he. It was not surprising that he could relate to his elders, for he was old beyond his years.

In that junior high year, all could see Ben's spirit beginning to flag. But still, he refused to give up.

10

After more than one quarter century of faithful service to his congregation, it was time for the Rev. Lester to retire. It was the opinion of many that his best before date had long since expired and a call was finally sent out for a new spiritual leader to replace him.

Morgan McCullough, a mild-mannered man in his early fifties, came to minister to the flock at a time when the church was undergoing a great deal of upheaval politically, socially, economically, and spiritually.

At that time, the congregation was predominantly elderly folk, though there had been attempts at encouraging young families to join the fold. Conspicuously absent from the congregation were those in between, middle-aged folks desperately needed to help relieve the older group of the burden of church affairs. Not that there would've been a mighty effort on the part of the elders encouraging such a move, for though many confessed to being tired of the work on all the boards and committees, it was obvious they'd never relinquish control of the small empires created over the many years. But if the church was to survive, there had to be some changes made.

Because Rev. McCullough fell into the age group most needed in the congregation, there was much hope he could salvage what was left of the organization, encouraging a more middle-aged membership and hopefully before all was lost completely. Those old folks who so resisted change were not going to last forever.

Keir and Grace were in their forties and had already taken on as much church work as they dared, given Keir was burdened with running a business and renovating their home (a project that never seemed to find a natural end), while Grace was busy running the household, keeping the company books, and shuttling the children around to all the things they needed to attend. And of course, there was the added concern over Benjamin's medical needs. That alone consumed much of the family's time and energy.

Grace liked Rev. McCullough from the very start. His sermons were from the heart, thought-provoking and, she thought, aimed directly at her. She took great comfort from his message each week and she and Keir were able to relate to the man from an age standpoint as well.

One afternoon, Grace stopped by the church to pick up some material for a bible-study session. She'd meant to climb the stairs to the second floor office but in an eerie flash of déjà vu, heard music coming from the sanctuary.

The strains of *Air on the G String* resonated throughout the hollows of the room, filling every corner with sonorous chords and Grace's soul, with sweet memories. She hadn't felt such emotion in that place for many years. Her palms began to sweat and a lump formed in her throat. Did she dare hope? It had been so many years.

She crept to the door and peered inside. Morgan McCullough was seated at the console running his fingers across the keys, oblivious to anything else around him. The music surged through her, mesmerizing her, and she had to hold onto the doorknob to steady herself.

He stopped playing, reset the stops, and turned off the air to the organ. He piled his music together and slid off the bench.

Grace could not decide whether to approach him or not but then, he saw her standing there in the doorway. She recalled that evening with Lee so many years ago when she'd stood still and wondering in the same place, moved by the magic of the music.

"I couldn't resist," he said. "Such a fine old instrument. Far better than I've ever had the pleasure to play on before."

"You play very well," she said, trying to maintain a formality with the man. He was after all, her spiritual leader and had thought himself alone in the hallowed place of worship. "We had no idea when we hired you Rev. McCullough, that you had such talent." She took a few steps toward him. He stepped down from the choir loft.

"Morgan. Call me Morgan please. No need to be so formal."

"And I'm Grace."

"Yes, I know who you are. Someone told me you used to be the soprano soloist a few years ago. You're not in the choir anymore?"

"No. That was a lot of years ago."

"But you still sing, don't you?"

"Some. I don't have a lot of time… You know… Life."

"Do you mind?" he asked, taking a seat on the piano bench. Fortunately, the rustic old piano on which Lee had struggled to play had been replaced by a much finer instrument.

"Oh, I don't know Rev…uh Morgan. I'm pretty rusty."

"You sure?" he asked, beginning to play one of her favorite hymns.

She moved closer and debated whether to take the offer. No one had heard her voice in that sanctuary for years, not since she and Lee had performed together. And then it all came back to her. The joy of singing a hymn of praise in the church she so loved. She began:

"Lord of all hopefulness, Lord of all joy,
Whose trust ever childlike no cares could destroy:
Be there at our wakening, and give us we pray,
Your bliss in our hearts, Lord, at the break of the day.
Lord of all eagerness, Lord of all faith,
Whose strong hands were skilled at the plane and the lathe,
Be there at our labors, and give us we pray,
Your strength in our hearts, Lord, at the noon of the day."

That verse always reminded her of Keir and the small shop he'd set up in the garage behind their home. He always seemed happy whenever he returned from working out there.

Morgan stopped playing and laid his hands on the ledge above the piano keys. "If that's rusty, I'd like to hear you at your best."

She blushed at his words.

He turned on the bench to face her.

"Why aren't you in the choir? Goodness knows they could use you." He gave her a grin that betrayed a slight embarrassment.

"You're going to think I'm awful. I could say I'm too busy with home and hearth, but we are in the house of God and I dare not...lie." She couldn't tell whether he knew what she meant.

"The truth is, well, I don't think I can match skills with the organist." Was that polite enough?

"Unfortunately, I know what you mean. She's a dear old thing and I would never want to upset her with any kind of criticism...but..."

They both burst out laughing.

"I'm sorry, Morgan," she began. "It's just that I sat in this church for so many years listening to the music coming from this magnificent old organ and now..." She gestured. "Well, there were times many years ago when the music was amazing. Exceptional. Frankly, until I heard you play today, I never thought I'd ever experience that again."

He chuckled and spoke modestly, "Thanks, I do love to play. But I doubt what I can produce is in any way exceptional. And of course, my first calling is the ministry. But you…you need to use your talent too, Grace. It's God-given." He sat for a moment looking at her.

She returned his gaze and studied him for a moment. He was a pleasant looking man, gray hair receding from his brow, and he had an endearing smile.

"This may sound a bit forward, and it may even be totally the wrong thing to do, but…if I played for you once in a while would you consider doing a little solo work? I can try to broach it some way with the organist and choir."

"I can't…Morgan. Those early days…the memories, well, I don't think you need to hear any of this."

"No?" He gave her a look she took as encouragement.

"All those many years ago," she stuttered. "So many years. It was all different then. The young organist at the time and I…we…there was…"

"That was Lee, wasn't it?"

"Yes, it was. How did you know?"

"I've already heard the gossip, Grace. There're no secrets in such a small congregation."

Grace rolled her eyes and knew exactly what he meant.

"Then you know he and I were… Well, it was before Keir."

"Grace. I'm not trying to make you uncomfortable, but your voice. It should be shared. You have a gift."

"Do I have to decide right now?"

"No, of course not. Why don't we just get together every so often, just to practice? Just you and me. No commitment. Would that be okay?"

"I-I suppose."

"Okay. Let's do that. Maybe we could get a few others together for a talent night, or something. Get this place moving."

Grace listened for a voice in her head, the one urging a second sober thought. Not that she always heeded the warning. She took a moment but heard nothing.

"Sounds good," she said at last and turned to leave.

"No pressure," he said.

"No pressure."

And that's how it began.

Grace knew Keir was not entirely happy with her decision to spend the occasional evening with Morgan, hoping he knew there'd never be anything except a mutual love of music between the two of them.

But Keir was still reminded of her history with Lee each time she left the house to practice. It was a part of Grace's life he'd never be able to share. And, of course, he heard the gossip as well. Those old folk, who couldn't even remember why they'd entered a room half the time, had sterling memories of the days when Grace and Lee were 'an item.' Even though at the time Grace had thought she and Lee had been completely discrete about their activities beyond the choir loft, she'd seriously underestimated the fact that everyone has a least a modicum of imagination. And the fact she and Morgan were now spending time together created a whole new opportunity for busybodies with too much time on their hands, to fantasize.

But it *was* just the music. And it gave Grace such a wonderful renewal after years of struggling with Benjamin's health issues. It was something that she could do for herself.

Eventually, she was persuaded to return to the choir loft a few times and on one occasion, she and her young son even performed a duet. No one knew until that time Ben had also been blessed with a beautiful, clear singing voice.

Predictably, Morgan took an overwhelming interest in Benjamin and his health problems. It was not surprising, for all who knew the lad could not help but love him. He had a charm about him that was inexplicable and in spite of his ill health seldom complained, remarkably able to roll with the punches.

Ben and Morgan would often sit and discuss life. They seemed to be on the same wavelength. Though Grace and Keir never asked Ben what the two talked about, they did notice Ben seemed much more at peace after spending time with Morgan. It cheered them that the two became close in a very short time.

* * *

In late summer of Benjamin's fourteenth year, he returned to camp much against his doctor's wishes. His health had deteriorated considerably despite all medical intervention. Doctors feared if he was allowed to attend the camp, he could possibly die there – a situation that would've been devastating for both campers and staff, to say nothing of his family.

"I want to go with him," declared Jane, who'd made plans to enter nursing school in the fall.

"I don't know if that's enough, Jane. They don't want him there at all."

"I was a counselor last year. I know the ropes."

Grace looked at her lovely daughter. Gone was the freckle-faced tomboy she'd seen just a few months earlier. Jane had blossomed into a stunning young woman with long wavy hair that had settled into a tawny color. She'd inherited Keir's height and his dark blue eyes.

Ben had begged to go to camp, as everyone knew he would, but there'd been much debate on the subject. The family knew he wouldn't be talked out of it but they more than shared the doctor's apprehension. In the end, the camp staff relented, though still seriously concerned the boy would need constant monitoring.

The moment that Jane and Ben boarded the bus for the camp, Grace broke down completely.

"What if he never comes home, Keir," she sobbed, not caring who else was around to see her display of tears.

Keir put his arm around her and led her back to the car.

"He'll come home. You know he will. He's Ben."

In addition to the regular camp activities enjoyed by all the campers, Ben endured regular blood tests and some transfusions. At the end of the first week, his condition had improved to the point where he was allowed to stay for a second week. He and Jane spent the weekend away from camp hanging out with other friends and a couple of staff members. They were able to have a 'normal' weekend, free of all the blood tests and medical intervention he'd had to endure the previous week.

The second week of camp was by far the best Ben had ever enjoyed even though he knew it'd probably be his last. It'd not escaped him that everyone was hovering over him most of the time, and he'd been in treatment long enough to know he was running out of options.

The last day of camp was always the most emotional for campers and staff, mainly because everyone hated leaving all the friends with whom they had shared so much. But in addition, there was one camp tradition called 'pass the stick.' It was a time of remembrance, campers sitting around a campfire, passing a stick from one to another, and reflecting on the experiences shared over the past few days. It was also a time to remember all those who hadn't been able to return to camp. Jane was late getting down to the campfire that last day, and as she approached, she encountered Ben heading back to the lodge. She turned and followed him and they sat for a time in silence on the back step. She waited for him to speak, though she was already certain of what he would say. She'd dreaded the moment.

"I don't want to be the one who they're remembering next year," he said at last.

Tears welled in Jane's eyes and she reached out to take Ben's trembling hand.

"Don't worry, Ben. You'll be coming back next year," she choked. And she hoped she could be right. His courage and determination had allowed him to spring back time after time, skirting one crisis after another over the years.

"You know that I won't be back next year. I know that. Mom and Dad know that. Everybody here knows that."

"Geez, Ben. It's just not fair. You. All these other kids," she gestured to the wind.

"Well, at least I'll know a few other guys when I get to heaven."

That remark was enough to make Jane lose it completely. She pulled a tissue from her jacket pocket and sobbed into it. Regaining her composure at last she said, "You're a pretty neat kid, Ben. You know that? One of a kind in fact. The world would sure be a much better place if you'd stick around."

Ben smiled at his sister. He knew how hard things had been for her – her needs always coming second to his.

"I'm going to miss you, Jane."

"I'm going to miss you too, Ben."

She squeezed his hand, and he put his head on her shoulder.

"Do you want to go down to the fire?"

"No, let's just stay here together. Just the two of us. Together."

They sat like that for a time, studying the clusters of stars overhead and listening to the chirp of crickets in the fields.

***

Jane and Ben returned from camp that year renewed and thankful for the time they'd shared. Although Ben had rallied somewhat, there was little hope of his recovery. Doctors admitted it was just a question of time. It was amazing to see how the lad refused to give up. He made it to school most days to the astonishment and admiration of all his teachers. They could not help but compare his amazing grit to that of some of the other students seen shuffling from class to class, barely putting in any effort at all.

Keir and Grace had taken to sleeping in Ben's room, alternating nights so as to keep an eye on him. Most nights he slept through the pain, but it finally became obvious he needed more relief than they could give him at home. They bundled him into his apple green afghan and placed him in the back seat of their car, cringing each time he moaned.

Staff at the hospital knew him well after all the times he'd been there. And he knew them all as well, trusting them to care for him with the compassion they'd always shown him. And the intravenous morphine gave him the comfort he needed.

Ben never lost his sense of humor, joking with nurses and others who came to sit with him those last few days. And there were many who came. Keir and Grace stayed almost around the clock though Jane's time was not as flexible since she'd begun her nursing studies.

Morgan came to the ward daily. He sat with Ben, sometimes for several hours at a time, praying with him, still holding out hope the boy would rally. At times, Morgan seemed tortured and once or twice when he was unaware of her presence, Grace noticed him weeping, his head cupped in his hands.

When the boy slipped into a coma, Morgan was there and he knew there was no further hope. His prayers had not been answered.

"Go to the light, lad," he whispered then. "Go into the light."

***

They moved dreamlike down the hall, the four of them – Ben's parents, his sister, and Morgan. They'd sat at the bedside in Ben's room after his death, Morgan offering one last prayer. They'd gathered up the boy's few things – cards, pictures, his Game Boy – and packed them in those horrid white plastic hospital bags with the drawstrings and glaring blue logos.

They moved towards the parking garage in silence, for what was there to say. Ben was gone. He would leave behind all the pain he'd endured during his short fourteen years, but now the pain had transferred ten-fold to all those he'd left behind.

Grace had never been fully able to wrap her head around the process of treating children like Ben. On one hand, she knew that with treatment, many children did survive and go on to live perfectly healthy lives. But for the others – the years of falling back into a pit with every relapse – grasping the hand holds on the walls of the pit, climbing up almost to the top and then losing the grip and plummeting downward again. Did it seem right to keep putting a kid through that time after time? And yet what was the alternative? As much as she grieved the loss of her son, she was grateful that he'd never have to repeat the cycle ever again. He'd fought the good fight and lived more in his fourteen years than most people might expect to live in the optimum three-score and ten. He'd taken advantage of every day he'd been allowed and was never afraid to ask for one more. He'd loved life and he'd loved all those around him. He'd inherited the adventurous spirit of his father and now for him, there were untold adventures yet to come.

No one will ever know how Morgan McCullough made it through the funeral service without breaking down. The church was packed with friends, relatives, medical staff, workmates, and families of other young cancer patients. One of his teachers gave a most touching eulogy, speaking of the time Ben refused to give up on a class trip to the mountains. He'd made it to the top of the mountain, surpassing the efforts of more able students who quit before they reached the top. He said he would never forget the look on the boy's face as he stood on the mountaintop and looked down at the rocky path he'd climbed, that arduous trip a metaphor for Ben's life. The teacher's voice broke a few times as he praised the courage of the young lad, but he was also able to inject a little humor as well, talking about all the times Ben had asked the teacher to stay a while longer so he could work on an art project. "Just five more minutes. Just five more minutes," he would say. Grace imagined Ben had made the same request of the Almighty when he'd been summoned home.

After the service, Keir and Grace followed the powder-blue casket holding their son, through the sanctuary and down the stairs to the street where it was placed in a waiting hearse. The hearse moved slowly away, followed the short street in front of the building, and joined the traffic on the main roadway, eventually disappearing from sight. They stood there, quivering with both the coolness of the day and the unbearable sorrow. Benjamin was gone before he'd barely had time to scratch the surface of life. The lad's needs had consumed the lives of his family. There would be no more clinic appointments, no more long days watching the toxic mix of chemotherapy drip into Ben's frail body and no more all night vigils in the ER.

Though neither spoke a word, both Keir and Grace were struck with the same thought. *What do we do now?*

11

Packing up some of Ben's less personal things took care of a few days for the family. A few more days were filled with the busyness of answering the many cards and letters they received, and another week was devoted to boxing up and storing some of the treasures and keepsakes the family knew they could never part with. There were frequent visitors who came with the offer of help and support. It was all part of the civilized ritual of dealing with the dead.

Keir spent a lot of time in his shop when he wasn't at work. In fact, he couldn't stop working. It was his way of dealing with the pain. He took on many contracts building and repairing furniture, and when he was not doing that he found busy work sorting screws or putting his tools in order. He began to complain of migraines, a condition Grace attributed to overwork and the fact Keir found it difficult to sleep at night.

Grace redecorated Ben's room right away. She was aware many parents left their kids rooms just as they were, as if they'd gone away on vacation and would soon pop in the door to resume life at home. But though she couldn't fault those parents for the manner in which they grieved, their kids were not coming back and all the fluffing of pillows, rearranging of stuffed animals and aligning of clothes in the closet, was ever going to change the fact.

She painted the walls of his room a pale peach, sewed up frothy lace curtains and bedding and piled a mountain of white and peach-colored pillows on the window seat, Laura Ashley style. She kept one of Ben's treasures, a ragged little blue bunny that he'd taken with him every time he was hospitalized. She'd patched and darned holes in the toy so many times she'd lost count. But with the redecorating, Blue Bunny now had the room and the bed all to himself. He sat alone and forlorn, nestled against the peach-plaid pillow shams.

It was hard for the family to have any conversation that didn't start with "remember the day that Ben…"

Jane continued with her studies and wasn't home much of the time. If she wasn't in class, she was engaged in patient care and took her studies very seriously.

She looked forward to graduating and perhaps going to work in Africa. *At least,* thought Grace, *she has a better plan than I did.* And Grace's father was happy to see Jane pursuing a career in nursing, something he'd wished Grace had done.

But Grace was about to receive another blow, one that took her completely off guard. She and Morgan had discontinued their musical times together when Ben's health had begun to deteriorate rapidly and they'd never resumed the practice. Not that Grace felt like singing in any case.

As she was leaving the church one Sunday morning, Morgan approached her and asked, "Have you got a moment, Grace? I need to talk to you about something."

"I can't do any singing right now, Morgan. I'm sure you understand."

"No Grace. It's not that. Can you come up to the office?"

"Sure," she said, a look of puzzlement crossing her face. "Just let me tell Keir." She turned away to look for her husband.

"Bring him too, Grace. That's all right."

"We'll be up in a minute then."

That's mysterious, she thought and retraced her steps to where she had last seen Keir. She found him deep in conversation with one of the board members. She waited patiently for a couple of minutes, tapped Keir on the shoulder, and nodded in the direction of Morgan's office. Keir looked relieved at the intervention.

Morgan's door was ajar when the couple approached and they tapped gently.

"Come in and close the door if you will," said Morgan. He was seated at his desk and indicated they should sit in the chairs opposite.

Grace sat and looked at the picture mounted on the wall behind Morgan. It was a drawing depicting the young Jesus in his father's carpentry shop, a picture that Ben had done for the minister a few months before. Morgan had had it framed professionally.

"I wanted to tell you two before I spoke to anyone else."

"Tell *us*?" Keir said.

"Yes," Morgan replied, holding up a sealed envelope. "I'll be leaving in a couple of months. This is my letter of resignation to the Board Chairman."

"You're leaving?" Grace gasped. "But why? I don't understand. You've already done so much for the congregation here."

Keir remained silent.

"There're a lot of reasons, some of them...personal." He avoided looking at Grace. "And at the moment, I don't like the direction the organized church is going. And there seems to be so much political upheaval right here in this little congregation. All the boards and committees are at odds with one another. It's been a very difficult time for us all."

"I can't disagree," ventured Keir, "but why don't you stay and help put some of it right? Everyone in the congregation loves you. What you've done for us so far is beginning to bear fruit."

"That's kind of you to say, Keir, but I may take a leave from the church altogether. I haven't quite figured it all out yet. But I do know I must leave."

"Oh, Morgan. This is awful. I had no idea. You've been such a good friend to our family – with Ben and all. We could never have gotten through the ordeal without you."

Morgan shifted slightly in his chair and was silent for a moment reflecting on her words. At last, he said, "I'm so sorry, but my mind is made up. I apologize for leaving everyone in the lurch after being here for such a short time."

"I don't know what to say," Keir managed. "I wish you…good luck with whatever you go on to do."

"Thanks, Keir. I'm going to miss everyone here, especially you two. I will remember you both as…'soul-mates.'"

At his words, Grace's eyes began to tear and she choked, "We certainly feel that way about you too, don't we, Keir?" She glanced at her husband who was absently straightening his tie. "It won't be the same here without you. You're sure you won't reconsider?"

"It must be this way. I believe the overall plan has a Divine purpose. I am so very grateful for the time I've been able to spend here at the church and with you and your family." He glanced over his shoulder at the picture the boy had crafted. "Ben was a very special young man. And he taught us all so much." He looked at Keir. "And he was also the son of a carpenter."

Keir was taken aback by that remark. He wondered if that was why Ben had chosen that particular subject for his artwork. Even with Ben's fragile health, he'd tried to spend time with the lad working on small building projects, just as he'd learned at his own father's knee. "Of course we always thought he was special as well, Morgan," he remarked, finally regaining his composure. And then he added, "But you know it means the world to us to have you say so. I don't know what we're going to do without him."

Silence fell in the room, and at last, Grace and Keir rose from their seats and looked at the man who'd come to mean so much. Morgan had come into their lives at just the right moment it seemed, helping and sustaining them during the blackest days that any family could endure. By God's hand he'd come to them and they'd be forever in his debt.

With nothing more to be said, Grace and Keir reached across the desk and shook hands with their friend.

"Grace and I do wish you all the very best," said Keir.

"Thank you. May the presence of the Christ Whose Name is Love – be with you now and always."

"And with you as well, Morgan," whispered Grace.

***

"What do you suppose that was all about today? With Morgan, I mean?" Grace asked her husband later as they sat down for dinner.

Keir looked at her as if to say, "Don't you know?"

She knew that look and fully expected him to say, *"You know. You and Morgan. The music. All the practice sessions. The wagging tongues."*

But she was surprised when Keir said, "It was Ben."

"Ben? How could this all be about Ben?"

"Morgan couldn't save him, Grace. I've never heard anyone pray as earnestly for a child's recovery as he did. And yet, Ben died anyway. If Morgan, a man of the cloth, the most devoted Christian man I've ever come to know couldn't persuade God to save him, then who could?"

Grace stared at the man seated across from her. He was running his finger back and forth along the edge of a pale blue placemat, waiting for her reaction to his comments.

"Is that what you really think?"

"I know it. I can hear it every time I listen to one of his sermons. I've watched his body language these past few weeks. His faith is beginning to flounder."

"But, Keir, that's ridiculous."

"Is it? Is it really?"

She pondered his words.

"But surely," she began, "there must have been others he prayed for in the past that didn't pull through."

"You heard him, Ben was special."

"Well, I know that. You know that. I just find it so incredible that someone who knew Ben for such a short time could feel so intensely about him. And to the extent that he's now willing to make a complete about-face in his ministry."

"Well, he did say there were other factors. Maybe Ben's death was just the tipping point for him."

"Do you really think so?" Grace rose from her chair and went to look out the window at the yard. Winter had descended upon the garden. The snow, pure and silent was covering every sign of life. It was as if nature was working in concert with every other loss in their lives. She turned at last and faced her husband.

"Well, all I can say is the church is never going to be the same without him. He tried so hard to get things sorted out there. And the music. Oh, Keir, the music. Morgan's the one who brings a sense of joy and life into the musical aspect of worship. Sometimes I just want to scream when old Florence fumbles through the hymns. I can't even bring myself to sing along with them."

Keir tried hard not to think about Grace's attachment to Morgan over the past few months, and the spirit of music they shared, something she chose not to share with him. And when thoughts of Lee suddenly flashed through his mind, it surprised him. He pushed the thoughts away quickly. *Why had that happened?* He hadn't given a thought to Lee in years.

"Hmm. Yes, the music," he mumbled.

"Well, at least we still have Morgan for a couple of months yet. I guess we should just enjoy things while we can. But I sure don't envy the committee that has to replace him. Those meetings will be nothing short of a three-ring-circus." For the first time that day, Grace gave a little chuckle.

"Boy, I'll say," he agreed.

***

Grace, Keir, and Jane waited until spring to take Ben's ashes to the mountains. They'd wanted Morgan to be with them, but he'd left the church a few weeks earlier. The skies were a stone gray and a gloom hung over the green lake where just a few years earlier Keir's brother, Ian, had begun his journey home. The family sat on the fallen log beside the water and listened to the slap, slap of the easy current against the rocky shore.

"Ian and I loved this place," said Keir. "We could hardly wait to come to the mountains every spring to climb and explore. This is the first time I've been up here in a while. I used to come up at least a couple of times a year."

"You should start coming again, Keir," Grace said softly. "The mountains are so peaceful and they don't ask for anything. They're just spread out here waiting for you to come to be refreshed and renewed."

"I sure wish I still had my side-kick to bring along though." He wiped away a small tear that'd formed.

"He'll be here waiting for you, dear."

"Shall I do this for you, Dad?" Jane asked taking the urn Keir was clutching.

"Thank you, Jane," he replied, surrendering the ceramic container to his daughter.

There were no ducks that day as Jane set the ashes afloat. A gentle rain began to fall, washing over the ashes like tears from heaven. A silent eulogy.

Jane returned to the log and sat for a few quiet moments of reflection while Keir and Grace went to stand at the shore.

"When Dad and I came up here with Ian a few years ago, I never thought I'd be standing here saying goodbye to my own son one day. You know what my dad said then?"

Grace slipped her hand into Keir's. "What did he say?"

"He said, 'It's not right that a father has to say goodbye to his son like this, that he should have been the first to go.'"

"I'm so sorry, Keir. This must be so very painful for you. Losing first your brother, then your father, and now your son."

"I'm the last of the line, Grace," he said. "Ian didn't have any children. I'm the last of the male line."

Grace could never understand why that was so important to men, but she dared not start down that road with Keir at the moment. She circled her arms around her husband and they stood for a time, welcoming the rain as it fell and blended with their tears.

"I love you, Keir," she whispered.

"I love you too, Grace. I love you so much."

They broke from their embrace and as they turned to retrace their steps through the forest, Grace's mind projected a strange image, an image from years past, the image of a country graveyard and the sight of stones marking the final resting place of infants and children. She'd been so young but had felt an overwhelming sympathy for the parents of those small souls. And at the time, she would never have imagined that one day she'd be saying goodbye to her own child in a similar manner. The remembrance of it all and the way she'd felt on that bright June morning brought renewed tears to Grace and she slipped her arm through that of her husband. As they walked slowly back along the path, she allowed the tears to flow unabated.

12

Grace and Keir returned to the church a few times but eventually stopped going for good. The situation within the ranks had not improved with Morgan's departure and a permanent minister hadn't been found. A series of interim pastors came and went – a situation merely adding to the upheaval. That was all bad enough but Grace and Keir were also angry with God.

Initially after Ben's death, the couple had sought comfort in one another's arms at night, but restful sleep was impossible for them, often causing one or the other to leave the bed before morning. It took considerable time for the couple to settle into a new pattern of life.

Grace finally took a job keeping books for a small business in town and found that was enough to take her mind off things during the day at least. But evenings when Keir worked late were another matter altogether. She wandered the house pulling out boxes of old clothing for disposal. She read book after book, often without retaining any of the material and kept the television blaring whenever she was in the house. *How did other parents handle it?* she wondered. It was probably easier if they had other children to care for. Jane came and went as her studies dictated and when it was time for her to graduate from nursing school, Grace rejoiced. At last a happy occasion to celebrate.

Jane and her fellow nursing students celebrated officially with diplomas, banquets, and all the attendant ceremony, but the following weekend, Grace and Keir hosted a party in their home. Grandparents, aunts, uncles, cousins, and friends attended to congratulate the young nurse.

Grace had spared no expense decorating, hanging silver streamers, and placing small round tables topped with snowy white and silver tablecloths, around the main rooms. Silver candles, alight in crystal containers, sprayed flashes of light against the facets of the glass. There were armloads of flowers in a kaleidoscope of colors and a caterer provided a five-course dinner for guests. Keir had thought the whole thing rather over the top, but since Jane had expressed a desire to leave the country soon, he gave Grace the latitude to throw such a grand affair. However, he wasn't sure how they could top it when Jane got married.

"Good career choice, Jane," crooned her grandfather." I always thought your mom should have gone that route."

"So she told me, more than a few times, Grandpa," Jane laughed. "But I think she got in enough nursing time having to look after Ben all those years."

"Never really looked at it that way," her grandfather mused. "You're probably right. What do you figure you're going to do now?"

"I've applied to go overseas with a couple of humanitarian organizations. I hope they'll take me. I want to go to Africa, but it could be anywhere I'm needed, really."

"Very adventurous of you. Stands to reason, you have a couple of adventurous parents. I remember when your mom went off to Paris after she finished university. And your dad went running after her a few weeks later. Couldn't wait to get her home to marry her. Ah, young love." He looked over to where Keir and Grace were talking to Keir's mother.

"That's not going to happen to me," Jane said. "There's no one in my life right now. I just want to get out in the world and try to make it a better place."

"Very noble of you, dear. I'm sure you'll do just fine."

"Thanks, Grandpa. Oh, excuse me. There's a couple of my friends just arriving. Talk to you later."

And she skipped across the room to greet two of her fellow graduates.

***

Jane was overjoyed when she was informed she'd indeed be off to Africa, Kenya in fact. Just as Grace had read everything she could before she went to Paris, so did Jane as she prepared for her resettlement. Before she left, she had to endure what seemed like a hundred immunizations and attended a few seminars to acquaint her with the practical aspects of her posting.

It was torture for Grace and Keir to see her off that September day. The nest was now completely empty and they were back where they'd started so many years before. Just the two of them. But now they were rattling around in a big house, half of which they never used.

"Do you think it's time to downsize, Grace?" asked Keir one evening.

"Sell the house? Oh, Keir, no. I don't want to do that. This has always been our home."

"Just a thought. We could get an apartment and do a little traveling. See a bit of the world. Go over to Africa and see how Jane's getting along."

"You think? We don't have to sell the house to do that. I don't…all our memories are here, Keir. Jane. And Ben."

"It's okay, Grace. It was just a suggestion. There's a lot of upkeep here, but if you're happy staying put…"

"I am, for now. As long as we're both healthy and can handle this big house and yard. We're handy to everything here. I can walk almost everywhere I need to go and the neighbors are great – well except for that lot across the street – the frat boys. They can move any time."

"Yeah, one more 3:00 AM yelling session and I will call the cops."

"I'm surprised someone hasn't done it before now."

"Me too. So…I guess we'll stay put, for now then?"

"For now."

'For now' turned into three years, as shortly after that conversation, it was determined Keir's mom could no longer live in her own home and needed constant care. Grace quit her job, packed up all her daughter's things, and moved Mom into the room Jane had vacated.

The woman tried to be pleasant enough though was persistent in her demands couched as questions. She kept apologizing for putting Keir and Grace out but had a market list of needs as long as her arm.

The linens were not quite right. What was the thread count? Were they really Egyptian cotton? The towels seemed to scratch when she used them. Was Grace using enough Fleecy in the rinse cycle?

She liked the meals that Grace prepared, but the doctor had recommended less salt, or was it less sugar? She couldn't remember.

Could she have another blanket? There seemed to be an awful draft in the room. Oh, it was a lovely room, though the décor was not quite to her taste, but she could probably live with it. When was the last time the drapes were cleaned?

It was so nice of Keir and Grace to take her out for a ride to the mountains, but you know, it was such a long trip and her legs were aching so badly by the time she got back home. Would she be able to make it up the stairs?

She was so grateful to have the small television set in her room, but her shows were much more enjoyable when she watched them on the larger screened TV in the living room. Would it be possible to get a different set for her room?

Grace wanted to go back to work. At least there she'd have people to talk to who didn't repeat the same conversation every ten minutes. But she held her peace.

And Keir, to his credit, would often praise her unfailing patience in dealing with the old duck.

"I take my hat off to you, Grace. I don't know how you do it," said Keir one afternoon as they stood in the kitchen preparing dinner.

"Yes, you do. This is where I get my patience." She reached for a bottle of wine and removed the cork. "And to think there was a time when a sip of wine would put me out of the picture almost immediately," she added. The wine was an inexpensive blend they jokingly referred to as the 'house white.' She poured two glasses and handed one to Keir, tapped his glass with hers and said, "Here's to endurance."

"Apparently, wine's good for the heart," he said and took a long sip.

"But murder on the liver, they say. So…here's to our hearts but not our livers." She raised her glass again and then matched his long sip.

Keir laughed, put his glass on the counter, and took her in his arms. "You are one funny broad," he said. "How I did I ever get stuck with you?"

"Well, you wouldn't take no for an answer, remember? You chased me till I caught you."

"I do remember," he said smiling at her. "Do you ever regret it, Grace? I know the last thing you were expecting back then was someone like me to ride in on a white horse, or in my case, an old broken-down black Ford… Well, after you and…Lee."

That'd been the first time in their marriage Keir had ever mentioned Lee.

She broke from his embrace and went to sit on the sofa in front of the fireplace.

"That was so long ago, Keir. I really haven't thought about Lee in years."

He sat down beside her.

"I know you saw him in Paris."

Grace felt a flutter in the pit of her stomach. "You knew…and never said anything all this time?" she stammered. She couldn't look at him.

"What was I supposed to say, Grace? I couldn't come right and ask you if anything happened between the two of you then. I know how hung up on him you were before we met. You never mentioned seeing him, so I just let it ride."

"Oh, Keir. We met by accident just after he arrived. He was just sitting there at an outdoor café drinking a cup of coffee. Isn't that just so cliché? Running into someone at an outdoor café in Paris – in April?" She laughed nervously. "He was there to study with some musical icon – a very great honor, I understand. I think he was just as surprised as I was that we met the way we did."

"You didn't know he was going to be in Paris?"

"No. I had no idea. It was all over between us. How would I have known? I even contemplated turning away when I saw him sitting there but he looked up and saw me before I could move."

"So…did you see much of him? You two were there together for months after I left."

"Keir. Do you really want to get into it? After all this time?"

"Only if you want to tell me, Grace."

She reached out, put her glass of wine on a side-table, and took a deep breath. She looked around the room. She and Keir had decorated it together in tones of ochres and orange to complement the cedar walls. It'd always been their favorite room in the house.

"He came over for dinner a couple of times. I went to meet his teacher – the maestro. He was a funny old thing – like an old eccentric elf with a thatch of white hair. He lived in this incredible apartment. It was like a museum – all paper and funny little tables. And the dust on everything was unbelievable."

How long could she drag this out before Keir could see she was trying to avoid the rest of the story?

He looked at her. Grace was still an attractive woman after more than twenty-five years of marriage. She never let the gray show in her hair.

She returned his gaze.

"Nothing happened between us, Keir. One night, I realized that as much as I was happy to have someone from home to spend time with…I…I…we… There was nothing left between us. I told him we shouldn't see each other anymore. It wasn't right."

Grace had seriously glossed over the real story but she was never going to tell Keir that she'd come within a hare's breath of sleeping with Lee that last night they were together in Paris. The night he came to the loft with dinner from a nearby bistro. The night she drank more wine than she should have. The night she found herself in Lee's arms on the bed, she'd shared with Keir only weeks before. The night she'd offered no resistance when Lee kissed her and stroked her breast. And if the moonlight hadn't bounced off the diamond in her engagement ring reminding her of her commitment to Keir, things may have turned out differently for all of them. What would her life have been like if she hadn't married Keir? Not had Jane. Not had Benjamin?

"Then…that was it?"

"Yes," she said with more emphasis than she'd intended. "There's no more to tell. That's really the last time I saw him."

"I didn't mean it to sound like an inquisition, Grace. I won't mention it again." He could see how uncomfortable she was with the conversation. And even though he knew there was probably more to the story than Grace was admitting, he also knew when to leave things alone.

"It's okay. Really. It was so long ago," Grace said. "And I've never regretted marrying you if that's what you think. Despite all we've been through the past few years…and it has been pretty rocky at times…we've had a good life together, haven't we? Our marriage didn't crater when Ben got sick the way we saw things happen to a lot of other couples. That has to say something, doesn't it?"

Keir didn't get a chance to answer for there was a loud call from upstairs.

"Keir. Keir, can you come and help me. Something's wrong with the TV."

"Better get on that dear. Mom probably pushed the wrong button on the remote control again," urged Grace.

He chuckled a little at the not-so-subtle way his mother commanded attention and rose to see to her needs. He was the good son. After Ian's death, the only one. He and Grace had been left to care for not only his parents, but hers as well. Fortunately, Grace's parents were still in good health and had been able to remain in their own home.

"Just a sec, Mom," he called. "Be right there."

Grace rose and poured herself another glass of wine.

***

She knew she'd lied to her husband that afternoon, not only once, but twice. Well the first time it'd been a lie of omission when she neglected to fully disclose what'd happened the last time she saw Lee in Paris. She wanted the memory of that night to remain forever buried. And as for the second lie, she felt she was merely stretching the truth a little. She had seen Lee a few years back, when he'd come home from his studies abroad. He hadn't seen her.

It was on the occasion of his father's funeral. Grace had merely gone to pay her respects to a man who'd always been kind and gracious to her. And she made sure Lee didn't know she was there. She'd taken a place at the rear of the church well out of sight of the family of mourners and planned to be well away before the reception began so Lee would never know. It had been a traditional service in the church Lee's family attended regularly and after the eulogy it was announced Lee would play a special piano selection in memory of his father – a piece that'd been one of the man's favorites. She'd watched as Lee moved slowly to the piano and taken a seat. She remembered tapping nervously on the edge of the hymn book in her lap and taking note of how tired Lee seemed to look. He'd been very fond of his father, she knew.

As soon as Grace heard the opening chords, she'd lurched in her seat, the hymn book on her lap nearly sliding off onto the floor. Grabbing it just in time and grasping it firmly, she'd glanced around to see if others had witnessed her unusual reaction. The music had stirred a profound memory in her soul. The haunting melody of *Paganini's Somewhere in Time* had echoed throughout the sanctuary and drawn her back to the night she'd first met Lee. She'd recalled standing mesmerized in the doorway, thinking she should leave but captivated by the music filling the night. How had it become his signature piece? In that moment at the funeral, listening to those few familiar notes, the years fell away. Hearing the haunting melody Paganini had written and Rachmaninov had drawn upon when composing his Rhapsody, had been surreal. Of all the pieces Lee could have chosen from the list of his father's favorites, did it have to be that one? Her hands had begun to sweat leaving telltale smudges on the navy blue hymnal. She'd closed her eyes, trying to quell the tears that threatened, though she knew those around her would assume she was just mourning the loss of a fine gentleman.

At the end of the service when the family retreated from the church behind the casket and the other mourners had begun to leave, Grace held back until she saw that Lee was preoccupied with those in the reception line, then slipped quietly out the side door of the church. The music was still resonating in her head, music soon replaced by something she hadn't heard much of late. It'd taken a few moments for it to come to the surface, but there it was, too clear to ignore. It caused her to stop dead in her tracks.

No more, said a voice in her head. *This is the last time.*

13

A few months later, a stroke felled Keir's mother and after a mercifully short time in hospital, she passed away. The funeral was held in her home church, the service well attended by her friends and fellow churchgoers. She was laid to rest in the plot with Keir's father, for there was to be no trip to the mountain lake for either of them. Once again, Keir and Grace were alone in their big house.

"Let's take that trip to Africa," Grace said one day. "Jane's written we should come and see her. She's only been home once since she went away. I miss her so much. We should go and see firsthand all the things she talks about in her letters."

"Yah, we should do that. It's time we had a new adventure of our own."

"I was hoping you'd say that. I've already called Penny at the travel agency and she's looking into a few things. Maybe we can even go on a safari."

"A safari? That is adventurous of you."

"Well, we can hardly go to Africa and not go on safari. We can imagine that we're Denys Finch-Hatton and Baroness von Blixen."

"Imagine we're who?"

"You know. Karen and Denys. Out of Africa. Theirs was the most romantic and compelling African love story of all time."

"Oh, them," replied Keir who was feigning ignorance. He knew fully well Grace was recalling her favorite movie.

"Remember?" she continued, "Denys was killed tragically when his plane crashed. He's buried on the crest of a hill in Kenya and the lions come to visit him there. You know."

"Yes, it's coming back to me now," he said with a grin.

"Oh – and remember the day they took the gramophone out to the meadow where the baboons were and Denys said, 'Think of it: never a man-made sound...and then Mozart!' I still get goosebumps every time I think of that line. He seemed to have such reverence for the music."

That Grace had swung the conversation to the mention of serious music and its effect on her was not lost on Keir, but he downplayed the remark by saying, "That was the Hollywood line, Grace. Do you think Denys really said that?"

"I hope so."

"You're an incurable romantic, Grace," he conceded, "but don't be mentioning plane crashes if you're trying to talk me into an eighteen hour plane trip."

"Roger that. I'll go call Penny."

***

The house was a flurry of activity for the next few weeks. With packing, immunizations, documentation, and paperwork complete, Keir and Grace boarded a plane with a stop in Frankfurt, Germany and a transfer to Nairobi.

Nairobi, popularly known as the 'Green City in the Sun,' was much larger and more modern than Grace and Keir had expected, having a population of just under two million people. Its name had come from a water hole known in the Maasai language as *Enkare Nairobi* and it had replaced Mombasa as the capital in 1905, growing as a tourist destination in large part due to big game hunting. Growth of the city hadn't been viewed well by the Maasai and the Kikuyu peoples as it'd encroached on their land. After the end of WWII, the dispute escalated into the Mau Mau Rebellion and eventually the British relinquished their hold on the area with Kenya becoming independent in 1963. Nairobi was named the capital city and became a well-established center for business and cultural concerns.

Jane's village was located some distance from Nairobi and after a couple of days in which to catch their breath in a modern hotel, Keir and Grace boarded a small plane to fly on to Kihara. Grace was sure the pilot was never in complete control of his faculties as the craft looped and dove during the hour-long flight. She'd looked to Keir for reassurance many times and clutched at his hand whenever the tiny plane lost altitude. When Keir glanced at her from time to time his look said, "So, what was that you were telling me about Denys Finch-Hatton's plane crash?"

Unfortunately, during the wild ride, there was no haunting musical score, not the slightest hint of Mozart, nor the glimpse of shrimp-colored flamingos skimming the water beneath them. Nothing at all to elevate the ride to a level one could call remotely romantic.

Grace was never so glad to set foot on solid ground as when the small plane skidded to a stop at the tiny airport near Kihara. The terminal resembled a squatter's hut and was pocked with what appeared to be bullet holes. She'd encountered sturdier structures back home when she and Keir hiked the mountains and had to spend their nights in rustic, isolated hostels.

"That was a barrel of laughs, wasn't it Denys?" she said when they stepped off the plane.

"To be sure, Karen," he agreed following her lead. "We wanted adventure, right?"

"Right. Adventure." She raised her eyebrows for emphasis.

The next leg of the trip was no better. They were introduced to Ita who was to be their driver for the rest of the journey. In all the years of bumping across rough terrain in the Canadian wilderness, the two had never experienced anything like the ride they took that day into the backcountry of Kenya. Grace bit her tongue as the Jeep hit a huge rock projecting from what passed for a road and tasted blood in her mouth for the duration of the trip. Oh yes, this was shaping up to be the adventure of a lifetime.

They caught sight of a number of animals along the way but Ita had no notion of stopping for them to take photos. They would have to wait for the safari for that opportunity.

At last, the village came into view and was more substantial than they'd expected it to be. Though the homes of the villagers were rude and without much style, the people who emerged from them were well dressed and appeared to be happy. Ita had stopped the Jeep in front of a large structure they presumed was the clinic. To the left of it there was a smaller structure. Perhaps the school.

Aching and covered in red dust, Jane's parents peeled themselves from the sticky leather bench seat in the rear of the truck. The first thing they saw was Jane flying down the steps of the hospital.

"You're here, at last," she cried forcing a group hug, "I'm so happy to see you. How was your trip?"

"Long and bumpy, but you probably know that," laughed Keir.

"Yes, the trip on that road is not for the faint of heart, I'm afraid. Come on in. There's someone you need to meet."

They followed Jane up the steps, through double doors, and along a short hallway. The girl tapped on a door at the end of the hall, then opened it to reveal a small office. Seated at the desk, sifting through a ream of sloppily piled papers was a man who appeared to be about ten years older than Jane.

"Mom, Dad, this is Scott."

"Nice to meet you Scott," said Keir extending a hand.

"Scott," said Grace. "Jane mentions you in her letters home. You're the doctor here?"

"Yes, that's right I am. And…"

"Scott is my husband," interrupted the young woman. "We were married a couple of months ago."

"You're married?" Grace gulped. "Oh, Jane. We had no idea."

"I hope you're not upset. It's just that I wanted you to meet Scott before I told you. I'm so glad you two decided to come to Africa."

"Well, welcome to the family, Scott," said Keir, thinking about the fact he'd saved a bundle of money on a big splashy affair.

But then Grace said, "Oh, Janey, we wanted to give you a big wedding. You're our only…daughter."

"We'll come back to Canada, Mom, one of these days so you can throw us a big shindig. But Scott and I…well, you know, we're here. We've been together for a while. It was time."

Time? Time, thought Grace. *That's a funny thing to say about settling on a life partner.* Her thoughts ran to her courtship with Keir.

"Shall we take a spin around the clinic?" asked Scott, changing the subject.

"Of course," said Jane. "You can see what we do here. There's a very small staff – just Scott and I and three of the villagers, but we're always busy. We not only provide medical care to those in the village but others in the vicinity as well, and for the most part, we've had adequate funding. We can handle most of the cases we get. Anything really serious we medivac out to Nairobi. We depend on Ita – your driver – to help out sometimes."

I'm surprised folks make it to the airfield, Grace thought, though she didn't give voice to that comment. She mentally bit her tongue, but dared not take it to the physical level, fearing another gush of blood in her mouth.

The trio made their way down the hallway to a large room holding twelve beds. All were filled but two – eight with adults and two with children. Her parents watched with admiration as Jane approached each bed enclosed in mosquito netting. The girl offered greetings to her patients in a combination of English and their native tongue. She seemed most fluent in their language.

Grace took the opportunity to observe her firstborn. She was tanned and beautiful and exuded compassion and confidence. A glance at Keir confirmed that he was thinking the same thing as Grace. They were both proud and happy at seeing their competent young daughter living the life she'd chosen. They must surely have done something right.

Scott too, seemed totally committed to his calling. As he stepped towards one of the patients, Grace studied her new son-in-law. He was about the same height as Jane, had long blond hair that he constantly tossed back, and a well-trimmed beard laced with threads of gray. He walked with a slight limp, a limp that would become more pronounced as the day wore on.

"Things are fairly quiet here today, but sometimes it gets a little crazy, especially if there are a lot of little kids who can't understand why they have to be here," Jane was saying. "It kind of goes in cycles and really keeps us on our toes when we're swamped. But Scott and I – our needs are few, though the hospital always needs something."

Grace made a mental note to look into ways to raise funds for the hospital once she returned home.

"You two are amazing," remarked Keir at last. "I'm blown away by all this…" He made a sweeping gesture. "Out here in the middle of nowhere. I had little idea." For a fleeting moment, his thoughts ran to Ian and his girlfriend and the way they'd lived in rural Australia.

"We're happy here, Dad. I mean really happy. We love it. There's nothing I'd rather be doing."

Keir stepped forward and took his daughter in his arms. There were no words needed. It was a beautiful moment, a moment Grace would often pull from her memory bank and savor.

Father and daughter broke from their embrace and Grace noticed tears in both their eyes. Jane sniffed and said, "Come on and meet some more of the gang. Bronwyn and George run the school. It's the other building next door, if you haven't guessed. They're a terrific couple. The kids love them."

"I'm sure the feeling is mutual," remarked Grace, "given that they've settled here so far away from the world."

"It's true. The two of them, like Scott and I, have fallen in love with this place and the people. It's a very rewarding life for all of us."

Can't say I blame them in some ways, thought Grace; they had real purpose in their lives.

They moved along the hallway and out into the heavy African air. There was a distinctive smell that Grace couldn't identify. It was a wild smell.

The little school was full of happy children, some sitting at crudely crafted desks, others cross-legged on mats. As they entered, George held up his hand to signal a break in the lesson and then converted it to a wave at the visitors.

He approached the group and a broad smile broke over his face. He was a large lumpy looking fellow and the grin made him look like an over-sized teddy bear.

"You've arrived," he said in greeting. "Jane's been positively giddy waiting for you to get here. I'm George." He extended a large paw to Keir. His grasp was firm and sincere. After releasing Keir's hand, he crushed Grace to him in a mighty bear hug. "It's so nice to finally meet you," he said then flipped Grace away from him.

"And you," said Keir, amused by the man's exuberance. "I understand you and your wife are both teachers here."

"Yah, that's right. She's not here at the moment. We kind of alternate – so one of us can deal with our wee one at home. She's just a few months old. That's our other one, Megan, over there." He gestured toward a small freckle-faced girl who appeared to be about four years of age.

"Of course," said Grace, following his motion. She hadn't even noticed the obviously paler child in the sea of dark faces.

"Both the girls were born here. They know no other life. It's going to be interesting to see what they'll choose to do once they're grown. Who knows what the world will be like then?"

"I dare say," remarked Keir, aware of all the changes that'd taken place in the world during his five decades.

"We shouldn't hold you up, George," said Grace. "Perhaps we'll see Bronwyn later."

"Of course," said Jane. "We're planning a little celebration in honor of your visit. Bronwyn and the girls will be over for dinner. You'll love her. She's one of a kind."

"That she is," echoed George. "Who'd have thought she'd pick up with a big lug like me and agree to live out here on the edge of nowhere?" He chuckled. "See you later, folks. It was a pleasure."

"And ours as well," said Keir.

***

"Can I help with anything, Jane?" Grace queried her daughter. Jane was busy preparing the welcome dinner in the couple's small quarters at the rear of the hospital.

"Nope. Everything's under control. I hope you'll like the meal. It's kind of a combination of western and African. We eat some fish and we do have the chickens out back. With that and the garden where we grow most of our own vegetables, we're pretty well self-sufficient. Sometimes one of the men will bring us some game, but I know you're not that fond of wild meat, Mom, so it's chicken tonight."

"Oh good. Thank you. Your dad used to do a little hunting with his friends when we were first married, but I was never much for eating what he brought home. But even though he brought back a few things from time to time, I think he was more interested in the camaraderie and just being out in the wild. Eventually, he just went out with the guys and 'hunted' with his camera. That solved the problem for me too."

"How are you both doing, Mom? Just the two of you now."

"We're doing well enough, I guess. I will admit there are days when I find it hard to come to terms with everything. It took Dad and me a while to find our way back to one another. We sort of ran out of things to talk about after Ben died. And then you left, too. We'd each withdrawn into our own little place – he spent a lot of time working, a lot of time in his shop and I – well, then I looked after your grandmother for a few years. And she was suffering too, you know. With Ian gone so tragically and then your grandfather as well. She turned into a demanding and cranky old thing. I hope I never end up like that."

"You and Dad still have a lot of good years ahead of you. I'm so happy you made the trip over here. You should do more traveling. Dad loves adventure. You too I guess. You did go off to Paris when you finished university."

"Ah yes, the year in Paris," sighed Grace, her mind pivoting to a sidewalk café and the memory of Lee's fingers pecking at his coffee cup. "Yes, Paris. Maybe your dad and I should go back there some time. Revisit some of the old…"

"Something smells delicious," said Scott as he and Keir appeared in the kitchen.

"Sure does," agreed Keir.

"Hope you like it, Dad. A little taste of Africa with a Canadian flair."

"George and the girls are on their way over," said Scott. "And I'm starved."

"Could you set the table, Mom?"

"Sure. Just show me where everything is."

"Plates and glasses are in here," gestured Jane. "Cutlery in that drawer over there. We're not much for show here." She was right. The dinnerware was plastic and the cutlery mismatched. Paper towel served as napkins.

No point in sending over a set of crystal for a wedding gift, thought Grace.

After a dinner Grace and Keir had to admit was delicious, the group went outside to sit on the veranda spanning the front of the hospital building. As day faded into night, the visitors enjoyed a performance of singing and dancing courtesy of the villagers. It was most unexpected and Grace and Keir felt much honored to have been gifted in such a way.

Bronwyn sat beside Grace holding her youngest daughter, Margaret, and Megan had found a place to snuggle on Grace's lap, somehow sensing the woman's need to try her hand at 'grandmothering.' Grace wondered if such a role

119

would ever be in the cards for her. And even if it was, her grandchildren would be thousands of miles away. She wondered how the rest of her life would play out and tightened her embrace on the child who was nodding off within the warmth of her bosom.

"She's really taken to you," remarked Bronwyn.

"It feels good to have a small child on my lap again. It's been many years. Oh, there have been children, grandchildren of friends and such, but we have no little ones of our own at home."

"Grace has mentioned Ben to us. I'm so sorry."

"It's been years, Bronwyn, and I still think about him almost every day. I wonder what his life would have been like. A 'normal' life."

"I'm sure he'd be a fine young man if he was anything like his sister. Jane and Scott are the best and so devoted to the people here."

"Thanks, dear," replied Grace. "It means a lot to me to hear that. And I'm sure Jane and Scott feel the same about you and George as well."

"And Grace…don't give up on the idea of a new little one coming along to sit on your lap." She gave Grace a wink and a smile.

Grace smiled back.

The day had been eventful for the couple. Travel to the village had been a challenge, they'd been able to observe first-hand the life their daughter had chosen and they'd even gained a son-in-law. And now with Bronwyn's remark about the possibility of a grandchild, Grace had even more to ponder. It was almost more than she could wrap her head around. And the prospect of a trip to Paris, indeed exploring any other part of the world with Keir sounded wonderful. But was it enough? Middle age had come to Grace and with it what she could only identify as a mid-life crisis, a wondering, a searching. Did all middle-aged women feel as she did? The natural progression of course, was to that of becoming a grandparent. But having seen how entrenched Scott and Jane were in their lives in this faraway land, she knew when there were grandchildren, she'd see very little of them. She looked down at the sleeping child in her arms and placed a tender kiss on the girl's fuzzy blond curls. Megan reminded her of Jane at that age and a tiny tear escaped and ran down her cheek. She was grateful that it was dark and no one was aware of her emotional moment. She shifted in her seat and the child awoke.

"I went to sleep, Grandma," said Megan.

"Yes you did, darling," replied Grace.

***

It was with extreme reluctance that Grace and Keir packed to leave the small village and their daughter behind. The visit had been an eye-opening and rewarding experience as they came to know the villagers there. And they'd leave with nothing but admiration for Scott, Jane, George, and Bronwyn, having seen first-hand the unfailing devotion they all had to the African people.

"Thanks for coming all the way over here you two," Jane said embracing her folks in a group hug. "But your adventure isn't over yet, is it. You're off on safari. How exciting!"

"Oh, Jane. Our time here has been so short, really. We're going to miss seeing you – and Scott – every day," Grace cried.

"That's for sure," agreed Keir. "But we can see how much you love it here and how much you're needed. We'd never wish any more for you."

"Thanks, Dad. I'm going to miss you both too. But I'll be coming home in a few months. Take care of yourselves and have a fabulous time on your safari."

Grace smiled and looked into the lovely face of her child and knew God had read her mind.

One last embrace and the couple stepped into the Jeep to make their way back to Kihara.

***

Safari! The very word had a magical ring to it. But after the bone-jarring Jeep ride back to the airport, Grace was beginning to rethink the idea of another 'adventure.' There was, however, no time for debate for their guide was awaiting their arrival outside the bullet-ridden terminal.

"Jambo. Hello, I'm Tebo," said the guide taking their suitcases from Ita. He spoke perfect unaccented English. "And you are..." He looked at the clipboard in his hand.

"Karen and Denys," put in Grace.

Tebo gave her a puzzled look, turned back to study the clipboard. He said, "It says, here you're, Grace and Keir, the..."

"We're traveling incognito," interrupted Grace. "It's Karen and Denys, if you don't mind."

Keir knew better than to interject, so he looked away and spent a few moments studying the dents in terminal's siding.

"Whatever you say," replied Tebo. He cared little about any felonious background his new passengers may or may not have had. Just as long as they behaved along the way.

"Our safari vehicle is this way," he nodded. "And you have a couple of traveling companions – the Browns." Under his breath, he added, "So they say."

"Thanks," said Grace, as she and Keir followed along behind the guide.

Tebo threw the luggage into the back of the vehicle, a large truck with an awning-like canopy for a roof, and opened one of the side doors for the couple. They stepped in. Seating was provided by benches along each side of the vehicle.

"Hi," said a voice. "I'm Marge."

"Hi," said another. "Bill."

"Hi, we're…Karen and Denys," said Grace, looking over at Keir. He gave her a wink.

"This your first safari?"

"Yes. Yours?"

"Yes. Hope we're in for a treat."

"For sure."

"First time in Africa?"

"Yes. We've just come from visiting our daughter. She and her husband run a small hospital way out there somewhere." Keir gestured wildly.

"Oh. Interesting."

There was some attempt at small talk. Actually Bill and Marge seemed pleasant enough, though Keir found them a little out of their depth when it came to discussing world travel, even though his own experiences hadn't been that numerous. But whenever he'd anticipated traveling anywhere, he did extensive research beforehand so he and Grace could get off the beaten track and avoid the usual tourist traps. He'd always liked the back roads. By the content of the conversation, it was obvious the Browns had no clue what they were in for.

They rode for miles, Grace and Keir trying to drink in every small morsel, every bit of wonder offered by the African landscape. Several times, they caught glimpses of the wildlife – colorful birds and small creatures they couldn't identify. At the entrance to the game preserve where arrangements for the safari had been made, Tebo stopped the truck and turned to face his passengers.

"Okay, folks," he began, "before we enter the reserve, I need to go over a few of the ground rules for the trip. The most important thing is that what we're going to see are wild animals. And I do mean they're wild. As cute and cuddly as you may think they are, there're not like your house pets. Rule number one is – always do exactly as I tell you, no matter what. I will never put you in harm's way. Rule number two – well there is no rule number two. Just remember rule number one and we'll all get along just fine. You may take pictures from the truck, but never leave the vehicle unless I tell you to. This kingdom is ruled by the male lion and he is king with a capital 'K.' Everything revolves around his comfort. All others out here are secondary, even members of his pride. The females hunt and provide. Nobody eats before the king has had his fill, especially the sons. Everyone else gets whatever's left over when he's done. And we all give the king a wide berth. By the way, it's illegal in Kenya for anyone to kill a lion, even the Maasai who've traditionally considered it a rite of passage for their young men. In fact, all big game hunting has been outlawed here since 1977. Are there any questions?"

No one answered.

"Okay. Just going to pop into the office over there and let them know we're here to begin 'the adventure.' And remember, if you want to live long enough to tell the folks at home about your trip of a lifetime, just remember rule number one."

Keir reached over, took Grace's hand, and grinned at her. "So, Karen," he said, "when do I get to wash your hair?"

"Right after the hippos pop their heads up out of the river, dear," she replied. "Did you remember to bring the shampoo?"

Grace glanced over at their companions, wondering if they were catching on to any of the banter. But all she saw was a look on Marge's face that said, '*I would never let Bill within ten feet of me with a shampoo bottle.*'

A few miles into the reserve, they caught sight of a marshy area.

"Without the marsh, there'd be no life here," pointed out their guide. "This is like a town square for the animals. Oh, and look over there. This is your lucky day. There's a sight we don't often see."

They followed his gesture and gaze to the edge of the marsh where a young lion lay in the grass.

Tebo pulled the truck to a stop and instructed the passengers to stay put. He moved slowly towards the immobile animal tapping cautiously at the side arm strapped to his belt. When he was close to the animal, he could see that it was indeed dead, though it hadn't been so for long. Large gashes and claw marks were visible and blood was beginning to dry on the tattered yellow fur. By the wounds he observed, he knew it hadn't been killed by any human hand. And he determined that it was in fact, a young male. With that, he returned to the truck.

"It's a male," he announced. "Probably killed by the dominant male because he got too close to one of the lionesses. The king has all the rights to the females and if the young males aren't chased off, they can be killed. I'll report it," he said picking up the radio's handset from the console of the truck.

When Tebo had finished his report Bill asked, "Will someone come and pick up the carcass?"

"Nope, nature takes care of all that." He popped his head out of the vehicle and scanned the sky overhead for vultures. "There's dinner waiting for whoever gets here first."

"Hyenas maybe?" asked Marge.

"Sure. Even other lions. Female lions are even known to kill the cubs of another lioness if they're very young and unable to protect themselves."

"Oh, my god," cried Marge lurching forward.

"That's nature way of ensuring the strongest survive," declared Tebo.

Marge slumped back into her seat.

The day was drawing to a close when the guide pulled the truck into a clearing. A campsite had already been set up by the tour company and the safari travelers were well ready for a rest and hearty meal. Tebo directed them to a table where chilled bottles of wine and beer awaited them.

"All the comforts of home, Karen," remarked Keir when the wine was poured.

"Indeed, Denys," she agreed. She raised her glass and said, "To a wonderful adventure."

"Right back atcha, Karen," said Keir raising his glass to her. And they both grinned.

The next time Keir glanced over at Grace, he had a difficult time controlling himself. With the wine and the warm night in the Kenyan countryside, he was becoming slightly giddy. He stifled a laugh that became a snort. During the rest of the trip, Grace and Keir continued to use only the names stolen from Karen Blixen's tragic tale of her life in Africa.

Night fell and Grace and Keir retired to their tent to the rabble of squabbling hyenas. They moved their cots close together and watched the fire outside as it danced and threw shadows against the side of the tent.

"Quite a day, eh?" remarked Keir.

"This is all kind of surreal, isn't it? Did you ever think when we met that frosty night in Jim's car that one day we'd be out here in the middle of Africa, huddled in sleeping bags and listening to the cries of wild dogs?"

"Nope. Not in a million years. But it is pretty special isn't it?"

"Something to tell our grandchildren about."

"If we ever see them. Besides, they'll probably have more stories to tell us, growing up here in Africa."

"Yah. That's something else I'd never have anticipated when we started our lives together. Funny how it's all gone, isn't it?"

"I guess you could say it's 'funny,' but I'd say more...well, unbelievable. But it does sound like we're about to become grandparents."

"Really. Jane told you that?"

"No, it was something Bronwyn said. Or implied, anyway."

"Well. A new phase of life for us, Grace. Grandparents, eh. I can't believe where the years have gone."

"Me either," she murmured and fell into a deep and satisfying slumber.

***

The following day, the group pressed on deeper into the reserve and weren't disappointed by anything they saw – Thompson gazelle, strolling elephants, and the comical stance taken by giraffes kneeling to drink at the water's edge. The usually exotic and graceful animals looked like a group of chairs with broken legs. And Grace was astonished at the sight of their enormous tongues. Keir took roll after roll of film from both the safety of the truck and away from it when permitted. Being so close to animals they'd only ever seen in zoos was worth every minute of discomfort, sitting cramped and captive with the Browns, a couple who had little to offer conversationally.

Sitting about the fire one night, Grace began to think of Keir's brother, Ian. She imagined him sitting as they were at that moment, in a lonely wilderness thousands of miles from home, his heart and mind set on adventure. She knew the trip with Keir was a far cry from what Ian had experienced, the young man having encountered strange tribes who'd reportedly never seen white people before he arrived, but this trip did seem to satisfy Keir's adventurous side. She wondered if in another life, he would have wanted to be like Denys Finch-Hatton – free and undomesticated. Her mind wandered aimlessly.

"What are you thinking about, Grace?" Keir asked, seeing the look on her face that'd been lit up by the flickering fire.

Fortunately, Marge and Bill had retired for the night and didn't hear Keir call his wife by her real name.

"I was thinking about Ian and how the adventures he'd sought out cost him his life. He was so young. Not even thirty. And here we are tonight, sitting on the African plains in quite a different circumstance, but living our adventure too."

"Funny, I thought of him too – back there when we were with Jane and Scott. I think he would have loved it here. I do. It's so peaceful."

"Like the peace we always find in the mountains at home?"

"Just like that."

"Keir. If life had been different for us, for you, would you have…?"

"I've told you before, Grace. I'm exactly where I want to be. Here with you, watching the smoke from the fire twisting up towards the African sky, listening to the calls of the night birds."

"Ian said he envied you."

"Yes, he did."

"Keir."

"Yes."

"Would you ever want to learn how to fly?"

"What kind of crazy question is that?"

"Yah, it is kind of crazy isn't it?" She chuckled.

"You are one funny broad, Grace."

"That's what you always say. That's why I married you. I thought you needed the amusement."

"Hah. And here I thought it was for the fringe benefits," he said, reaching over and kissing her sweetly.

"That too," she replied and kissed him back.

***

The days in Africa would be some of the most memorable Grace and Keir ever shared. Awakening in the mornings to the sounds of Africa; the very smell of the land; the songs, roars, and wails of the wildlife; and sitting at the end of the day, drawing close to one another, gazing at the galaxy from a perspective seen nowhere else on earth – those were the things that would live in their memory. It was indeed, another world.

But they were not to leave before one last memory found entrenchment in their minds. They'd arisen on the last morning of the safari, eaten a satisfying breakfast, packed up their things and said farewell to the others staying behind to break-down the camp.

"All set?" asked Tebo, ushering his four charges into the Jeep.

"Sure thing," answered Bill, though it'd been a rhetorical question.

"Did everyone have a good time? Was it the adventure you thought it would be?"

"Definitely," replied Keir. The safari had been right up his alley. Suddenly Grace understood Jane's penchant for a non-traditional life-style. The girl was more like her father than Grace had ever realized.

The trip back through the game reserve passed quickly, Tebo stopping just a couple of times to allow for the last few photo-ops.

"I'll be stopping up ahead at the depot to let them know we're leaving the reserve," he announced turning back to his passengers. "It won't take too long," he continued as he pulled over in front of the small service building. "Just a bit of paper work." He opened the door and hopped out, but stuck his head through the window and said, "Stay put."

"I can't wait to take a shower," said Marge. "And sleep in a decent bed."

"Sounds heavenly," agreed the rest as they watched Tebo pass through the door of the building. Keir opened his camera bag to check for any unexposed film he might have left. He was sure he'd used at least ten rolls, but it'd been totally worth it. He'd captured many one-of-a-kind images, from spectacular landscapes to the live action of exotic wildlife.

While Tebo was busy, Grace tried to make small talk with the Browns, thankful that she would soon be relieved of their company.

"K-uh, Denys and I think we may have a grandchild on the way. We're so excited, though we'll probably not see much of him…or her."

"Really?" replied Marge, a note of detachment in her voice. "We're not likely to ever see that happen."

Grace gulped. Had she innocently opened a can of worms? She hesitated with her reply.

"You mentioned once or twice…that you had kids," she said, hoping Marge would either give some clarity or change the subject. It was an awkward moment. They were confined to a small space and Grace knew silently ignoring the Browns in these last few moments together would have been extremely rude.

"Two," volunteered Marge at last.

"Uh. Boys? Girls?" asked Grace, picking up the thread on what she'd anticipated might have been a dead conversation.

"One of each."

But then…crickets. Grace could see Keir staring out the window of the truck leaving her to deal with the Browns and their unfailing ability to shut down any meaningful exchange.

"Oh," she replied, not feeling the need to mention she and Keir had once had a son in addition to the daughter they'd mentioned to the Browns. The subject of Benjamin's death was something Grace rarely shared with strangers. And, at that moment, most especially the Browns who epitomized the expression 'strange.' Besides, it was becoming obvious the other couple would never be so much as a blip on Keir and Grace's radar in the future. No long Christmas letters. Calls to visit them in their home. Where was it again? And hadn't she and Keir been living under assumed names all week? That thought brought a tiny smile to Grace. She was startled when Marge opened up.

"Blaine. Well he's just downright odd. No sign of a lady in his life. Bill and I think, well, maybe he's, you know…"

"Marge," cried Bill. "Shut it. That's a private matter. You know we never discuss it with anyone else, especially strangers." He threw a caustic glare at his wife.

"Well, who on earth are they going to tell, Bill? Heaven knows it's been on our minds for years now."

"End of subject, Marge," he declared.

Keir and Grace shared a look of embarrassment. Grace had never meant to end the trip with the other couple on this low note. Their remarks had come as a surprise given how little they'd shared over the past few days.

"What's taking Tebo?" cried Bill. "How the hell much paper work can there possibly be?" He reached for the handle of the vehicle, opened the door, and stepped out, taking his camera with him.

"We were told to stay put," yelled Marge after Bill's retreating form.

"Don't be pissy, Marge," he yelled over his shoulder and strode off across the grass.

"Now what's he up to?" asked Marge as though to ask would prompt a skywriter to scrawl the answer against the cloudless African sky.

Bill disappeared into a copse of trees leading into the dense jungle. The others tried not to consider the dire consequences he was inviting, not the least of which was a tongue lashing from Tebo.

"We can't go after him," declared Keir. "Maybe I should go get Tebo."

Grace was saved from comment as Tebo emerged from the service building. He hopped in the front seat.

"Sorry about that, folks. Took a little longer than I anticipated. The station's short-handed today – one of the fellows is off sick."

"Bill's not here."

"Say what?" Tebo responded, turning to see just three passengers.

"He took off over there," said Marge pointing to the clump of bushes across the grassy area.

"What were my parting words?"

Marge began to cry.

"Oh hell!"

Keir and Grace looked at one another, eyebrows raised in mild amusement. Amusement, however, was the last thing on Tebo's mind. He started the truck, threw it in gear, and sped off in the direction Bill had gone.

"One simple rule. Just one. It shouldn't have been that hard to remember."

Grace had taken a tissue from her bag and handed it to Marge who'd advanced to a full-blown howl.

Dust kicked up behind the vehicle, now off the hard surface of the road. Tebo was muttering under his breath. A series of curse words inaudible to the rest. They could only imagine what he was sputtering. It seemed impossible Bill could have disappeared so quickly in so short a time. The truck slowed as it neared the treed area and then stopped.

"Rule number one!" cried Tebo. And he stepped from the truck.

"Righto!" chimed the remaining trio in unison.

The guide slammed the door of the vehicle, took his sidearm from its holster, and disappeared into the scrub.

Marge's crying jag subsided and she sat, soggy tissue wadded in her hand.

"Why does he always have to be so…?" she moaned.

Though Marge hadn't completed the sentence, Keir and Grace could think of a few descriptive phrases.

Ten minutes passed. Then twenty. At last, Tebo emerged alone. He stepped into the truck and reached for the radio's hand set. He turned to the others.

"He's okay. Took a bad spill over some deadfall and probably broke his leg. I'm sending for help."

Marge began to cry again and Grace reached into her bag for more tissue. "He's lucky it wasn't worse. Who knows what might have happened to him if I hadn't found him." He radioed the authorities.

"It's okay, Marge," soothed Grace. "Everything's going to be okay now."

"He's so bull-headed. Never listens to anyone. Always thinks he knows best," sobbed Marge taking a swipe at her runny nose. Marge had one of those faces that contorted into true ugliness when she cried.

Neither Grace nor Keir offered any comment. Bill's impulsive action had brought what had been a very wonderful few days to a less than pleasant conclusion.

It was a full hour before medical help arrived to transport Bill to the hospital for the surgery he'd require. And because the station was short-handed that day, Keir, Grace, and Marge were forced to sit in the truck while Tebo returned to ensure Bill didn't invite any further trouble. Marge continued to prattle on with a litany of Bill's failings. And later, because Bill was no longer within earshot, she launched into a long and embarrassing account of why the Brown's would never see any harvest from their daughter's womb. Keir and Grace stopped listening after a while and prayed for the arrival of the rescue vehicle.

During the wait, Keir searched his camera bag for more film, hoping to take the last few random shots of whatever happened to wander by. The only thing he saw was something resembling an over-sized rat, the sight of which stirred up the memory of a garbage-filled alleyway behind a Parisian walk-up.

***

Africa had been an exciting interlude. A wonderful visit with Jane and her new husband, Scott. The safari had offered intimate interaction with exotic wildlife – something most people could only dream of experiencing. There'd even been a little unexpected drama courtesy of Bill's reckless behavior. But more than that, the trip had brought about a new perspective for the couple. Spending the past few days together in a different setting had been very good for them. The trip had refreshed and renewed them and had made them feel almost young again. And there was something about Africa itself, the way the land throbbed with mystery. Their time there had been restorative and so much more than Keir and Grace could have hoped for.

And of course, there'd been the added fun of assuming new personas. Yes, they'd never forget their time in Africa or the alter egos they'd taken on, those of the long-suffering Baroness von Blixen and the love of her life, Denys Finch-Hatton.

14

Back home, Grace imposed a deadline on herself and her husband. The woman didn't have a definite time frame as to when a possible grandchild might arrive, but that was inconsequential. She had a mission.

Jane's room hadn't been touched since Keir's mother had occupied it, but now there was an excuse to renovate and update. Not that she and Keir ever needed an excuse. It seemed they'd been renovating for most of their married life. One of Keir's favorite lines to friends was that once Grace found out he was a carpenter there'd been no rest for him.

"Can we take out this storage closet so we can have a bigger bathroom?"

"Sure. We can do anything. The question is…should we?" Keir replied.

"We've wanted to do this bathroom over for years, Keir."

"We?" he asked. "There's nothing wrong with the way it is."

"Well, if we take out the closet, we can have a free-standing shower as well as a tub. That's how everyone's doing it now."

Keir had to smile at Grace's logic. He would let her beg for a while and then indulge her whims. That's how it'd always been with most of their projects. And Keir knew any improvements would pay dividends when it came time to sell. In the end, their combined talents for design and practical application usually resulted in a pleasing product. But there had been the time they'd tried to install glossy wallpaper in the hallway and came as close to divorce as they ever wanted to. What'd begun as a plan to create a beautifully patterned accent wall became a disaster when the sopping, sagging, and shredding paper refused to adhere to the wall no matter what they tried to do. In the end, when the last slippery piece of paper slid onto the floor to join its mates, Keir and Grace knew their days of hanging wallpaper were over. Without a word, they gathered up the remnants of the project, trotted them out to the back lane, and deposited them into the yawing jaws of the metal garbage container. Peace was restored in the household and the event was never mentioned again.

For the most part, Grace had never minded the upheaval during renovations, primarily because she knew when finished the result would be worth it all. But Keir had told her many stories of those for whom he'd worked – stories of folks who'd come near to a breakdown once a wall in the house disappeared. It was as though it'd been a barrier between them and some unseen supernatural force or alien invasion, even though in some cases it'd been an interior wall. For others, it was just the fact that their daily routine was disrupted and one woman even asked before the project was begun if there would be any dust. Keir had an answer for her but his conscience wouldn't allow him to express it.

Once Keir had acquiesced on the bathroom renovation, it required Grace to relocate all the sundry items in the storage closet. Some things unearthed from the tomb had long ago outlived their usefulness for the family and had more or less been forgotten about.

"See," Grace said after pulling several boxes out of the closet and piling them in the hall, "most of this stuff we can get rid of anyway. What were we keeping it all for? Look. Here's a box of Jane's dress-up clothes."

"Seems to me I've been saying that about a lot of things around here. What if we do ever want to downsize?"

"Not yet, Keir. Not yet."

He looked at her fondly. "Remember when we were happy living in one little room in Paris?"

"Yes. We didn't need much. We spent most of our spare time in bed," she said with a giggle.

"We did, didn't we? Ah, the good old days."

Grace sat down on one of the cartons. "They were good days, weren't they Keir? The two of us, young and in love, wondering what was in store for us. Life was a clean slate then, waiting to have our story written on it. Now here we are, just the two of us again. The only difference is we're here in a big house with a lot of 'stuff.' But we've worked hard for it all, haven't we?"

Keir put down the box he'd taken from the top shelf. "Yah. Hard to believe so much time has passed. And think about it. In the first half of our lives, we fell in love, got married, had the kids, and accumulated a bunch of stuff. Now here we are in the second half – big house, the kids are gone, and we're stuck trying to figure out what to do with all this clutter. Quite a life cycle."

"That's kind of a cynical way of looking at it. But you're right."

He chuckled. "But we're not so old yet, Grace. There's still time to get more stuff. Where did you say you wanted me to put all this?"

"In the garage. We'll have a garage sale one of these days."

"Okay. Take off that trim while I'm schlepping these boxes. And keep it intact. We can use it to match everything when we put the place back together."

"Righto, sir," she answered mockingly. She'd lived with Keir long enough to know everything he did when building was carefully thought out well before hand. She watched him stack a couple of cartons together and head down the stairs. She sat for a moment pondering the words he'd spoken about the years ahead of them. She hoped he was right.

Grace stood up, took a chisel and hammer from the toolbox, and began to pry at the trim, trying to separate it from the wall. A gap began to open up. She repositioned the chisel and continued, tapping it gently with the hammer, prying carefully. After a few such moves, the trim released intact. She turned it over, pulled out the finishing nails one by one, then laid the piece along the wall out of the way. She continued with the next piece of trim.

Keir had taught her well.

***

The trip to the airport the day Jane and Scott were to arrive from Africa, was filled with major excitement. Though Jane's letters home had said nothing about the arrival of a child, Grace was certain that her daughter and her husband were coming home to present their new offspring. And a surprise is still a surprise even though everyone knows that everyone knows that everyone knows. There were just a few details that needed to be revealed.

The family finally emerged from the security of the international arrivals area, Scott pushing the luggage cart and Jane clutching a tiny bundle in her arms. The baby was wrapped in a blanket showcasing a wildly colorful African print. At the sight of the group, Grace immediately felt tears spring to her eyes and she threw open her arms in welcome.

"Oh," was all she could utter as she flung herself at her daughter.

Jane had teared up as well. "This is Theo," she managed with a choke. And then – "Theodore – after Scott's father. Hope you don't mind, Dad," she said pulling herself from her mother's grasp and turning her attention to Keir.

His reaction was a gentle smile and he wrapped his arms around them all in a group embrace, temporarily forgetting Scott, the luggage bearer.

Finally breaking free Kier said, "Oh, Scott. Good to see you again. Welcome."

Grace peeled back the baby's cover and peered at the little cherubic face of her grandson. "Oh, he's just beautiful, Jane. What a sweet, sweet little fellow. And not such a surprise, really." She laughed a nervous little laugh.

"Bronwyn told me she let the cat out of the bag. She saw how much you enjoyed being with her children. And it all went well. He was a healthy nine pounds. And he's the darling of the village, let me tell you."

"Here, let me take him from you. I need to get in all the grandmother time I can with him."

"Good. He eats a couple of times a night."

***

With reluctance, Grace placed Theo into the car seat they'd borrowed for use during Jane and Scott's visit. Theo dozed off by the time the family reached home.

"You're going to notice a few changes in your room, Jane," her father announced. "Your mom has been keeping me busy the last couple of months." He looked over at Grace and winked.

"Come on through," said Grace. "Though your dad would never admit it, he enjoyed getting things ready for you as much as I did."

Jane would discover that with the removal of the storage area and a complete gut of the old bathroom, a new and spectacular space presented itself. There was a glassed-in shower separate from a gleaming new soaker tub. An antique cabinet had been repurposed as a vanity and was fitted with a modern sink and fresh brushed nickel hardware. The tile floor was warm with in-floor heating and a glass table holding a porcelain jug of white chrysanthemums brought regal elegance to the new room. The scent of jasmine wafting from a bowl of potpourris on the edge of the tub claimed ownership of the air.

"Wow," exclaimed Jane upon viewing the well-appointed space, "can we put in a bathroom like this back in Africa?"

"Wouldn't dare," replied her husband. "We'd never be able to use it. Everybody for miles around we be in there just to play with the taps."

Theo began to fuss in the car seat they'd placed on the floor. Grace released him and steered the group towards Jane's bedroom.

"We've changed a couple of things in here too. I hope you like it. Your 'little girl' room has been given a face-lift."

"Oh, this is lovely, Mom," cried Jane as the tour continued.

The room, like the bathroom, was an easy mix of modern and traditional, with white furniture and luxurious fabrics patterned in green and turquoise. In the corner stood a white crib dressed in bedding matched to the rest of the room.

"And there's the crib, too," Jane giggled. "You thought of everything."

"Of course we didn't know whether to expect a boy or a girl," said Grace, delighted with her daughter's approval. "So we went with something that would work either way. And it's not too…cute. It should do for a few years whenever you come home."

"It's just perfect. Theo and I might just move in for good," said Jane. "What do you think Scott?" Grace knew her daughter was just kidding, but in her heart, she wished it could be so.

"It's pretty nice," replied Jane's husband. "But no deal. What do you think if we get new curtains for the kitchen at home?" He said 'home' like he meant it.

Theo began to fuss in Grace's arms and she laid him the waiting crib.

"I think he's looking for dinner," said Jane reaching into the crib to adjust the baby's blanket. "And then a nap." Turning to her parents she said, "Thanks for all this you guys. Everything is lovely. I'm not going to miss the old 'little girl's room.'"

I might, thought Grace.

As expected, the few weeks spent with Jane, Scott, and Theo went all too quickly. Relatives and friends came and went to ooh and ah over the baby, give updates on their own lives and generally wreak havoc on any order in the household. But it was all good. Grace and Keir would not have had it any other way. Over the next few years, Jane and Theo would visit, Scott remaining behind in Africa for the most part to continue ministering to the villagers, and giving the grandparents the opportunity to mark the stages of their grandson's life. But the departure of their daughter and grandson was always a time of sadness, for there were no other children or grandchildren on whom they could focus attention. And though they never said so to Jane, Theo did remind Keir and Grace of their son, Benjamin. He had the same blond curls, laughing eyes, and sweet personality.

15

Grace spent a few years dealing with her aging parents. Though they'd remained relatively healthy for most of their lives, their last few years saw a rapid deterioration.

"At least there're two of them," Grace remarked to Keir. "And they can complain to one another." She feared a reprise of the days with Keir's mother, having to endure a move of one or the other of her parents into her home. She loved them dearly, but even with time on her hands, her last wish was to have to spend it providing yet more nursing care. Thankfully, with visits from a home-care worker, Grace's regular delivery of meals and attention to their clinic appointments, the couple was able to remain in their own home. And Grace knew they wouldn't have had it any other way. Just as Grace loved her home, her parents also loved theirs. They would have been hard-pressed to give it up.

On a dreary day in mid-February, a few days after he was hospitalized, Grace's father passed away. He was close to ninety and had lived a full and productive life. Grace was beyond grateful that he'd not suffered in any great way. His mind had been sound and he'd never lost his sense of humor. *Just like Ben,* she thought. When Grace and Keir went to tell Grace's mother of her husband's death, it was clear she had little understanding. The woman was so frail and all knew she wouldn't last long without her mate of over sixty years. The two had been devoted to one another, had raised Grace and her brothers in a decent, loving, and Christian home, and had worked tirelessly throughout their lives together. The day before the funeral for Grace's father, her mother was admitted to the hospital where she passed away shortly thereafter.

Folks would often say to Grace that they'd seen it happen many times – mates who'd been together for so long unable to survive without one another. Grace wondered how she would survive if anything happened to Keir. She was realistic enough to know that statistically women most often outlived their husbands. She recalled the letters she and Keir had received so many years ago. Letters in which

Ian's girlfriend had mourned his loss and tried so valiantly to carry on in the face of his tragic death.

After dealing with her parents' failing health for years and then their back-to-back funerals, Grace was exhausted. All she wanted was to sleep for a week. But in the end, she knew she needed something to fill her life. Just as when Benjamin had died, she was overwhelmed with emptiness. Once again she was without a purpose. Without a mission.

She took another part-time job. It wasn't very challenging but it did get her out of the house for a few hours a week and she liked and respected the people with whom she worked.

Keir continued to work at his trade, slowing down only when Grace insisted they take time off for vacations. Cruising became a practical and relatively inexpensive way to see the world. It satisfied Keir's adventuring spirit and provided the comfort and safety of lodging. The added bonus, and the reason many folks chose to travel that way, was of course the ample supply of fantastic food. Keir and Grace were well past the age of backpacking and sharing uncomfortable space with others in foreign hostels.

A twenty-one-day cruise would take them across the Atlantic from Fort Lauderdale to the Azores then on to several other ports in Europe. It was the trip of a lifetime, but the most anticipated docking was at Le Havre where the couple planned to board a bus for a day trip into Paris. Keir and Grace had always promised themselves they'd return to the city where they'd shared so many wonderful days as young lovers. Though the trip would give them just a short time in the city, even that prospect was a major factor when choosing that particular cruise.

Excitement began to mount as the ship neared port, Grace especially looking forward to the overland trip to the City of Light. Le Havre is a modern rebuild of an older city destroyed during the invasion of Normandy and from that port city, it's about a three-hour bus ride to Paris.

The morning the ship docked, however, Keir awakened with an excruciating headache, a condition he'd suffered from over the years. And from past experience, he knew his only option was to spend the day quietly in a darkened room. If Grace wanted to take the trip into Paris, she'd most certainly have to do it on her own.

She'd risen and gone to shower, eager for the visit to a city holding so many romantic memories for her.

Keir could hear her crooning the sweet French love ballad she used to sing to him years before.

"You're not up yet," she said coming from the shower and shedding her bath towel.

"Oh…I'm so sorry, Grace," he moaned. "I seem to have one of my migraines this morning. Not great timing, eh?"

"Oh, Keir! Not today of all days. We were so looking forward to going into Paris together, seeing how much it's changed since we were there all those years ago. Going there is one of the main reasons we chose this cruise. Are you sure you're not up to it?"

"Oh, I'm sure. My head is on fire. Why don't you go, though? The tour is all booked and paid for."

"Are you kidding? I can't go to Paris alone!"

"You did it before."

"Keir, you know that was different. I was working there. And we just have this one day to go and feel like kids again. To feel the old thrill of walking hand in hand along the boulevards. And there's lunch. And free wine!" she said by way of enticement.

"You know I can't eat anything when I have one of these damn headaches. I doubt I'd even be able to walk any distance without throwing up. I'd be lousy company."

"You can say that again. On a scale of one to ten, throwing up all day is about a minus something on the 'romantic-day-in-Paris' meter. Oh, I'm sorry, Keir. I'm sorry you feel so terrible. Really. And it would be mean of me to go without you."

"No go. You should. You can't do anything for me here anyway. I just need to sleep this off."

Grace drew out some clean lingerie from a drawer and began to dress.

"Are you really sure?" she pressed. "I hate to leave you here all by yourself. It seems selfish of me."

"Just go, Grace. It would be selfish of me to expect you to stay here. And stop talking. It's not helping."

Grace moved towards the bed and took a seat, gently so as not to jostle her husband. By the look on his face, she could see how much pain he was in.

"It won't be the same, Keir," she said softly taking his hand in hers. "We had such plans for today."

Keir sighed loudly, closed his eyes, and hunched into a fetal position, an indication that the discussion was at an end.

Grace rose from the bed, finished getting ready, and stuffed a variety of items into a large colorful bag. As much as Keir had always warned her about carrying such a bag when they traveled, fearing her vulnerable to loss of valuables such as her passport or wallet, she flatly refused to wear one of those ridiculous zip-up fanny purses favored by many tourists.

She scrambled through the carry-all bag again, taking a second look at the items she'd packed. She went to Keir's bedside and kissed the back of his head then went to the door of the stateroom, opened it, and placed the 'do not disturb' card on the outside handle. She tried to close the heavy door gently but as usual, it slammed shut with a resounding thud. In her mind's eye, she could see Keir recoiling at the impact of the door's hardware against the metal frame.

No time for more than a cup of coffee she realized, after hearing the announcement for the Paris-bound tour bus. It promised to be a scenic drive from Le Havre through the French countryside.

Grace searched for her ship's card, pulled it out, and went through the security exercise at the top of the gangway.

On the bus, she searched for an empty seat beside another solo traveler. She spied a woman she'd seen aboard ship a few times and wondered why she was sitting alone. She knew the woman was traveling with her niece.

"Is this seat taken?" she asked the woman.

"No. It's all yours."

"Thanks," Grace said settling her bag under the seat in front of her. "I thought you may be taking the tour with your niece."

Grace noticed the woman was sporting a nasty shiner.

"Uh, no. She's gone off with that fellow she picked up with on the ship."

"Oh. She met someone?" asked Grace, smiling inwardly. She and many of the other passengers had been following with amusement the fledgling, though on-again-off-again romance, throughout most of the voyage. Today it must be 'on.'

"Yes. You'd think they'd have wanted to take this trip into Paris. It is after all, known as the city of lovers," remarked the aunt.

"Yes, it is," replied Grace. *If you only knew,* she thought stifling a tear. *If you only knew.*

"Your husband didn't come today?"

"No. Unfortunately, he suffers from migraines. This one couldn't have come at a worse time."

Grace looked over at the woman, her gaze settling on the black eye. It was so blatantly obvious despite auntie's attempt at artful makeup.

"Fell down the stairs," the woman said, aware that Grace was inspecting the bruise.

Not surprising, thought Grace unkindly, given that every time she'd seen the woman she was putting away a highball. But she couldn't think of a polite response and turned her attention to the window and the changing landscape beyond the outskirts of Le Havre. She sighed as the bus passed through acres of green fields, age-old woodlands, and small French towns. And try as she might, she couldn't control the tiny rivers of tears escaping from her eyes every few moments. She drew in a self-pitying sniff and pulled out a tissue to dab away the tears and blow her nose. Her make-up began to run, and she hoped the mascara rimming her eyes didn't resemble the same black smudge worn by her traveling companion.

How long ago she and Keir had traveled in cheap and uncomfortable tour buses through similar fields, forests, and villages. Another tear rolled down her cheek and she saw it reflected in the window. She was almost sorry she'd come, but what had been the alternative? A day in the ship's library? Silly games on the lido deck? Lying on a lounge on the stateroom's balcony waiting for Keir's headache to subside?

But the thought of making small talk with this stranger for the duration of the bus ride was beginning to give Grace a headache as well. She turned from the window, reached for her bag, and pulled out a guidebook. It was the one she'd purchased so many years ago and she knew nearly every paragraph by heart. That didn't stop her from leafing through it, feigning interest so as to avoid attention from her seatmate. From time to time, Grace returned her gaze to the window and the scenes running by. Perhaps it was her state of mind, but she couldn't help comparing the rural landscape to that of western Canada – especially the sight of fields brimming with crops of canola. But any comparison to the Canadian countryside fell well short as Grace was treated to the sight of crumbling castles and a forested area she knew was obscuring a view of the Palace of Versailles.

At last, they were in the city. The traffic was bumper to bumper, a function of the morning rush hour, and the guide, Evelyne, began a recital of the group's itinerary. They'd hit the highlights, she explained, stopping for a few moments to allow for photo taking and then proceed to a designated restaurant for a typical French lunch.

Whenever she and Keir had traveled, it always amazed Grace how the large tour buses were able to negotiate the roadways and lanes originally designed for carts and foot traffic. And she wondered at the life-span of a tour bus driver. It had to be one of the most stressful jobs in the world, ferrying assorted oddball tourists through cramped alleyways, listening to them complain that 'it wasn't like this at home' and waiting endlessly as guides searched and rounded up stragglers who couldn't follow instructions. She thought of the Browns and wondered what life had brought to their doorstep. But then, did she really care? No. She didn't.

Though Grace had packed her travel bag and checked it more than once, she found she'd managed to forget her camera. But in the end, what did it matter? *How much could the popular tourist sites have changed anyway*? she wondered. She'd seen them all before, first with Keir and then again with Lee, and now without Keir by her side, it didn't seem necessary to document the trip in any significant way.

The bus rolled by the Eiffel Tower and many aboard stood to snap pictures. Then there was L'arc de Triomphe and later, the Louvre. Snap, snap. They stopped for a tour of the Notre Dame Cathedral and Grace stood for a few moments in the shadow of a large tree waiting for the rest of the group to emerge from the church. She and Keir had toured the magnificent structure on more than one occasion and she didn't need to jostle amongst the crowds yet another time, elbowed by rude camera-wielders. She wondered how the saints on high were now viewing such commotion in an edifice built in their glory.

The guide was finally able to 'herd the cats' and they all boarded the bus to head off for lunch at a small restaurant near the center of Paris. After leaving the bus, several passengers peeled off to take advantage of the facilities and the guide directed the rest into a small space at the back of the establishment where they were crammed onto bench seating at a long table. It reminded Grace of the pizza joints she and others in the young people's group had frequented so many years ago. She and her bus-companion were shoehorned against a sloping wall and couldn't have moved if the place suddenly burst into flames. Those who'd gone off in search of the bathrooms fared much better, for they were seated on the outer side of the tables where there was at least, a little more headroom. *Must remember that for next time*, thought Grace.

Elbow to elbow the tourists struggled to enjoy the salad of greens and a tasty dish of roasted chicken smothered in a delicious cranberry-red sauce. In the awkward confinement, someone spilled a flask of less than exceptional wine and though it was noted, the wait-staff failed to replace it. Dessert was an apple crepe, and Grace declined the offer of coffee.

Thankfully, lunch break came to an end, and the guide hurried them along for the rest of the tour. Grace slid along the wall to freedom.

"You have two options," the guide announced when the group had gathered on the street near the bus. "You can continue on in the bus or you can go off on your own to do some shopping or sightseeing, meeting back here at three o'clock. But bear in mind, if you're not back here when the bus leaves for the ship, I cannot be responsible. The ship departs at six thirty and will not wait for you."

Grace knew immediately she was not getting back on that bus until she absolutely had to and duly informed the guide of her plans to strike out on her own.

"Don't get lost, ma'am," ordered the guide, noting Grace was planning to go it alone in a strange city.

"It's all right. I used to live here."

Grace couldn't help but notice the look on the face of the woman with the black eye. She was shuffling towards the steps of the bus, her backward glance at Grace pleading, "Take me with you."

"Three o'clock," repeated the guide pointing at her watch.

"Three o'clock," said Grace who knew exactly what she was going to do until that time.

The first thing she did was slip into a small shop nearby to purchase a tie for Keir. It was silk and stitched with small images of the Eiffel Tower.

Next, she found a taxi stand and instructed the driver in her rusty French to take her to the area in which she'd once lived.

After a short trip, the building came into view and Grace felt a slight lurch in her stomach. She paid the driver and stepped out onto the sidewalk. She stood for a few moments, studying the way the stones of the façade fit into one another. The building hadn't changed at all that she could see. The ledge where Keir had waited for her to come home was the same as it'd been that day he'd arrived to surprise her. She closed her eyes and imagined him sitting there now. She took the two shallow steps to the front door and reached for the latch. The door was shedding patches of the many coats of paint it'd endured over the years.

Inside, the stairway looked much the same and exuded painful creaks with each step she took. How many times had she made that climb? Hundreds she guessed, over the course of a year. And in much prettier shoes. She looked down at her feet now. She was wearing a pair of sturdy and comfortable shoes, the kind favored by aging tourists. She remembered her red sandals, the *prostitute* shoes. She'd never worn them again after that last night with Lee and had finally thrown them away before leaving Paris. As she climbed, she remembered the way Keir had always flown up those steps with such ease and how Lee had always come to her door out of breath.

I wonder what the inside of the place looks like now these many years later, she wondered as she approached the landing. Did she dare be so bold as to knock on the door and ask the present tenant if she might impose on him – or her? She gazed at the door for a few moments then turned away and took a couple of steps down. She reconsidered and moved back to the doorway. She'd come all this way. What harm to ask?

Grace tapped at the scruffy old wooden door and heard a shuffling from within. The door opened a crack and she glimpsed a head peeking through. The head sported a tumbling of dark, wavy hair belonging to a young man.

She began, speaking in English, hoping she wouldn't have to revert to French to make herself understood.

"I'm so sorry to bother you," she began.

"Yes?"

"It's just that…well… I used to live in this apartment. A long time ago. A very long time ago. I'm just in Paris for the day. I-I… I wonder if I might impose on you. Could I just step inside for a moment? You see, I lived here at a very special time in my life." She was trembling.

The young man blinked a few times. She could see she'd caught him napping. He opened the door a little wider and she noticed he was barefoot, wearing boxers and a well-worn T-shirt.

"Excuse me a moment," he said, "While I put on some pants." He closed the door.

As she waited, Grace looked down the hall and saw another tenant exiting the bathroom. *Guess things haven't changed too much*, she thought.

The door opened again and the young man gestured her inside. The room was an untidy jumble of clothes, books and newspapers, but not much had changed. The furniture, now a blend of Ikea and thrift store, was still sitting in much the same arrangement as before. *But in truth given the size of the place*, she thought, *there were few options for creative decorating.*

She glanced at the bed. It was unmade, the patchwork quilt sloughing off one side, half on the wooden planking of the floor. Her eyes moved toward the kitchen space that had been upgraded somewhat. Another nod to Ikea. The window had been hung with a paper pull-up blind hiding any view of the filthy alley below. Overall, the room still exuded an air of shabbiness and probably always would. But she'd loved this place, the first place she'd lived on her own and one that held so many romantic memories.

"When were you living here," he asked.

"When I was very young – in my twenties. I worked at the Canadian Embassy."

"You're Canadian, then?"

"Yes. Right now, I'm on a cruise with my husband. We stayed here together for a few months. It was a lifetime ago."

"He's not with you?" asked the young man, a look of confusion crossing his face.

"No. He's not feeling well today, unfortunately. I've come alone. You're very kind to allow me to come in. I shouldn't take up any more of your time."

"It's no problem. Would you perhaps like a drink? I have a little wine."

That remark struck Grace as quite funny and she chuckled.

"I'd like that," she said. "I had my first glass of wine in this very room." She laughed softly.

"Sit. Sit," he commanded, clearing the sofa of its toss of newspapers.

Grace sat down and watched her host pull a bottle of red wine from one of the cupboards. He poured two portions into juice glasses and handed one to her.

"Welcome back," he said raising his glass to her.

"Merci," she answered raising her glass in response. She took a sip and savored the distinctive taste of the French wine.

The young man's name was Alain and he was a student taking courses in Hotel Management. He'd lived in the apartment for about a year, but was contemplating a move into a larger place with Yvette, a girl with whom he was desperately in love.

"I envy you Alain," commented Grace after listening to the young man's story. "You and Yvette. This is a very special time for you. You're young and in love. On the brink of life. Treasure this time, for you'll never see it again."

Alain looked at the woman sitting next to him and smiled at her. She'd offered what seemed like a very personal comment to someone who was a virtual stranger. "You must have been…very much in love like that once yourself," he said.

"I was. It was the most wonderful time of my life." She hesitated and then added, "But now, I shouldn't take up any more of your time."

As much as Grace was enjoying the wine and conversation, she was also conscious of her timeline. She still had a couple of things to do before the clock struck three, the time when metaphorically she'd turn into a pumpkin.

"Thanks for your hospitality, Alain," she said placing her glass on a side table marred with scratches. "I've only got a short time here, but it's been such a pleasure meeting you. Good luck with your studies."

"It was nice meeting you as well, Grace," he responded. "I hope your husband is feeling better soon."

"Oh, he'll be fine. Thanks again." She extended a hand and he shook it warmly.

Grace closed the door of the apartment behind her, knowing it would be the last time she'd ever do so and took the stairs down towards the front stoop. She took them slowly, blessing each step with a memory. When she opened the outer door, the sunlight glistened on tears that'd appeared on her cheeks. She'd already checked and refreshed her make-up once that day and knew she'd have to do so again. She turned and walked along the street towards the small café where she'd seen Lee when he first came to Paris. It wasn't there anymore, but the space had been repurposed as a souvenir shop and stocked with every kind of tacky tourist trinket imaginable. She choked back the lump in her throat and retraced her steps to the front of her old apartment, then crossed the green space towards the building where Lee's maestro had lived. She would most certainly not venture inside that day, but took a seat on the bench facing the building. It was a different bench, the old one she was sure, long since retired. Years ago, she and Keir had talked about coming back one day, to sit together in that place. But today she'd come alone.

A passage from William Shakespeare's *The Merchant of Venice,* stirred in her mind.

> *"Here we sit and let the sounds of music*
> *Creep in our ears: soft stillness and the night*
> *Become the touches of sweet harmony."*

Funny, she thought to herself, *that those words should come to her then*. They spoke more of memories with Lee than of those with Keir.

She let her mind wander, allowed it to recall the words the eccentric old musician had spoken to her the day they'd met. He'd presumed she and Lee were a couple. I wonder if Lee ever set him straight, she asked herself. Lee. Lee. And she allowed her mind to wander further, recalling that last night with him. What would her life be like today if she and Lee had made love that night? Oh, that night.

For the most part, she'd tried not to think about Lee and where his life had taken him. It didn't seem right to think about him somehow. Her life had been full – motherhood, traveling, dealing with aging parents, and building a home and a business with Keir. But at that moment, she couldn't help herself. It all came flooding back. She couldn't help wondering about Lee. She'd heard from time to time that he was traveling, performing, and teaching. There'd always been those who felt the need to update her on his activities.

She'd fallen in love with Keir, borne his children, and dedicated her life to his needs. She'd spent most of her life with him and loved him more than life itself. That would never change.

But being in Paris, sitting on that bench on an April afternoon, staring at the maestro's apartment building, brought it all back to Grace and tears welled up once again. Had she really been so in love with Lee? Had she ever fallen 'out' of love with him? Had he ever loved her? She searched her bag for a tissue, dabbed at her eyes, and did a quick repair of her make-up. She rose from the bench and went in search of a cab to take her back to the restaurant. She had just enough time.

***

"Keir?" she called entering the stateroom. He was laying on a lounge on the balcony, sipping a scotch.

"How are you feeling?"

"Much better. Just needed to sleep it off. You know how it is. How was your day? How was Paris?"

"Oh, we went to all the predictable places. The tour guide was okay. Lunch was nothing that special." She hesitated. "The city hasn't really changed...that much. Well you know. It was just... Paris. I brought you a tie."

He took a sip from his glass, gave her a peculiar look, but said nothing.

Grace returned to the stateroom, opened the small bar fridge, and took out a bottle of white wine. She poured herself a glass, took a long slow drink, and welcomed the taste. She turned and studied Keir sitting there on the balcony then went to join him, taking a seat on the lounge beside him.

She turned to him and said, "It was *just* Paris."

16

Though Grace would always feel some regret that Kier missed spending time with her in Paris, she was happy he was able to enjoy the rest of the cruise. The real high point was the day they spent in St. Petersburg.

Entering the city at 6:00 AM, the ship passed a series of docks sprouting rows of cranes loading and unloading cargo, an activity made possible by the early sunrise north of latitude 60°.

St. Petersburg has an immense port area stretching for miles along the Neva River and in the gray morning light all one can see is row upon row of dreary looking utility buildings, the sight of which brings to mind images of the multiple housing units built years ago for the proletariat. But those buildings in no way represent what is seen throughout the rest of the city. In fact, when Peter the Great designed St. Petersburg, he did so with the intention of turning some forty islands into the most beautiful city in the world, one to rival Venice. As one might expect, this is a city of bridges – some 350 of them. The impressive Holy Trinity Bridge was designed by the French engineer Gustave Eiffel. And driving through the city one cannot help but notice the preponderance of yellow buildings, so designed in order to bring a little light to long, dark and dismal winters.

As the ship docked, passengers were met with a brass band playing the theme from the movie, Dr. Zhivago. Debarkation was not as complicated as one might think, Russian authorities merely concerned that the appropriate paperwork was in order.

Keir and Grace were eager to begin a tour of this most fascinating city. The first stop was the Fortress of St. Peter and Paul where many of Russia's royalty rest in tombs in the fort's cathedral. Grace had always been fascinated by the story of the Grand Duchess, Anastasia, and the way several different women had come forward over the years, all claiming to be her. They all professed to having survived the assassination of Czar Nicholas and his family on July 17, 1918. However, the guide assured everyone the family was intact, buried there in a common tomb. Anastasia, the Czar's youngest daughter, was indeed with her family, her remains having finally been located, authenticated, and eventually interred in the church.

Though the ship had sailed into port on a Monday, the day the Hermitage Museum is traditionally closed, by some stroke of serendipity the doors were opened to allow a tour by those from the cruise ship. Even more good fortune prevailed in that because the tour was limited to those people, attendance was extremely light. And passing through the galleries displaying so many priceless works of art, was an experience Grace and Keir would never forget. They'd later describe it to friends and family as mind-boggling.

The museum, composed of a series of five connecting palaces, is over-the-top opulent and houses so many spectacular sculptures and artistic renderings it's impossible for one to take it all in. Looking at the intricately painted ceilings, gold leaf applications on tabletops, and columns and urns carved from semi-precious stone is enough to take one's breath away. It's truly hard to know where to look next. One is overwhelmed with the realization there's more than two dozen Rembrandts housed in the same gallery in which one is standing. It's said it would take nine years to see everything in this museum. And the total value of it all is, of course, incalculable.

"That was an incredible day," declared Keir once they were aboard the bus for the return to the ship.

"Can you believe that museum? That was three-and-a-half hours of my life I will never forget."

"And to think that people actually lived in those palaces in the day. And they didn't even make us take off our shoes or put on those ridiculous booties to walk through."

"Amazing. All those inlaid floors. I don't even like people walking on our floors at home when they're wearing shoes."

"But you know what was the best, though?"

"What was that?"

"There were so few people, we could just walk up and stand in front of a painting with no obstructions. We could've probably reached out and touched any of them except for the babushkas sitting there watching our every move."

"Yah, those old ladies are probably tougher than they look. Wouldn't want to tangle with any of them. But you're right about the accessibility. They say that on a regular day people line up for a couple of hours waiting to enter."

"Yah, and we just walked right in."

"Wow. What a day. Living through the Cold War like we did, did we ever think we'd be able to come to Russia? To see all that magnificent artwork? And walk up the same staircase that Czars walked on? I still remember the day the Americans almost invaded Cuba because of the Russian installation there. And now here we are today – in Russia. How about that?"

"Yeah, how about that." He took her hand and gave it a gentle squeeze. "We've come a long way baby."

"Thank you, Phillip Morris."

He grinned at her reference to a cigarette ad from the 1960s.

The final port of call on the cruise was Stockholm, Sweden, a stop allowing the couple to spend more than just one day exploring an area. They checked into a quirky little hotel a short distance from a cobblestone square, a square featuring a modern mall. It was a significant contrast as the site was otherwise filled with old-world charm. It was getting late in the day when Keir and Grace reached the square and many folks were gathered there after work. Some strolled about while others sat at small tables enjoying cold refreshments. They chose one of the empty tables, ordered a couple of beer and watched a group of dancers in native costume perform traditional folk dances.

Later, they explored the mall and looked for somewhere to pick up a bottle of wine to take back to their room. This was a process that proved to be more difficult than they'd imagined, for liquor laws in Sweden are very strict – a move at encouraging sobriety in this traditionally tankard-tipping culture. At liquor stores, one has to look through a catalogue, make a selection, and order it from the merchant who retires to the warehouse to retrieve the order. It's not possible to order large quantities this way and therefore not uncommon for Swedes to commute regularly to nearby Denmark in order to satisfy their alcoholic needs.

Though the hotel had many failings and appeared to be lacking somewhat when it came to regulating egress, it was conveniently located and gave the couple easy access to the main area of the city. The *'hop-on-hop-off'* bus allowed them to see many attractions, though after a while it seemed to Grace all the opera houses, museums, concert halls, parliament buildings and palaces melded into one big overwhelming blur of stone and brick.

But one museum away from the mainstream fascinated Grace much more than the others, the one that'd been built to enclose an old ship, the Vasa. It had taken over 1,000 oaks to build the ship, and it was one of the most expensive and lavish vessels ever built in Sweden at the time. After completion, the Vasa was launched in 1627 but on her maiden voyage in August of the following year, she was struck with a heavy gust of wind and capsized in the harbor. The death toll was said to be about fifty people. There were attempts to salvage some of her guns a few years later but it was not until early in the 1950s any attempt was made to raise the ship from her watery grave. By 1961, 333 years after she went down, the Vasa was raised, still fairly intact, and along with her contents exhibited as a virtual time machine, the brackish, deoxygenated water and mud having acted as a preservative.

The days in Sweden had been very interesting, but the impression Grace and Keir took away from the time there was that the country was experiencing a population explosion. Almost everywhere they looked, someone was pushing a baby carriage. Grace could not help thinking about her grandson, Theo.

Just as in St. Petersburg, daylight comes early to Stockholm. By 3:00 AM dawn begins to break, though it seemed to the couple the birds had been up chattering since twilight.

They rose with the dawn, packed up, and bid adieu to the unusual space they'd called home for the week. They boarded a train bound for Malmo, a destination allowing for a transfer to one traveling into Copenhagen. Train travel, a very common and convenient mode of transportation in Europe, fascinated Grace who'd never traveled by train in her life. It also fascinated her that there was so much open space in Europe. They traveled through many forested areas and land devoted to thriving farms.

The Danish hotel they'd booked sight unseen was just marginally better than the one in Sweden. The room was spartan with little thought given to furnishings, though it was somewhat more modern than its counterpart in Stockholm. The upside? It was a mere one-half hour train ride into Copenhagen's central station.

"It's like we're back on the ship, Keir," remarked Grace wandering back into the room after checking out the bathroom. "You can shower and brush your teeth at the same time without moving an inch. The closet in our bedroom at home is twice as large."

"Thought you'd like that. Leave it to the Danes to use every square inch of space prudently. This is a very small country, you know. But love it or hate it, it's 'Home Sweet Home' for a few days."

Grace picked up a small suitcase, propped it on the shelf designed to serve any one of a number of uses in the room, and began a search for her nightwear.

"Yes. Home Sweet Home. I'm trying not to sound like all those folks who travel and then complain that *it's not like home*. It's why we travel, right?"

"It is. And here's something you're not going to hear at home." He stepped to the window and pushed it open. "Listen."

"What is that?" she asked, a strange look crossing her face. "It sounds like a cuckoo clock. Remember, my mom had one. And remember how I used to stop it before we went out so my parents wouldn't know what time I came home?"

Keir chuckled at the remembrance and said, "That's no clock. It's a real cuckoo."

"Cuckoos are real birds?"

"Yah. They are."

"Really? I never knew that. How did I get to be this old without knowing there was such a thing as a real cuckoo bird?"

Keir laughed again and laid a hand on her shoulder. "Guess I can still teach you a thing or two, eh?"

They took in the scene beyond the window. A few yards from the hotel was a small pond surrounded by a marshy area and beyond that a clump of forest. Two swans drifted lazily on the pond.

"You've taught me a lot over the years, Keir. You've certainly broadened my horizons. When I look back now I realize how naïve I was. And it hasn't just been the travel. We've had to face a lot in life, haven't we? And we've survived."

"Yes we have. And I've learned a lot from you as well, Grace. It hasn't all been one-sided."

She laid her hand over the one he'd placed on her shoulder. The cuckoo continued his call; Keir gave her hand a squeeze and turned from the window.

"Well, there's more to learn on this trip. And tomorrow is another day. I'm bushed. Which bed do you want?" he asked flipping an arm at the basically appointed twin cots.

"Neither looks terribly comfortable. They almost look like the ones we had on safari – which reminds me…"

"I know what you're going to say. Hold onto that thought." He moved from the window and sat on one of the cots. "I'm taking this bed," he said giving an exaggerated yawn and adding, "the bathroomette is all yours."

After Keir had folded his six-foot frame onto the five-foot cot and fidgeted a moment to find comfort, Grace bent over and gave him a hasty kiss. She dragged a nightgown from the suitcase teetering on the shelf then headed for the bathroom, ready to meet the challenges of Danish plumbing.

In Copenhagen the next day, the couple eschewed the use of a tour package and took advantage of shank's pony. They both loved exploring the central areas of the European cities, areas where many attractions could be accessed on foot. And no trip to Copenhagen would've been complete without a visit to the bronze statue of the *Little Mermaid*. Both were surprised to find the world famous statue so accessible.

The sculpture sits upon a rock at the water's edge off the Langelinie promenade and has been a popular destination for tourists since 1913.

Unfortunately, because of its accessibility, the statue has been the victim of many acts of vandalism over the years.

"You've got the guidebook out again, Grace," remarked Keir as they prepared to take the few steps down to the rocky shore.

"Just wanted to read up a little," returned Grace, a little defensively. "It's not so much compulsion as it is mitigation." She flipped through the book until she found the right page. "It says here the 'mermaid' was commissioned by a man fascinated by a ballet and asked the ballerina, Ellen Price, to model for the statue. She was the model for the head but wouldn't model nude so the sculptor used his wife for the body."

"Wonder who modeled for the tail," quipped Keir.

Grace raised her eyebrows, shrugged and then gave her husband a look. She snapped the book closed and shook her head at Keir's resistance when it came to using such material. She put the book back in her bag then scrambled down the embankment leading to the tumble of rocks on which the mermaid was perched. She stood dutifully and waited for Keir to snap a photo of her with the famous icon.

Back on the promenade, they purchased a miniature sculpture of the *Little Mermaid* then walked back through a beautifully kept park area.

"Rumor has it the statue is just a copy, anyway. The creator's heirs have the original hidden away somewhere," reported Keir.

"Hmm. I guess that's a good thing then. Considering all the times she's been defaced. She's had her head and arms chopped off more than once. I don't know what's wrong with people."

"Me either. There're a lot of people who think the sculpture needs to be moved further out into the harbor to protect her. You may never get another chance to get up so close to her."

"It's such a shame everything has to be rearranged to accommodate those who can't control their destructive urges. Yes, I guess we could very well be some of the last people to see some of these treasures – while they're intact and within our reach. That's one of the things I loved about the Hermitage. Being so close to everything. It made me feel like the old masters were there in the room with me, just ready to pick up a paint brush and make one final definitive stroke on their work of art."

"Another memory to cherish then, I guess," he said wistfully, "before it all changes. That's really the only constant in life, isn't it, Grace? That there *will* always be change."

"We'll never change, Keir," she said. "I'll always love you. We'll always be together."

"I'll always love you too, kiddo," he said with a slight chuckle, feeling the need to lighten the mood. "So what's next on the agenda?"

"Lunch."

Lunch that day, however, was unimpressive, though expensive and Keir and Grace quickly moved on to the Glyptotek Museum to view a collection of art and sculptures. Some had belonged to Carl Jacobsen, son of Denmark's famous brewer.

This collection is enough to overwhelm the most zealous art student and includes original works by Rodin, most notably, *The Thinker*, in both bronze and marble. Once again, the couple found themselves among very few guests in the museum and marveled at how close they were able to get to works of the masters. But a display of noses prompted giggles from Grace. The disembodied appendages were housed in a framework, row upon row, small and large, awaiting reattachment to the various statues missing that vital part of their anatomy. Another giggle escaped her as she imagined drawers full of more *delicate* body parts awaiting a similar restructuring. She'd heard that many male parts had fallen victim during periods in history when a display of such manliness was socially and religiously unacceptable.

Later, in Denmark's Natural Museum and while considering nothing could rival the Hermitage, they were impressed to see innumerable artifacts rescued from peat bogs. These included immense rocks carved with hieroglyphics, runes, coins, axes, and mummified remains. And once again, it was far too much to take in. The following day they decided to make a return visit before heading off to the Christianborg Palace.

They began with a tour of the subterranean foundation where their guide announced Denmark's queen was in the palace for the day, though her official residence is located elsewhere.

"Do you think we'll see her?" asked Grace, aware that Danish royals were somewhat less formal than other European royalty.

"Not likely," replied Keir.

"Well, we can go and take the tour of the palace, anyway, can't we?"

"Sure. We're here. Why not take it all in. Did you check the guide book?"

That remark was ignored and they returned to ground level, purchased tickets for the tour, and put on matching pairs of protective booties. No sign of Her Majesty.

The following day was less formal, Grace and Keir anticipating a trip to 'Legoland,' Denmark's answer to Disneyland. By Canadian standards, the trip by bus would probably have taken about half the time. Two trains and a bus ride later Keir and Grace were deposited in an area that seemed virtually in the middle of nowhere. They had, however, enjoyed the trip as it'd taken them through many subdivisions and small villages in the Danish countryside. But by the time they arrived, they had about one-half the three hours it'd taken them to get there. Still, they marveled at the ingenuity crafters had used when combining the colorful bricks into a myriad of different forms – everything from the Statue of Liberty, to quaint little villages with working water-wheels, to a flock of pink, spindly-legged flamingos. Some displays almost rivaled the sculptures seen in art galleries in the rest of Europe. But at the end of the tour, the trip back to the hotel was no less arduous and the couple arrived back exhausted and clutching packages of precious cargo that would eventually be dispatched to a lad in Africa.

One more day and one more castle. This one Kronberg, in the town of Helsingor. It was once a strategic fortification overlooking the water between Denmark and Sweden and is often referred to as Hamlet's Castle, having been immortalized in Shakespeare's famous play. It is also a World Heritage site.

After a tour of this most impressive structure, surprisingly still very much intact, Keir and Grace wandered the town.

"I absolutely love these old buildings and the little hideaway lanes here. Each one has a fascination greater than the last. Everything at home seems to be laid out in such straight lines, strewn with twentieth century buildings with no magic or mystery. Don't you just love following these little winding passageways into alleys where we find such quaint little shops? You know, like that little hidden bookstore we saw back there, the one only the locals seem to know about. It's such an adventure – getting off the beaten path, I mean. You've done that for me, Keir. I know we do all the 'touristy' things, but we always seem to find so much more. Things most other folk might not have nerve enough to venture out to see. Things that aren't in the 'guidebook.'" She said the last word using air quotes.

He had to smile at her sarcasm. "It's a good thing I've honed my sense of direction over the years or we might never get out of some of these hidden alleyways."

"I'm never concerned when I'm with you. You've always been able to find your way around ever since I've known you. Like in the mountains back home. And even in the city, you always seem to know exactly where you are."

"You'll never be lost when you're with me, Grace. And I'll always be with you, showing you the way."

She smiled but didn't reply. She had no idea she'd have cause to reflect on those words in days to come.

"Lunch?" Keir asked as they wandered back into a more populated part of the village.

"Lunch sounds good."

And it was. Two delicious open-face sandwiches – slices of heavy rye topped with filets of delicately fried sole, asparagus spears, and slices of hard-boiled egg. They washed it down with a couple of Tuborg beer. It was a fitting lunch for a day of adventure in a most charming Danish town.

But the last day in Denmark was the one that Grace had most looked forward to for it was the one that would take the couple to a museum in Rungstedlund, the home of Karen Blixen. According to brochures (which seemed to be in short supply), the trip could be made on the same train they'd taken to Helsingor. They expected to transfer along the way to a bus running near the home, now a museum. Unfortunately, one finds things are not always as written in the brochures. For some reason known only to the Danish rail authorities, the train did not stop that day at the appointed station and continued on along the line depositing Keir and Grace back in the town they had visited the previous day. At the station, they were advised by the agent to take the train back down the line and change to another train, one that would take them to their desired destination. Since the train was not due to depart for some time, they wandered the streets, eventually visiting the tourist center. It was there they were advised it was much more convenient to access the museum by bus. That had some appeal despite the lengthy ride they'd had to *Legoland*, but nonetheless, they purchased two tickets and hoped for the best. Aboard the bus, they were once again able to take in views of the Danish countryside – both rural and urban. Since they'd no idea what route the vehicle would take or how long the trip would be, they'd asked the driver to announce the stop when they arrived at the museum.

"There it is," cried Grace as the bus cruised right on by a sign indicating the site.

"What," said Keir, who'd been peering out the window on the other side of the bus?

"The museum. It's back that way," said Grace flapping her arms.

Keir rose and went to the front of the bus to check with the driver. He appeared not to understand, but stopped to let the couple disembark.

"Good grief," said Grace. "It's blocks back. It's like no one cares if we see this museum. In the first place, we could hardly find a brochure on the place. Then the train whistled right by the station we were supposed to get off at, and now the bus driver didn't want to stop here." The level of her voice had risen with her level of frustration, for this museum had been at the top of Grace's list of things she wanted to see while in Denmark.

Keir shrugged. "How many miles have we put on these shoes this month? A couple more miles isn't going to kill us. Come on Karen. Suck it up."

She was still not amused but followed her husband the few blocks back to the entrance of the estate. Karen Blixen had been born in the home, lived most of her life there and died there in 1962 at the age of seventy-seven. Her life on a coffee plantation in Kenya from 1914 to 1931 had inspired a book chronicling events with both her husband Baron Bror von Blixen-Finecke and her lover Denys Finch-Hatton. The book was subsequently turned into an award-winning movie in 1985 and featured Robert Redford and Meryl Streep in the starring roles.

More booties were handed out before Keir and Grace were allowed to take the tour, view the desk on which Karen penned her famous book and listen to the guide review details of the author's life. But it'd been worth the trip for Grace after all. After a tour of the inside of the home, she and Keir ventured out into the garden, a large meadow dotted with groves of aspen and ash and beds abloom with a profusion of colorful spring flowers.

"How beautiful," declared Grace as the two strolled through the garden hand in hand. They stopped for a moment to view Karen Blixen's gravesite. The stone marking her burial place sat solitary and plain at the base of a large tree. Someone had sprinkled a few pink flower petals on the gravestone etched with her name.

"Having read the book, seen the movie and now seeing where she lived and is buried – we've taken it all in, haven't we? The whole story," she continued.

"Yes, Grace. It's all here," he agreed. His voice had a ring of sadness to it. "It's all here."

Grace pulled her hand from his and stopped. "This is having a weird effect on you, isn't it Keir? What are you thinking about?"

"Well – you know. Coming here – it reminds me of the eternal circle of life. Karen Blixen's life, no matter what she found in Kenya, Finch-Hatton, the love of her life, the hardships she endured. Well, she ended up right back here in her home in Denmark. Just like Ian did – all those years searching for a life, trying to carve out a career, looking for – and I guess finding love. Eventually, he came home – full circle back to the green lake he so loved."

Grace glanced at the man, the man she loved and with whom she'd spent decades. A man who'd given her a life she could never have imagined. *Why had Keir become so unsettled that day? Was he beginning to feel his own mortality?* she wondered. That was the last thing she wanted to think about on this trip. The holiday had been wonderful, full of fabulous memories – just the kind of adventure they both loved. They'd be leaving Denmark to fly home the next day and she wanted no sadness in the last few hours.

She pulled her gaze from him and looked beyond to a gray wooden bench sheltered by the branches of a towering oak. She took Keir's hand to guide him to it, intending they should sit quietly together for a few moments. She'd been so moved by his words and felt the need to compose herself, never having expected the visit to Karen Blixen's museum to have had such an effect on her husband.

"Oh, my god," she cried.

"What. I'm sorry, Grace. I didn't mean to be so…"

"No, Keir. Look. Look at this bench. Look at the name on it. It has my name…"

His gaze went to the plaque riveted to the wooden framework.

"Huh. So it has. How odd."

"What do you suppose that means?"

"Hell if I know. Do you really want to read something into it?" His demeanor had changed quickly after his reflective words about Ian.

Grace pulled a tissue from the pocket of her sweater, dabbed at eyes that'd begun to sting with tears and said, "I traded names with Karen when we were in Kenya, Keir. And now here we are in her garden and my name is on this bench. That's got to mean something, doesn't it?"

Keir looked at his wife of so many years. They'd had the best of times and the worst of times. He loved her so. She meant everything to him.

"Come, Grace. Let's just sit a while and admire the garden. Reflect on the past month and all we've shared on this trip. We'll remember Denys and Karen and the profound love they had for one another."

"Like us?"

"Yep. Just like us."

"Do you think they'll ever make a movie about our life?"

"That would be something, wouldn't it? Do you think Redford will be too old to play me?"

Grace didn't answer but gave her husband a fond look, a look tinged with playfulness.

"I love you, Denys," she said.

"I love you, too, Karen."

Karen and Denys sat on the garden bench until a custodian came to announce the museum was closing.

"How do we get back to Copenhagen?" asked Keir of the woman, fearing another meandering bus trip.

"Just walk to the end of the garden," she said indicating a pathway. "There's a fence and then beyond it a couple of blocks you will see the railway platform. Catch the train there and it will take you back into the city."

"No way," groaned Keir.

"Well, come on, Denys," Grace said rising from the bench. "We're just a hike through the forest, a fence vault and two train rides away from those safari cots and the mini bathroom. Life is good."

Hand in hand, they retreated from the beautiful garden and memories of the woman who'd inspired a spate of role-playing understood by only the two them.

Love and memory – what wonderful gifts the universe has given us…

17

The trip to Europe had been memorable and Keir and Grace returned home refreshed and eager to plan for more adventures abroad. Grace had saved every ticket, coupon, and receipt and put them together with Keir's photos into three large albums.

The following year, they restricted themselves to some mini trips, sightseeing close to home and taking occasional 'mental health days.' They traveled to the mountains a few times, but never went to the green lake.

But there was no argument from Grace the next year when Keir suggested another cruise. The plan was to fly to Istanbul and tour the area for a few days before boarding a ship having stops in Athens, some of the Greek islands and Israel.

Every time they planned such adventurous excursions, Grace was reminded of the days when they were young and could barely afford to put gas in the car. She was also reminded of the few months she'd spent with Keir in Paris and how he'd had to sell his car to pay for his airfare.

It was mid-September when the couple boarded a plane bound for Toronto with connections to Munich and Istanbul. After an exhausting eighteen hours, they reached their destination, fortunately during daylight hours. After paying $60.00 each for visas, they passed easily through customs and out into the exit area of the airport. They'd arranged for a driver to take them into Istanbul, some distance away, but had no idea how they'd find him. What they did find, seemed like it might have been an episode of a Turkish game show. Lined up in the entranceway were dozens of drivers and tour guides, each one holding up a card. This required those who'd deplaned to walk up and down the rows of the taxi drivers until they found a card bearing their name.

And so began the quest, the couple jostling amongst other tourists, all trying to pick their driver from a throng of dozens. Eventually they were matched with their driver, one who spoke perfect English, and began the trip into the city for their Turkish adventure.

Istanbul is a huge and fascinating city – a mix of ancient and modern. One inescapable feature is the abundance of old stone walls everywhere, a sight causing one ponder their origin and wonder about those who'd labored long and hard to place those thousands of stones.

Grace knew Keir would've read everything he could about the history and culture of the land and could give her a thumbnail history lesson if ever she queried him.

For most of the long trip from the airport, they'd traveled modern highways but once into the heart of the city the roads narrowed into lanes winding through small markets and apartment complexes. Clotheslines strung between the buildings sported all manner of apparel, women walked the cobbled streets toting purchases from the markets, and children dodged traffic while chasing mangy scrap-scrounging cats.

One lane led to another and then another and Grace knew that even with Keir's keen sense of direction, he would be challenged to find his way back through the labyrinth. At the bottom of the last lane, the driver put the vehicle into reverse and backed up a small hill to the front door of the hotel. It seemed they'd come to the end of the world for it was impossible to access the building in any other way. What lay beyond, the couple could only guess.

"Oh my gosh, Keir," declared Grace. "Where on earth are we?"

"Isn't this crazy? Do you think we'll ever get out of here?"

"Not without a rescue team."

They stepped out of the taxi; when the driver had unloaded their luggage Keir pulled out his wallet and paid him in US dollars.

"Ready for an adventure?" Keir asked Grace.

"Well, I'm not sure about this one. It kind of reminds me of our trip to Africa. I wonder how Penny ever found this place out here in the middle of heaven knows where."

"Oh no. Don't do that. Don't go all *tourist* on me." He gave her a grin. "And there's no turning back now." He picked up a couple of pieces of luggage leaving the lighter bags for her.

"Well, it doesn't look too bad from the outside," she ventured, glancing at the white stone and glass exterior.

And there was a certain charm about the small hotel, the balconies and arched windows typical of other buildings they would see in Turkey.

A revolving door led them into a large reception area.

"Oh my god, Keir," she gasped. "Look at this place." The sight before them had taken her breath away for it was far from what she'd expected. White marble flooring stretched from wall to wall and was strewn with colorful Persian carpets. Pillars of polished white marble soared upward supporting the twenty-foot high ceilings, ceilings hung with crystal chandeliers. Brocade sofas and armchairs were clustered around glass and wrought iron coffee tables and the reception desk to one side rivaled every piece of amazing furniture Grace had ever seen. It'd been built from an array of exotic woods inlaid in an intricate pattern. It seemed too beautiful to serve such a utilitarian purpose.

"That's it. I'm never leaving here," she declared, carefully setting down her two bags on the brightly patterned carpet. "Really, Keir. I'm staying here forever. This is what I always envisioned a hotel in Casablanca would look like."

"Of all the gins joints in all the towns in the world…" began Keir. "Do we have to pretend we're Rick and Ilsa this time?"

"Boy, do you know your classic movies."

"Well how many times have you made me watch that old flick?"

"Good afternoon," interrupted the hotelier.

"Yes, good afternoon," replied Keir approaching the desk to attend to the practical matter of check-in. He handed the man the couple's documents while Grace continued to take in the opulence of the hotel lobby. While the look of cool marble dominated the space, the placement of plush furnishings and scattering of carpets gave it a sense of homey comfort.

"I can't get over this space," Grace declared when Keir returned to her holding keys to their room. "It's just so…grand. It's wonderful. Remind me to tell Penny when we get back home. Oh wait a minute, I said I wasn't going back home."

"You haven't seen our room yet."

"Well, if it's half as nice as this I'll be ecstatic. Besides I'm so tired after all the traveling, I just want to take a shower and sleep for a few hours."

"The concierge advises against that. He says we should try to stay up so we can get our internal clock to reset to Turkish time."

"Yah, he's probably right. Just a shower then. Hope the bathroom is decent."

They followed the hallway to the bank of elevators and proceeded to the third floor. Their room was large and immaculate with doorways arched in Moorish style. The king-sized bed was firm and the pattern on the heavy bedspread reminiscent of the carpets in the lobby. The bathroom was well appointed, with sparkling fixtures and an abundance of soaps and creams on the marble countertop.

"Wow. How is it that the Turks can get things so right? In all our traveling, this has to be the most fabulous bathroom ever. Look. The taps are shaped like little ducks. And the bathtub is big enough for three people. Remember Denmark? The whole bathroom would have fit into this tub. Yup. Never leaving here."

"I'm so tempted to lie down but our tour starts at 9:00 AM tomorrow," said Keir. "I'm whacked after that trip. I think I'll just have a shower too, some supper and then see how I feel."

"Sounds good. I can't think when we last ate. On one of the planes I think. Whatever it was it was so underwhelming I can't remember." She moved to the small desk near the window and pawed through a series of brochures." It says here that dining is on the roof. Can this place get any better?"

"We'll see. I'm off to the shower. See if you can find me something to wear."

The rooftop restaurant was enclosed with a glass screen allowing diners a bird's-eye view of a nearby white stone mosque and the tops of neighboring buildings. And from this vantage point, it was also possible to see in the distance, the Bosporus, the body of water separating the continents of Europe and Asia.

The waiter handed each one a menu featuring North American cuisine and gave Keir the menu devoted to alcoholic beverages.

"That's interesting," declared Keir when the waiter had left. "In a country that doesn't encourage the consumption of alcohol, there seems to be no problem for tourists to order what they want. Remember the process in Sweden?"

"Sure do. But that was a great trip, wasn't it? Hope this one turns out as well."

"Me too."

He turned his attention to the wine list and when the waiter returned ordered a bottle of medium priced white.

"I'm really looking forward to tomorrow. Penny certainly outdid herself on this hotel. Let's hope the tour goes as well."

"So far so good."

The waiter returned, opened the wine, and allowed Keir a taste. After approval, he filled two wine glasses half full.

Keir took his glass, raised it to her, and said, "Here's loo…"

"Don't say it. Don't say it."

"…looking at you, kid," he finished. Then, a grin.

Dinner was delicious, the service excellent, and the brush of calm breezes chasing away the heat and humidity of the day, refreshing.

A short walk after dinner took the two beyond the hotel where they discovered to their surprise and delight they were virtually in the heart of the city and not in some remote location where they'd never get their bearings. A busy thoroughfare nearby featured a rapid transit line and small shops and restaurants abounded. Feral cats lay like corpses along the walkways and hidden within the plantings in the parks. No one discourages the presence of these creatures, most grateful they help keep the city free of rats and other vermin. This city of fifteen million human souls is indeed considered very clean.

It was still early in the evening and the city crackled with energy. Keir and Grace listened as impatient drivers who apparently had little understanding of basic traffic rules, opted to use horns rather than signal lights. And they watched with horror as pedestrians flung themselves with happy abandon, out into breaks in traffic.

A stop at the *Million Stone* provided Grace with the first of her history lessons. This stone pillar is a small fragment of the triumphal arch monument erected by Constantine the Great to mark the starting place of distances to all cities in the Byzantine Empire.

Their stroll eventually took them to a small park where they sat observing others who'd ventured there. A beautiful water feature, the Fountain of Sultan Ahmet III, dominated the space and tossed a cooling spray of water droplets onto all nearby. Vendors sold cobs of corn and watermelon from small wagons.

"Look at those boys there, Keir," said Grace, with a slight nod. The children were five or six years old and dressed in sultan-like costumes of white and silver. They carried small, jeweled scepters.

"Hmm. Wonder what that's all about. No one else seems to be dressed up in any way."

"I guess we can ask at the hotel when we get back."

"Speaking of which, I think it's time. Let's go; we've got a busy day tomorrow."

"So far this has been so fascinating. I love this city. It's so vibrant and there's so much to see. I don't know what fascinates me the most – the mosques, the people, the shops. I'm really looking forward to the tour."

"Me too. But first a good night's sleep."

They rose from the bench and headed back the way they'd come. At the hotel, an enquiry about the costumed children had the couple both fascinated and a little disturbed. It was revealed the evening out for the boys was in preparation for an event they'd probably remember with little fondness – their upcoming ceremonial circumcision.

By the light of a new day and after a well-deserved sleep, Keir and Grace were anxious to experience more of Istanbul's colorful spirit. They walked down the hill and met the young man who'd be their guide for the next two days. In his van sat two other couples who'd also signed on for the tour. Keir looked at Grace for guidance as to which names they'd use for the tour but a slight shake of her head told him there'd be no new identities that day.

The driver retraced the confusing system of alleys they'd traversed when accessing the hotel the day before, and once again, Keir and Grace were captivated by the charm of Istanbul's quaint laneways.

And no tour of the city can begin until one has had a cup of Turkish tea, a delicious black blend served in tiny glasses set on miniature saucers. After the refreshment, the guide moved his charges through the monument area and gave a detailed recitation of the city's complex history. Keir was able to ask some intelligent questions of the guide, while the rest of the group, completely confused by the enormity of the information, pretended to be thoroughly engaged and made no comment. Everyone snapped dozens of pictures and Grace knew she would easily fill several more scrapbooks.

The lunch included in the tour package was a serious affair, a seven-course wonder in fact. A salad of lettuce, tomatoes, cucumber, and grated carrot was followed by thin saucer-sized pizzas, a loaf of puffy bread called lavash, a vegetable plate, cheese blintzes, a mixed grill of three meats, rice, and garnishes and finally a plate of delicious fresh fruit. And there was no problem ordering a glass of wine or beer to accompany the feast.

By the time, the tour arrived at the Blue Mosque where predictably the use of protective booties was required, Grace and Keir were on sensory overload. The travelers were informed that the pattern on the wall-to-wall carpeting in the mosque was arranged to facilitate correct alignment to Mecca, though they found it note-worthy there were relatively few worshippers present. Here, visitors began to hear what was to become a recurring theme, a theme giving the term recycling a whole new meaning. Marble in the building had been recycled from the Hippodrome, an ancient track facility for horse and chariot racing that'd finally fallen into ruin by the fifteenth century.

Standing behind the barrier separating worshippers from others, travelers looked up in awe at the domed roof supported by four immense pillars. Shafts of light spilled through stained-glass windows throwing shards of color onto thousands of blue tiles on the walls, tiles giving the building its modern-day name. It appeared that no expense had been spared in Sultan Ahmet I's monument to himself. It was his intent that this mosque rival the grandness of the Aya Sofya, a church constructed centuries earlier and the next stop on the tour.

The Aya Sofya is Istanbul's most famous landmark and had been built in 537 as a Christian edifice. It survived as such until 1453 when it was converted to a mosque. It was subsequently declared a museum in 1935. A hybrid, if you will, it is now a curious mix of Christian and Muslim relics, and like the Blue Mosque features a dramatic dome, this one supported by dozens of decorative ribs. More than twenty restorations have been required to maintain this amazing structure.

"I'm without words, Keir," breathed Grace upon entering the church. "Even as I remember marveling at other churches in Europe this has to be the most unbelievable place I've ever seen."

"Better buy some postcards, Grace. We're never going to capture the magnitude of this place with our little digital – especially with all these other folks milling about."

"There must be thirty or forty chandeliers – and look at that dome. It's hard to imagine anyone could engineer a structure like this way back in the sixth century."

"Why, Grace. Have you been reading the guide books again?"

"Just wanted to keep a little ahead of you, dear."

The day's tour continued with a trip to the Basilica Cistern, built in 532 as water storage for the palace and other state buildings. After taking the steps down into this subterranean wonder, one first encounters a small café. On occasion visitors may listen to a concert or watch a fashion show while enjoying a cup of Turkish tea here. Understandably, acoustics experienced during such events are unlike those found anywhere else on earth. And it is not unusual for couples who want a memorable day to be married in this most unique setting.

"Many of the columns, plinths, and capitals used in the construction of the cistern were rescued from demolished Roman buildings," announced the guide.

"Wow. That's recycling to the nth degree," said Keir as the tour group traversed the boardwalks stretching deep into the cool hollow.

"How awesome is this?" replied Grace, gazing at the ancient columns supporting the structure. She pointed to four stone columns supported at the base by carvings of Medusa, the quartet of inverted snake-covered heads emerging from small pools of water.

"And naturally, anywhere where pools of water abide folks are tempted to toss a coin or two," continued the guide. "These coins are retrieved, washed, and used to buy food for the many carp that swim and thrive here."

After returning to ground level, everyone was ready for a cup of tea before the next stop on the tour, the Topkapi Palace. It was interesting to Grace that in many of the large cities she'd visited the main attractions were clustered near one another. It made sense of course, for when they were built movement for the masses was mainly by foot-power.

Topkapi Palace, a display of sheer opulence, was over the centuries the scene of much drama including unbridled debauchery, imprisonment and continual and brutal power struggles. Viewing the entrance to the palace for the first time, visitors may be reminded of Cinderella's castle in Disneyland. The palace is built around a central courtyard surrounded by pavilions, kitchens, audience chambers, and sleeping areas and requires some length of time to see in detail. The guide led the group through a series of courts, each one seemingly more unique than the last, and then announced the final stop on the tour.

Although she did not recognize it for what it was, it was here on this stop in a palace conceived in 1453 by Mehmet the Conqueror, that things would begin to change for Grace and Keir.

"Our next stop on the tour is the Treasury where you'll be able to view one of the world's most fabulous collections of jewels and artifacts," announced the guide. "I guarantee you've never seen anything like it before."

"Sounds fabulous," said Grace.

"You go on, Grace. There's too many people lined up there. I'll take a little breather."

"Really, Keir? It's once in a lifetime," replied Grace giving her husband a curious look. She knew jewelry was probably not his thing but thought he might've found some of the artifacts of interest.

"No, you go on ahead," he said casually. "I'll just stroll around outside here. Take a few pictures."

"Okay. If you're sure. Come find me if you change your mind."

"Will do," he said taking a seat on a small bench.

Once inside, Grace realized it would have been impossible for Keir to have joined her. She'd been forced into a throng of people moving slowly through the display, stopping periodically to view more closely the priceless gemstones, the jewel encrusted swords and pots, and the oversized caftans designed to make the sultans look larger. It was an unparalleled display of wealth worthy of any powerful ruler.

Keir was still sitting on the bench when she emerged from the building and she went to join him there.

"That was incredible. The guide was right. I've never seen anything like it. There's even a display of Christian artifacts – Moses' staff if you please. I wonder if it's really genuine. And how on earth do you suppose the sultan came by it?"

He smiled at her childlike excitement and the quizzical look on her face.

"Guess we'll never know," he said. "Oh, here's our guide rounding everyone up. What a day, eh. Grace? Bed will feel good tonight."

"Yes, it sure has been a day. I hope I can remember everything the guide told us about the palace. This city has the most fascinating history. You know it's one thing to read about it in a guidebook but quite another to hear the tidbits offered on a tour. You know – the more intimate stuff." She rambled on as they moved to join the others returning to the tour van.

"See what I've been telling you all this time?" said Keir. "Put away that guidebook."

"You're right, of course. There's a lot more to the story than what's written in the guidebooks. Like here in the palace for instance. It took four hundred cooks working in the kitchen to feed 4000 people living in the court. And a fire in the kitchen predicted bad luck for the household. And the eunuchs in the harem were from Sudan and were chosen for their ugliness. Hmm. But there were also blond women in the harem brought there as slaves. And get this – the sultan could only visit the harem at the discretion of his mother."

"Hmm. Yes, I heard that. Good thing we don't have that policy back home."

"Yes, well…we also discourage harems," she said sarcastically.

"Oh, right. What other tidbits of info have you squirreled away today?"

"Oh my goodness, there was so much packed into such a short time. And tomorrow is another day."

"Right, Scarlett. We need to get back to the hotel and rest up."

She gave him one of those looks.

***

Back at the hotel Grace and Keir kicked off their shoes and flopped onto the large bed for a well-deserved rest. It'd been an exhausting but extremely interesting day and that preview had made them more than anxious to see whatever else was in store. They drifted off into a light slumber, and arose looking forward to another delicious evening meal on the hotel rooftop.

***

"Would you like a bottle of the same wine you ordered last evening?" the waiter enquired.

"Yes, that would be great," replied Keir, impressed by the gracious service. When the wine was served, Keir took a sip from his glass and spoke softly.

"Even with all our traveling I don't know when I've had a more interesting day, Grace. What about you?"

"It was amazing. It's all here isn't it, Keir? The history. The fantastic buildings. The people. Hearing the ancient and haunting call to prayer echoing from minaret to minaret. These are moments we'll probably never experience again."

"You're right. I don't think we'll ever find anything to compare to this. Come sit beside me, dear so we can watch the sun go down. It's part of the whole magic of this place."

Grace moved to sit beside Keir and together they watched as the sun, a solitary white orb ringed in pink, made its last appearance of the day before surrendering to the quiet waters of the sea.

"Happy?" he asked.

"I am. This has been like a dream, Keir. I don't want it to end."

He drew her close to him and kissed her softly. And in those magical moments, Grace fell in love with Keir all over again.

***

The following day the adventure continued with a trip on the Bosporus to view the many spectacular waterfront buildings. One stop was at the summer palace, an impressive structure that reportedly houses the world's largest chandelier weighing four-and-a-half tons. Other points of interest included the suspension bridge connecting the continents of Europe and Asia and a long distance view of Robert College, the largest American school outside of the United States. Grace wrote furiously in her journal recording the details of these sights to pair them later with the many photos Keir was snapping.

And no trip to Istanbul would be complete without a visit to the bazaar and the spice market. These places are always crowded elbow to elbow and like the roadways, there's little polite regard given to space occupied by others.

Though Grace found the atmosphere exciting, the variety of items for sale intriguing and the method of bartering challenging, she did note that Keir was less than enchanted. She knew crowds had never really been his thing, a hike in the great outdoors much more to his liking, but he had always been thoroughly engaged in the culture of an area on their previous trips abroad. *Perhaps he's still a bit jet-lagged,* she thought to herself as they returned to the hotel after the busy day.

Before Grace had finished packing away the souvenirs they'd purchased that day, Keir had fallen into a deep sleep. When he awoke, they ate a light supper and retired early in preparation for the trip to Ephesus the following day.

***

The ancient city of Ephesus, once the capital of the Roman province of Asia, was excavated over a period of 150 years and has been well preserved. But, it's believed 80% of the city has yet to be uncovered. A quarter of a million people once called this city home making it the fourth largest city in the Roman Empire. A visit here gives one some insight into the way of life experienced by those living in ancient Greece and Rome.

The day was hot and throngs of folk were emerging from the many buses and vans in the parking area. Grace and Keir's tour began at the Magnesia Gate and the two began to work their way downward along the Curetes Way. One stop was Mary's house or rather the church built atop the foundation of the home Mary was alleged to have lived in after the death of her son, Jesus.

"Wow, Ian would have loved this place," remarked Keir as they moved along the uneven roadways. Large pieces of marble such as that seen in the Blue Mosque were evident everywhere, scattered amongst the pillars, porticos, and archways. "It must have been quite the experience to be in on a dig of this magnitude."

"I'll say," replied Grace. "We have nothing like this at home. It seems like we demolish everything over a hundred years old there. I guess that's why we love to come to Europe – to see all the history. But it's hard to take it all in sometimes, isn't it? "

A nod from Keir.

The guide chattered away as they approached the Great Theatre, a U-shaped structure rising high above the stage. The stone-tiered seating had been designed to accommodate thousands of people.

"Archaeologists," said the guide, waving his pointer finger at the tiers, "often use structures such as this to estimate the population of cities. For instance, this theater would hold approximately 25,000. The rule of thumb then is to take that number and multiply it by ten to get the approximate population of the city. In this case the estimate is 250,000."

"That's interesting," Grace remarked turning to Keir. He'd moved from her side and was sitting on a small ledge formed by broken stone. "It's pretty hot, isn't it," she continued, moving to his side and noting his demeanor.

"Yah, I guess that's it. I just want to sit down for a bit."

"We're moving on, Keir. There's still more on the tour."

"You go on, Grace. I'll either catch up or I'll meet you back at the bus."

"Are you sure, Keir? This tour was one of the main reasons you wanted to come to Turkey. You don't seem to be enjoying it that much."

"I'm fine, Grace. Really. Go on. You can fill me in on the details later. Here, take the camera."

"You know I take lousy pictures."

"Then we'll buy some postcards later. Go on now."

"Keir."

"Go."

"Okay, see you in a bit. Keep your hat on and have some water."

"Don't nag me, woman. Go."

"I'm going. I'm going." She took the camera from him and moved to join the rest of the tour.

Grace found her husband a short time later. He was slouched up against the side of the tour van sipping on his bottled water.

"Are you alright, Keir?" she asked. "You seem kind of pale."

"It's the heat. You know how it gets to me sometimes. I'm a cool climate kinda guy. That's why I finally left Hawaii, you know," he said defensively. "It was way too hot for me there."

"So you've said more than once. Are you're sure that's all it is?"

"I'm fine. Really."

"Too bad you had to miss some of the tour. What an awesome place. I could've almost fancied myself an ancient citizen walking through the city."

"Were you a great female warrior – an Amazon perhaps? They're reputed to have founded this place, you know."

"No. I didn't know that. They didn't live in the Amazon?"

"Nope. The word amazon has something to do with breasts."

"Breasts? Hmm. That's interesting. Did the Amazons really live apart from men?"

"They did. Most of the time. Or so the legend goes. It's all legend. "

"Well I could never do that. I'd be lost without you, Keir."

"I'm not going anywhere, Grace. We'll be growing old together in the 'home,' playing canasta, trying to remember where we put our teeth." He gave her a grin. "Oh, here's the driver. Not looking forward to the long drive back but thank goodness the van has air conditioning. It's a cool shower for me and a glass of that stuff we keep in the fridge in our room. And I may not necessarily do it in that order."

"A glass of wine sure sounds good to me," she agreed. And they stepped into the van.

They boarded the ship the next day, bound for the port of Mandraki and a tour of several of the Greek islands. Grace was watchful of Keir as he seemed to be having difficulty keeping up with the rest of the group during the tours. Keir, the man who'd once scaled mountains with such ease could now barely climb the stairs to enter an ancient church. And it began to seem to Grace that everything worth seeing was situated at the top of a stone stairway or on a mountaintop. Couldn't these people build anything on a flat surface?

Leaving the Greek islands behind, the ship moved on to Cypress. Though to that point, most of the tours had been fascinating and everything the couple could have wanted in terms of historical interest and friendly interaction, the same could not have been said of Cypress. Most of the island seemed to be torn up for roadwork, the van driver was belligerent and testy and the museum uninviting. After an hour on shore, the couple and many others returned to the ship and Keir spent the balance of the day on the balcony of their floating home nursing a glass of scotch.

For Grace, Israel was every bit as fascinating as Turkey had been. Fortunately, they were able to view many of the tourist attractions during short stops on a bus tour, and Keir was able to manage the walking during those times.

One thing that came as a surprise to Grace was that the town of Bethlehem is actually in the Palestinian area, the West Bank, an area held separate by a huge cement wall topped with barbed wire. Traveling towards Bethlehem, the bus headed into the Judean Mountains and passed through the valley where Goliath met his end at the hand of the young shepherd boy, David. At the checkpoint between the two areas, bus passengers were treated to a visit from authorities who came aboard and walked the aisle carrying machine guns, for there are very stringent procedures in place regarding who is allowed to cross the border. Apparently, all requirements were met that day and the bus moved on to the Church of the Nativity.

This Catholic Church is significant for having one of the lowest doorways one could ever encounter, a huge problem for those like Keir who hovered over the six-foot mark. Even those of shorter stature were required to stoop, the move forcing exaggerated bows of reverence. Once inside Grace and Keir were pushed into a throng of other pilgrims, many hoping for the ultimate mystical experience, a view of the grotto in which the Christ Child was thought to have been born. Given the number of people crammed into the space, it was apparent the fire marshal had few powers of enforcement here. After a few moments in the place Keir begged off and told Grace he'd wait for her outside the door, that egress point also seriously non-compliant when it came to fire-codes.

Grace pressed forward for a few moments hoping to get a glimpse of the grotto, but with the many people sitting in prayer on the steps leading down into the chamber, it was impossible. In the mayhem, priests above tried to conduct mass and security guards attempted to silence the chattering tourists and guides. Outside, the heat of the day was much less oppressive than the atmosphere in the church and when Grace was finally able to emerge from the congestion she informed her husband she'd been unable to experience anything close to a moment of epiphany within that stifling place.

And so it went, Grace trying vainly to enjoy the trip, while Keir, a man who'd always traveled with such enthusiasm for adventure, declined so many opportunities. He'd always had a thirst for learning about the world, absorbing every detail during their travels together, shaking his head in amusement at Grace's naïve excitement over discovering new things. This trip had taken a turn neither had expected.

The ship would eventually dock in Athens where Keir and Grace spent a few days before returning home. From their hotel, located centrally, they were able to walk to the Presidential Palace and many other points of interest, though they found the unrest in the city disconcerting. A heavy police presence kept marchers and protesters under watch and large black military buses were parked everywhere. With Greek citizenry apparently unhappy about European monetary conditions, many were choosing to express their dissatisfaction by staging large, noisy marches and strikes involving transportation in and out of the city. It was with relief that the couple departed Athens just hours before the airports were closed by striking workers. It was the last trip they would take.

18

Grace unpacked the many treasures collected by the couple on their latest trip abroad and then set about putting right the house that hadn't seen their presence for many weeks. It was good to be home, but the homecoming was marred by a feeling of unease. Keir hadn't been himself on the trip and as much as Grace wanted to put it down to jet lag and extreme heat, deep within her she knew something was very wrong. It reminded her of when Benjamin had first been diagnosed. Doctors had tried to quell the couple's worst fears when examining the large swelling on the child's neck, had even mentioned a number of possible reasons for the swelling. They'd carefully avoided the word 'cancer.' But in the end, it was apparent any supposed alternative to the obvious was moot.

With reluctance, Grace picked up the phone and made an appointment with the family's physician. Keir had always been healthy, rebounding from illness and most physical injuries quickly, and when he did complain it was usually about migraines or a nagging backache, the result of a fall during his early years in the construction industry. On the trip, it'd been difficult for Grace to watch her husband struggle with activities he'd undertaken with ease in the past.

The next few weeks were consumed with visits to clinics, labs, and diagnostic facilities. There was a sickening feeling of déjà vu for the two, sitting for hours on the world's most uncomfortable seating, watching other folks wander about in hospital smocks clutching fistfuls of lab forms and dreading news that was sure to bring about a change in their lives.

Keir's lungs and heart had been seriously compromised the specialist advised. He'd seen it before in men who'd worked in construction, men who in their youth had worked unprotected when handling toxic materials such as formaldehyde, asbestos, and creosote. They'd unknowingly been at serious risk in an era when wearing protective gear was never a consideration. Keir had also been a smoker in his younger days and that'd most certainly impacted on his health as well.

He was put on a series of medications to help alleviate some of his breathing problems and irregular heart rhythm and advised against aggravating his condition by indulging in a lot strenuous activity. And above all doctors stressed, a bout of pneumonia could be deadly. It was not a comforting message Keir and Grace received from medical personnel.

Keir had all but retired from his trade, content to putter in the garden or patch up small pieces of furniture for friends, but he was restless. He'd always been extremely active and had always answered the beckoning call of the mountains, forests, and back roads. But now, he had to find contentment with short trips, walking the easy trails with Grace, listening to the birdsongs and savoring the soft kiss of mountain breezes wafting over them as they munched their favorite picnic fare – French bread, cheese and wine. He'd never give up wine despite the doctor's instructions but he was able to say no to the scotch.

But the call of the wild, the lure of a difficult climb, memory of what a thrill it was to discover a hidden waterfall at the end of a new trail, these things nagged at Keir like one of his migraines. It was almost more than he could bear. And what of the travel – the adventure he and Grace had come to enjoy?

"I know we talked about going back to Turkey, Keir. You wanted to go to Cappadocia, but I don't think you could handle the walking there. What if we went back to France?" she asked one day as they sat on their back deck. She'd helped him with the planting earlier in the season. The yard was a mass of color. Brilliant purple and scarlet petunias bloomed in boxes and decorative pots on the deck, and the flowerbeds spilled a cascade of colorful perennials.

"I'm just looking around at all the flowers we've planted here and I suddenly had a memory of springtime in Paris. How one day everything sprang to life with the promise of new beginnings." She tried not to think of Lee sitting at the sidewalk café, toying with his coffee cup, glancing up to see her standing there before she'd a chance to move away. "You'd come back home before springtime. You really only saw Paris during the dreary weather. And then you missed seeing it again when we were there on our cruise. Remember? You had such a migraine that day. I really hated going into Paris without you. We'd had such a wonderful time there when we were young. I'd so wanted us to relive it together. Maybe we can still do it."

"Maybe. I guess we'll have to see what the doc says. It would be fun though, wouldn't it? The two of us back in Paris. We were so young and so much in love. But I'll never make it up the stairs to our old apartment. I wonder who lives there now."

"I wonder," she said reflectively. She'd never told Keir of her visit to their old apartment when she'd gone to Paris alone. She'd never said anything about Alain and the wine she'd shared with him. She'd never mentioned sitting on the bench

174

in front of the maestro's building wondering if she'd ever really been in love with Lee. It had all been so long ago with Lee, hadn't it? Another lifetime.

"I hope it's a couple just like we were, young and in love," she said, breaking from her memories.

"A lot of things have changed in our life, Grace. But that's the one thing that hasn't – and it never will. When I look at you, I still see the same pretty girl who was there in the front seat of Jim's car that first night. The night I fell in love with you. And I have loved you all these years."

"And I love you so," she choked. She looked into the face of her husband and just as he'd mentioned her youth, at that moment she didn't see him as the aging man he was, the man with the dull pallor of infirmity. Rather, she saw the tall, handsome, and athletic boy she'd fallen in love with. The young man who could see from the very beginning that the two of them were meant to be together.

"The years have slipped away, haven't they?" he said. "And here we are, grandparents. How old is that boy anyway?"

"He's sixteen. A young man. Tall and handsome like his grandfather."

"It has been good, hasn't it, Grace? Our life together."

"Yes. It has, Keir. All of it – the ups and the downs. And there's still more ahead."

"I'll drink to that," he said.

"I'll get the wine."

When she returned a few moments later, Keir was busy pulling weeds from one of the flowerbeds. The garden had never looked better.

They sat together on the deck's comfortable old lounge. She raised her wineglass to him and said, "Here's to what's yet to come."

"What's yet to come." He took a sip and smiled at her. She smiled back but a small tear escaped from the corner of her eye.

19

It was different when Benjamin died. In the beginning anyway, when the grief was raw. Grace and Keir had lain together in their bed, clinging to one another, wetting each other's faces with tears, the kind of sloppy, angry tears known only to parents of a dead child. Many nights one or the other would rise, pad out to the living room, turn on the TV and watch the motion and listen to the sound, little aware of the content. The one left in bed would arise at dawn and find the other stretched out on the sofa, put on a pot of coffee and shuffle to the front door to retrieve the morning paper. But there was always the reassurance that when bedtime came they would begin the night again in the comfort of one another's embrace. That had been the way it was in the beginning, but then one night, Grace found herself going to bed alone when Keir began to suffer serious insomnia. Months passed before they were able to establish what they called a new normal, able to retire together at night.

But now once again, Grace's bed was empty. It felt like a cold and friendless foreign country where she was a stranger and had no understanding of the language being spoken to her.

Keir had succumbed to pneumonia just as doctors had feared he might. Though they'd put him on a course of heavy antibiotics shortly after his admittance to the hospital, he'd slipped into a coma and passed away soon thereafter. Keir and Grace had not had a chance to say goodbye to one another nor had there been time to send for Jane.

After his passing, Grace had remained at the bedside, sitting rigid and numb. She'd sat there wondering if there were any comfortable chairs anywhere in any hospital or any clinic in the world. She wondered if should she say something important to mark the moment. This had been her life partner for nearly fifty years. What should she say? She'd never had a problem talking to her husband throughout the many decades of their time together, but everything that came to mind at that moment seemed so trivial and meaningless. Finally, she'd taken her husband's hand in hers and murmured, "You were a good husband." She'd laid his hand gently by his side, arisen, and gone to the door. A nurse there motioned her to wait while she went in to wrench Keir's wedding ring from his finger. In one final medical intrusion, the woman had put a stethoscope to Keir's chest to confirm his passing. She'd returned to Grace, handed her the ring, and said in a cold and dispassionate voice, "There are papers you need to sign down the hall." Grace had watched the nurse retreat to a computer station and then gone to join her brother and his wife who'd been hovering a few feet away. She hadn't cried.

Her brother and sister-in-law had taken her home. No one had been able to find any words to say as they traveled along the familiar streets and avenues of the city. Other family members and friends had arrived, teary and overwhelmed by the suddenness of Keir's passing. He'd been in the yard fixing the fence mere hours before his death.

When all had left, Grace stood in the middle of the living room and looked around. Everything in the house had felt the touch of Keir's hand, he and Grace having built most of the home together, renovating, redecorating and refurbishing with a vigor many folks would've found daunting. Memories screamed their presence from every corner.

She'd gone to the fridge, taken out a nearly full bottle of white wine, and pulled a wineglass from the oak china cabinet Keir had built. She'd filled the glass and gone to sit on the sofa. Before she'd taken a sip, she'd turned and looked at the photo of Keir that was sitting on the end table. She'd taken a long, slow breath.

"Here's looking at you kid," she'd said, tilting the glass. "There are new places waiting for you to discover, new mountains for you to climb." When the glass was empty, she'd risen and gone to refill it.

"I hope there's wine in heaven," she'd breathed. "You'd like that."

Grace made a few funeral arrangements but waited for Jane and Theo to arrive before finalizing everything.

"I'm sorry I didn't get a chance to say goodbye to Dad," sobbed Jane. "How could it all have happened so fast?"

"I didn't get to say goodbye either, Jane. He just slipped away. But at least he didn't have to linger for months in a nursing home like some people do. Going quickly like that was a blessing for him."

"Of course it was. He was always so strong and such an outdoorsy guy. He would've hated being cooped up in a care facility, depending on strangers to look after him."

"That's for sure. But he'll have one final trip to the mountains. To the lake. But not just yet. I think I'd like to wait a few months. Gosh, how he loved those mountains. He taught me to climb and hunt for fossils on those slopes when we were young. That kind of life had never been on my radar before we met. I was mostly focused on my music." She sighed and looked at her daughter. Jane was a very attractive woman in the throes of middle age. Threads of gray were trying to hide within the two braids she wore.

"It was such a long time ago and yet I remember it all so clearly. Now my whole world has tilted on its axis. I don't know which direction to go. I guess I've come to the proverbial fork in the road, haven't I?"

"No, not really, Grandma," spoke Theo, who'd been sitting perched on the arm of the sofa nursing a can of Coke. It was an indulgence his mother allowed when they were away from home. "You know there really isn't a fork in the road."

"What do you mean, Theo?" asked Grace looking at her grandson with a frown. The lad was, as she'd remarked to Keir weeks earlier, tall and handsome. He had a head of unruly blond hair and was slight of build. *He was in fact the image of Keir,* she thought, recalling pictures she'd seen of him at that age. She wished Theo had not lived so far away and that he and his grandfather had been able to spend more time together hiking and exploring the wilderness, the way Keir, Ian, and Ben had done.

"If you choose a path and follow it, you can't go back and unfollow it. You just continue on a path. You can't reverse time."

"Well, that's an interesting perspective," agreed Grace. "That sounds like something your granddad might have said." She laughed a gentle little laugh. "It kind of makes sense when you think about it, I suppose. How did you get to be so wise at such a young age?"

"Good genes, I guess." Then, a shrug.

That response garnered more chuckles from the grandmother. Grace realized she hadn't laughed in days.

Grace eventually went to sleep in Benjamin's old room where there was less chance the smaller bed could scream *"cold and empty."* She tried to imagine she was back in her youth, single and able to nestle amongst frilly pillows and bed coverings in room decorated exclusively for her.

After Jane and Theo left, the house was like a tomb in its silence. Friends came and went for a few weeks, helped her with the garden and repair of the fence, but Grace was well aware that eventually she'd have to face the loneliness and all the attendant responsibilities that came with maintaining a large home and yard. It was too soon to consider selling.

She could cope with the financial affairs, for she'd always done so, even saying to her banker it was a good thing she'd not died first for Keir would've had no idea how much money they had or where it'd been invested. He'd never been interested in their financial affairs, trusting her to take care of those aspects of their life together.

And Grace considered herself better off than some widows – oh, how she hated that word – for at least she was capable of performing a few household repairs. She'd watched Keir over the years as they'd renovated and repaired their home and was not afraid to turn her hand to a few small tasks.

She smiled to herself one day heading out to the garage. She'd planned to do a repair job in the yard and the anticipation of it had somehow buoyed her spirit.

She opened the door of the workshop and looked at the place where Keir had spent so many hours crafting items for their home, building furniture, and repairing things for friends and relatives. It was a place where he'd often sat in quiet reflection. His tools were there just as he'd left them, expecting him to return and pick up on a project he'd left unfinished.

She found a small skill saw, a tape measure, screw gun, and a box of two-inch wood screws and took them to the backyard. She set them down near a stack of 2x6 planks treated with a chemical preservative and went back to the garage for the small aluminum sawhorse.

She'd already torn up the old planking on the wooden walkway to the back gate, a task that Keir had planned to tackle before he died.

She measured carefully – *"measure twice, cut once,"* she heard Keir's voice say in her head. Funny, that was the first voice in her head she'd heard in years. And this time it had been Keir's. Then she recalled the words he'd spoken the day they'd come away from a small bookstore in a Danish village, the fascinating little shop hidden away in a winding alley. *"I'll always be with you, showing you the way,"* he'd said. Grace took a moment to ponder that and knew that Keir's would be the only voice she'd hear in her head from that moment on. That he was still with her, watching over her.

She took a board from the pile, laid it out, and measured – *twice.* She drew a line on the lumber, set it on the sawhorse, and took the small skill saw in hand. It was a little intimidating at first but once she got the sequence of the start button and the hand motion, she found it almost exhilarating. She was a bit wobbly, the first cut not quite true, but she figured she would improve with practice.

She set the plank in place over the edge strips of the walkway, picked up the screw gun, and inserted a screw into the bit. The screw flew off with the first few attempts but was then finally grabbed and drilled into the plank with a scream. She could hear Keir groaning at the sound of the gun struggling with her efforts. But just as with the saw, Grace eventually got the feel of the tool.

When she'd put down a half dozen pieces she stood back and looked with pride at the sidewalk. It was a little crooked, but nonetheless functional and better than the old one with boards that'd begun rotting through in many places. She finished the job and went inside well satisfied and feeling confident enough to take on other household repairs.

She knew other women whose husbands could barely screw in a light bulb and she was grateful she'd learned a few things over the years. She was not about to let the place go to wrack and ruin after all Keir's dedication to building and maintaining the home.

The first summer did not seem so bad. She made sure she kept busy. Very busy. She recalled the letters she and Keir had received from Ian's Australian girlfriend after he'd been killed so suddenly. After Ian's death, the woman had also engaged in a manic busyness to distract herself from her grief.

Grace knew the young woman had eventually married and had a couple of children, but she also knew Ian's girlfriend would always wonder what her life would've been like if Ian had not died.

Winter, however, was a different matter. Being shut up in the house with nothing but memories began to gnaw at Grace. She repainted a couple of rooms and bought some new furniture. That helped fill a few hours.

She tried to read but couldn't concentrate on any serious material and found fluff novels irritating. The characters were one-dimensional, the plots predictable, and the dialog banal.

"Life is not all happy endings," she would scream and throw the offending novels across the room.

And worse than anything, Grace couldn't listen to any music. Every note conjured up a memory. The house remained silent for much of the time.

It came as something of a shock to Grace that many of her friends disappeared after their initial expressions of condolence. Couples that'd been faithful over the years seldom called her, the dynamics of their previous relationship with 'a couple' seemingly evaporated now that Grace was single. She'd heard that did happen in the case of divorcees, friends never sure which of the partners to align themselves with, but she hadn't realized that would be the case after the death of one's mate. But it was confirmed when she spoke to other friends who'd been widowed as well.

Grace searched her memory. Had she and Keir been guilty of the same thing in the past when others in their acquaintance had found themselves in similar circumstances? She realized that in some cases, they had.

Not everyone disappeared from her life like that however, and Grace cherished the friends who remained steadfast. But she found herself spending most of her time with other single women, widows and those divorced. It was a tremendous adjustment for her because she and Keir had always done everything together. She'd never dared think forward to the day when they wouldn't be together, neither of them having given serious consideration to the 'till death do us part' words mentioned in their marriage vows.

She didn't know where she fit anymore.

She felt like she was trying to fly with one wing.

She was alone. Alone. The very word had a paralyzing hollowness to it.

Should she go back to work? Volunteer? She supposed that was why so many single women did engage in those pursuits. Especially older ones. Women need to nurture. To help.

Should she travel? She and Keir had always enjoyed the adventure. But what good was an adventure if you had to do it on your own. She was reminded of words from the song in the John Wayne movie *McClintock* – 'what good is a memory a loved one can't share?' Yes. What?

And she hated trying to navigate through airports on her own. The few times she'd had to do it, she'd been completely intimidated. No, traveling was out of the question.

Grace almost wished there was a fork in the road. At least then there would be some options.

20

The second winter after Keir's death the loneliness became so unbearable Grace considered returning to church. Others had been urging her to get out more, to join a group, participate in something. Would returning to church be what she needed to do? And what about her old church? Was it the right place to go to try and fill up the emptiness she felt? She was aware many changes had taken place there over the years, some of which had driven her and Keir away in the first place. But she was feeling an intense need to make some sort of spiritual connection, for she'd even fallen out of the habit of regular prayer. She hoped if she was able to spend some time with God in a formal setting it might assuage some of the sadness she felt. She meant to put aside her feelings about all the chaos that'd taken place in the church those many years ago and vowed to concentrate instead on the spiritual message.

She dressed with care that morning, choosing a gray wool car coat and black knee-high boots. She couldn't say why she was so obsessive over her choice, for she was not going out to impress anyone in particular. But it did seem the proper thing to do. She knew lifestyles were becoming more casual, but church had always been to her a place to put one's best foot forward. And did she really expect to see a single soul she knew after all this time? She was well aware the membership had changed drastically during her absence.

Grace parked a couple of blocks away and made her way through the old familiar neighborhood, noting some of the changes that'd taken place there as well. New condos had sprung up to replace some of the older homes and a trendy boutique now sat on the corner once occupied by the neighborhood's grocery store.

She approached the old brick structure and stood across the street for a few moments studying the building. The church had stood on that same spot for close to one hundred years. It still looked the same as she remembered. The concrete steps leading to the front door were cracking, the cracks running vein-like on most every tread. The somewhat wobbly wrought-iron railings had been worn smooth over the years at the hands of the faithful coming and going.

The bell in the tower hadn't rung in years. She'd heard it said the ringing of the bell on Sunday mornings bothered the neighbors, those new urbanites who'd come to inhabit the now revitalized area surrounding the church.

She took the steps slowly, still not sure if she'd made the right decision in coming. She'd climbed those same steps on a rainy afternoon as a young bride, her heart aflutter at the prospect of marriage to Keir. And then years later, she and Keir had descended them in sorrow, moving slowly, trancelike behind the casket bearing their only son. The years between those events had been filled with both joy and sorrow – baptisms, Christmas concerts, funerals for elderly church members and friends, and the unrest brought about when a political agenda began to transcend the spiritual enrichment expected to be found in a house of worship.

Grace had often remarked that if the walls of that old place could talk, the stories told would fill many volumes.

At the top of the stairway, she pulled on the handle of the heavy oak door and stepped across the threshold. How many thousands of footsteps had that slab of oak endured? She looked inside. Folks were milling about holding white-capped Starbuck's cups and patterned coffee mugs. The logo on one mug read: *"Elvis has left the building."* A few folks were seated in the pews, bent in quiet reflection, perhaps anticipating moments of joyous hymn singing or a message of inspiration from the pulpit.

She wandered amongst the crowd of people filling the aisles and her eyes were drawn to a place in front of the choir loft. The old upright piano had been replaced with an electronic keyboard and a young man was deftly running his hands across the keys, entertaining the crowd with a piece of jazz that would have been more at home in a piano bar. The louder he played, the louder the hubbub, as the milling folks were forced to speak over the music. She elbowed her way through the coffee-guzzling crowd being careful not to jostle anyone's cup. She moved to stand behind the young man as he played. It was the place she'd stood the first time she'd met Lee and he'd asked her to sing for him. She remembered how he'd been practicing a difficult composition by Rachmaninov, and how that particular music had come to mean so much to her.

The man played on, pretending not to notice her hovering at his elbow. The crowd continued their social chatter.

She willed herself to move away and looked towards the front of the church to the place where as a young woman she'd pledged her love to Keir. It seemed like just yesterday. And there was the baptismal font where they'd brought each of their tiny children, committed them to the faith, and prayed for a good future for them. She thought of Benjamin whose life had been cut short and of Jane who was living a life of service in a distant land.

The woman blinked once or twice wondering if she'd perhaps wandered into the wrong venue. Surely, this could not be the church of her youth, the scene before her so incongruous with the memories flooding her mind.

Her gaze moved towards the choir loft and in her mind's eye, she could see Lee sitting at the console of the organ, playing with such passion it'd often brought tears to her eyes. She saw herself standing there too, hymnbook in hand, on the brink of life, falling in love for the first time and thinking she had her life all figured out. And then her mind took her to thoughts of Morgan McCullough, the fumbling-in-faith man who'd so loved her son, Benjamin. The gentle and sensitive preacher who'd reawakened her love for music.

She thought to leave. But then something made her stay. Would the service offer her something? Words of comfort? A purpose for her life? After all, something had drawn all these people to this place.

She found a seat and took a hymnbook from the rack in front of her, opened it and found the hymn she'd sung that first day with Morgan. It was *Lord of All Hopefulness*.

The verses spoke to her of the four stages of life. Yes, hopefulness. What would life be without hope?

Lord of all hopefulness, Lord of all joy,
Whose trust, ever child-like, no cares to destroy,
Be there at our waking, and give us we pray,
Your bliss in our hearts, Lord, at the break of the day.
Our waking – when we are young

Lord of all eagerness, Lord of all faith,
Whose strong hands were skilled at the plane and the lathe,
Be there at our labors, and give us we pray,
Your strength in our hearts, Lord, at the noon of the day.
The noon of the day – when we embark on the life we've chosen

Lord of all kindness, Lord of all grace,
Your hands swift to welcome, your arms to embrace,
Be there at our homing, and give us we pray,
Your love in our hearts, Lord, at the eve of the day.
The eve – the later years

Lord of all gentleness, Lord of all calm,
Whose voice is contentment, whose presence is balm,
Be there at our sleeping, and give us we pray,
Your peace in our hearts, Lord, at the end of the day.
The end of the day – our last moments

Grace felt some peace as she sat reading the hymn. But hopefulness? She wasn't sure what to hope for.

With little formality, a few folks straggled into the choir loft and took their seats. They were wearing street clothes. The minister wandered about for a few moments greeting some of those gathered and then took the three steps to the pulpit. He was wearing chinos and a beige pullover. Gone were the austere black robes of the choir and clergy. Grace's gown had had a label with a number sewn inside the collar. That number corresponded to the one in the cabinet in the choir room where she'd stored her music. Traditionally, when the choir members had taken their places, it was a signal for the congregation to rise in respect as the minister entered the sanctuary. Lee would then have played the chord for the doxology and all would sing:

Praise God from whom all blessings flow;
Praise Him, all creatures here below;
Praise Him above, ye heavenly host;
Praise Father, Son, and Holy Ghost.

When had that formality been abandoned? That musical prayer had always seemed to set the mood for worship.

This minister greeted the congregation collectively and welcomed any visitors attending. His gaze seemed to settle on Grace and she felt a pang of guilt at having invaded his space. The service proceeded with a short prayer and a modern-style hymn.

But the magnificent organ, the instrument that'd always had such a powerful presence in the sanctuary and had over the years cost the congregation many thousands of dollars in maintenance, remained abandoned, silent, and alone in deference to its modern cousin, the electronic jazz machine.

"Just one more time," Grace pleaded silently. "I need to experience that old feeling. I want to hear the sound of wonderful music resonating from that stately, old instrument. I want to feel the floor shudder beneath my feet with the dramatic chords of Handel or Bach." But the pipes were silent. She remembered the day

Lee had taken her through the small door behind the choir loft to see the inner workings of the organ. That was where most of the magic happened, he'd said, for the pipes visible in the sanctuary were mostly decorative. It was a large room and was filled with pipes of all sizes. She'd thought they looked like rows of oversized whistles hiding out in that secret place behind the wall.

When the text of the sermon was announced, Grace had to chuckle to herself. At least she hoped she'd not laughed aloud, there amongst a group of strangers.

"You cannot plow a straight furrow," spoke the minister, "if you're always looking back over your shoulder."

The message could not have been more clear. Grace had spent the past thirty minutes looking back at everything the church had meant to her – the family ties, her friends, the music (especially the music), the joys, and sorrows. Lee. But now as she sat in the once comfortable pew, she knew there was no longer anything connecting her to those memories.

There had been no bell to announce the joyful assembly of worshippers. There was not one face she recognized in the crowd gathered. The harsh sounds emanating from the keyboard had failed to stir any emotion within her breast and she wanted to cry for those in this House of God, for they were missing those fundamental elements of worship that Grace had so loved.

She asked herself what she'd really come seeking that day. Was it God? She was sure he was there somewhere, nursing his own cup of java. No. She knew she needn't have come there to find Him. He was with her at all times in everything she did.

No, it was not God. What she'd really come there seeking was herself, her youth. But that person was no longer there.

The old church was no longer the place of inspiration it'd once been. It had been for Grace a place to experience the dawning of adulthood with a group of like-minded friends. It had been a place to set a family on a course of spiritual enlightenment. It had been a sanctuary of peace and love. But now, sitting there, Grace felt nothing.

She rose at the end of the service knowing it was the last time she'd ever sit within the walls of that sanctuary. She passed through the oak door at the rear of the church and took the crumbling steps down to the sidewalk. The frigid winter air greeted her. It was fresh and alive and offered…could it be? Did she dare feel…hopefulness?

She did not look back.

21

The following summer Jane, Scott and Theo arrived to spend two weeks in Canada. They'd planned to spend some time helping Grace with the garden and some of the heavier household chores, but the main thrust of the visit was to take Keir's ashes to the mountains. It was time.

"I'm so excited to see you all," cried Grace as the family cleared the custom's area and fell into her arms. "I'm so glad you were able to get away too, Scott. It's been awhile since you were here."

"I'm sorry I wasn't able to come when Jane's dad passed away, Grace. I just couldn't leave at a moment's notice," replied Scott, loosening himself from the woman's clutches.

"Oh, I understand completely. I know how important your work is. Jane did convey your regrets when she came for the funeral."

"You're looking good, Mom," Jane interjected as she pulled away from her mother's embrace. "You must be spending a lot of time in the yard. You've got a good tan."

"Oh yes – the yard," laughed Grace. "It's like painting the Brooklyn Bridge. As soon as I finish weeding all the flowerbeds, it's time to start all over again. Your dad did love his garden, but I never realized how much time it took to keep it up."

"We're looking forward to seeing what you've done with the place," said Jane. "It will be good to be home for a while."

"So, Theo," said Grace looking up at her grandson. "I think you've grown three inches since I last saw you. I think you may even be taller than your grandpa was."

"Maybe you can measure me on the wall in the basement like you did last time I was here, Grandma."

"Of course I will. That wall's the only place in the whole house that's never been renovated or had a new coat of paint in all my years in the house. I may have to take it with me if I ever move."

"Lots of luggage this time," announced Scott, adjusting the bags threatening to free themselves from the baggage cart.

Grace missed the wink he gave to Jane.

Once everyone had taken stock of the house, Scott and Theo trucked the luggage upstairs and began to sort it out for placement in the two spare rooms. Grace directed Jane to sit down and then went to put on the kettle for tea.

"The house looks great, Mom. You've kept everything up so nicely. Dad would be proud of you and especially proud of the way you've kept up the garden."

"It's a lot of work, but honestly, what else would I be doing? Anything I can't handle I bring someone in to deal with it – like the grass and the heavy things. I love this house. Your dad and I put so much of ourselves into it."

"Then you don't want to sell it just yet?"

"No I don't think so. I think I'll know when it's time to sell."

"Well…then."

"Well then…what?"

"Well, that leads me to the next topic of discussion. There's something I need to ask you."

Grace gave her daughter a curious look, half expecting her to say the family would like to return to Canada to live with her. But Jane threw out a completely new twist.

"It's Theo. He's applied to the university here in town. Your old alma mater in fact."

"Oh, that's wonderful, Jane. What a change for him after living in Kenya his whole life."

"He's made application for the pre-med program. He hopes to follow in Scott's footsteps to become a doctor. Eventually, he hopes to return to Africa and work at the clinic."

"What a fine idea. He'll make a wonderful doctor if he's half as dedicated as you and Scott are."

"Well, we're not going to live forever. It would be nice to hand over the reins to someone who knows the people the way Theo does. And so I guess the next thing that needs to be addressed is his accommodation while he's going to school."

"Oh, Jane. You know you don't even have to ask. Of course he'll stay here. The university is so close he'll be able to walk there in good weather. I'll be delighted to have him here. But you're really going to miss him aren't you?"

"Of course, But we have to think of the future. And I think it will be good for both of you for him to stay here. He really has lived a very sheltered life. I don't know if he can go from the quiet of a small African village to a big city campus full of strangers all at one fell swoop. At least if he stays here he'll have a bit of a buffer for a while. Maybe in time he can adjust to more independence."

"Well, this is a terrific surprise. And it will be wonderful to have someone else in the house. It's been a while. I really do miss your dad. Especially after supper when the day is waning and I have time to sit and reflect. Oh, there's the kettle boiling. I'm so happy at the prospect of Theo being here. I'm almost giddy," said Grace as she hopped up to brew the tea.

***

They chose a beautiful day in early July to go to the mountains – the kind of day Keir would have loved. They parked the car and stood for a few moments to admire the sight of the ancient crags surrounding them. The rocky peaks rose to meet a cloudless sky and the air was fresh with the pungent fragrance of spruce. The family had chosen that particular time of year hoping to spot a few Lady-slipper orchids along the pathway to the green lake. They made their way in silence for a few moments, each one drinking in the peace and serenity that only the mountains can offer. A spirited chipmunk darted across the path and disappeared behind a fallen log.

Theo was the first to speak. "Oh look, guys, there's one – to the left," he said, pointing. "Oh and another there as well."

They had timed their visit perfectly. The brilliant yellow flowers, such a contrast to the thatchy brown of the forest floor on which they lived, waved like royalty in the soft mountain breeze.

"Good eyes, Theo," spoke his father.

They approached the lake and saw the fallen log still sitting on the spot it had claimed so many years before. It'd been overtaken with moss though still appeared sturdy enough for one to sit upon.

Jane set the urn containing her father's ashes on the ground and took a seat on the log. "This place is so beautiful, isn't it? I still remember like it was yesterday – the day we brought Benjamin here for the last time. And here we are again. This time with Dad."

"I don't know if it will be right for you to bring me here one day," sighed Grace, moving to the water's edge.

"Mom, why would you say that? You'd want to be with Dad, wouldn't you?" cried Jane.

"These mountains were never really mine, Jane. Some people belong to these mountains. And some, not so much. I remember coming up here so many years ago. It was before I met your dad. I was with a young man. I cared about him but he didn't have the soul of a mountaineer. He called these mountains old rocks and didn't really seem to feel the spiritual connection I thought he should when we were here. He was a wonderful musician though. A quiet, gentle fellow." Her voice had faded to a whisper.

As she'd spoken, she'd been peering into the green water. She'd never before mentioned Lee to her children and as she stood scuffing her boots back and forth on the rocky shore, she was struck with a pang of guilt. Why had she picked that particular moment to remember Lee? She turned to look at Jane. Her daughter was holding her hand to her mouth, the young woman trying vainly to hold back tears.

"This place belongs to those who have been one with it," Grace said. "Keir, Ian, and Ben. Ben spent a lot of time here with Dad – hiking and climbing even when he wasn't feeling that well. He always seemed to be refreshed when he came home. But I think some of us were just tag-alongs, weren't we?"

Jane did begin to cry then. She'd thought she'd be able steel herself when the time came to deliver the ashes to the water but her mother's words had taken her off guard. Theo sat down on the log, put his arm around his mother, and fumbled for a clean tissue in his jacket pocket.

"Oh, Mom. This is so hard," sobbed Jane.

"Let me, Jane," said Scott softly, picking up the urn. "Let me do this for you. Do you have something, Grace?"

Grace looked at her son-in-law and smiled. He was a member of her family but a man she really knew little about. She pulled out a small card and beckoned Scott to the water's edge.

The ashes floated easily on the quiet lake and drifted away in a small gray cloud.

With quiet reverence befitting the day, Grace spoke these few simple words.

> *The water is wide,*
> *I cannot get o'er,*
> *Neither have I wings to fly,*
> *Give me a boat that can carry two,*
> *And both shall cross, my true love and I.*

Grace recalled the words Jane had spoken a few moments before, the response she'd given when Grace mentioned it wouldn't be right for her to find a final resting place at the green lake. She reflected on the words and watched the ashes disappear.

"And both shall cross, my true love and I," she whispered. She crumbled the card and put it her pocket. It was finally over. Keir was joining his son and brother on the final journey home. She turned and looked at Theo and wondered where his earthly journey would take him. Back to Africa when he finished school? Or did a different adventure await him? Only time would tell.

22

Grace was ecstatic when Theo was granted acceptance at the university and after she'd settled him into the home, her thoughts returned to the spiritual emptiness she felt. But the quest for a comfortable house of worship became a daunting experience as she ventured into new churches, spoke with new people, and tried to acquaint herself with different orders of service.

Folks at some of the Protestant churches were friendly enough and the order of service and hymns quite familiar, though she found music in the Lutheran churches less than joyful. The slow and dirge-like hymns were an effort to sing and the music in the liturgical settings seemed quite unmelodic. Even with her musical ability, she found the responses difficult to manage.

"Must be getting old," she muttered to herself one morning. "This shouldn't be that hard to follow."

She ventured into Roman Catholic churches on a few Sundays and did love the ritual and formality, the beautiful vestments worn by the priests and the fact that participation by the choir was a large part of the service. But she had a hard time with what she perceived to be a rote and mechanical approach to worship. She could not get used to just reading the same material from a service book week after week while the priest offered marginal personal input. She'd so loved the old ministers from her youth, men who added folksy tales from their own life experience to blend with the biblical text.

And she was not sure what to make of the charismatic churches where spontaneous shouts of hallelujah made her jumpy. The practice seemed rather theatrical after the more sedate approach to worship she was used to. The intrusive practice soon drove her to explore other options.

Grace came and went from different churches, despairing that she would ever find what she was looking for. She wasn't really able to put her finger on just what that was but reasoned she'd know when she found it.

One day, while skimming the local newspaper, she came across a small article about a local spiritualist church located a short distance from her home. She'd never been convinced such organizations were in fact 'real churches' but decided to take a chance and step out of her comfort zone.

An old storefront with large, partially covered windows was home to the church. It had been renovated to accommodate a congregation of perhaps a hundred people, though there were less than fifty attending the morning Grace arrived. At least she was not to be intimidated by large numbers as she'd been in some of the other churches, but neither was she able to slip into the group unnoticed.

The church itself did not have much going for it in terms of style or decorative appointments. And of course there was in the corner, an electronic keyboard. On the raised platform at the front of the room was a wooden lectern and behind it two wooden chairs, their seats padded in a royal purple fabric. At the far left of the lectern sat a small table spread with a white lace cloth. It held a variety of candles and an offering plate.

The seats for the congregation were those one might find in any high school gymnasium, the metal stacking variety that cause one to squirm in discomfort after about ten minutes into the program. Each seat was supplied with a photocopied booklet containing the words and music to a few familiar hymns and some short non-denominational prayers.

ANNA

I watched her moving along the aisles looking for the right place to sit. She passed me by, then turned, and retreated, as if to leave. She walked back towards the door looking a little lost, checking each row before deciding on a seat. Then she picked up the booklet from the seat next to mine, sat down, and turned to me with a hesitant smile.

"Hi. I'm Anna," I said to her.

"Hi. Anna." She placed her large black handbag on the floor and shifted out of her coat. "I'm Grace."

"Nice to meet you, Grace."

She extended a hand to me, and I felt a warm sincere handshake. "You haven't been here before, have you?" I asked.

"No. First time for me. I'm not sure what to expect."

"I don't come that often, but something directed me to come today."

She smiled again. I had the feeling we were both searching for something.

The service was simple enough – the recitation of the prayers in the printout, a couple of hymns accompanied on the keyboard by a slightly lethargic middle-aged man. The electronic device produced neither the thundering chords of a pipe organ nor the unnerving assault Grace would forever associate with the last painful visit to her home church. The message of the day was delivered by one of the church's members, a woman whose age I've never been able to gauge. There's no designated clergy in this small informal church, but the speakers are knowledgeable and very well respected.

Listening to the woman seemed to bring a measure of comfort to Grace and I could see from the odd glance I shot in her direction she was beginning to relax and respond to the positive energy in the room. The message enshrined the belief that everything in the world is a network of connections and that each one of us dwells upon the earth to fulfill an ordained purpose. It was a simple yet powerful message and I could see it was resonating with the woman at my side. At the end of the service, she appeared more refreshed than she had upon her arrival and rose from her seat, picked up her handbag and coat and made ready to depart. She threw me another smile.

"Would you like to go for lunch?" I asked impulsively, for something about this woman had struck a chord with me.

Grace turned and gave me a thankful look. "Lunch? Oh, Anna, I think that would be lovely."

"There's a little place I like to go to a couple of blocks from here," I said. "Would that work for you?"

"Of course. Shall I meet you there? My car is just down the street."

I gave Grace the directions and we headed for the door.

The small restaurant I'd invited Grace to is housed in an old bungalow, a building that like the church had been repurposed during revitalization of a tired old neighborhood. The front door had been painted a glorious, sunny yellow, and blue gingham curtains hung on the single-paned windows. The door always squeaked its protest when pried open.

"Gotta put some oil on those hinges," announced the owner passing by when I entered.

I watched for Grace and waved to her from the table I'd taken near the back of the room. The restaurant's charming and colorful theme continues throughout the place, the tables sport blue and white gingham tablecloths and are centered with cheery pots of blue violets. Grace would later tell me the sight of those violets spirited her mind back to days in her garret room in Paris. But that was not a story to be told during our first meeting. Now, you see I've begun to run ahead of myself again.

"I didn't know this place was even here," she commented, taking a seat across from me. "Something smells wonderful."

"I think it's the home-made bread. It reminds me of my mom."

"Your mom baked bread?"

"Every other day. We lived on a farm and there always seemed to be someone extra at the supper table."

"My dad was the bread-maker in our house. His father owned a bakery and put him to work there at a very young age. He used to tell us stories about hauling water from a spigot on the street each day because there was no running water in the store. Everyone in the neighborhood got their water from that tap on the corner."

"The world has come a long way hasn't it?"

"It sure has. And I'm not sure it's all been for the better. But best not to go into that right now I guess – after the message this morning. It was very inspiring. I like that little church."

"Good," I replied. "I like it too."

"The luncheon specials look terrific. Anytime I don't have to cook a meal after all these years I'm only too happy."

"Do you live…alone?" I ventured, not sure how much to probe, we two having just met?

"Well not at the moment. My grandson lives with me, but he's going to university and isn't always home for meals. I was widowed a few years ago. It was a hard time for me. Keir and I were together a long time. I was so lonely before Theo came to live with me. His parents, my daughter and her husband, run a clinic in a remote area of Kenya. Theo was raised there. What about you?"

"Divorced. My two kids live in another city. Have you been to Kenya?"

"Yes, my husband and I were there some years ago. But it's not an easy trip to get to where they are. Although I'm told the road has been improved some since we visited."

The waitress, a young girl of about eighteen, stopped by the table with menus and two glasses of water.

"What do you like to eat here?" Grace asked me, picking up her menu.

"Everything is good – it's all 'like Mom used to make,'" I said with a little chuckle. "But I'm partial to the chicken pot pie."

"Sounds good – I think I'll have that."

And that's how it all began. We talked for hours through cups of soup, leafy salads, and chicken pot pie just as delicious as I'd promised. We split a piece of homemade apple pie and after two cups of coffee, felt we'd had enough to satisfy us until well into the next week. It was as though we'd been separated at birth and were making up for lost time after all the years of separation.

Grace explained how she'd been searching for a new spiritual home and had just run across an article in the newspaper inspiring her to attend the service that day. She confided to me some of the disappointments and concerns she'd had searching for a connection to God.

"Well, I like some of the new age philosophy of the spiritualist church, though I still miss the old days when going to church with the family was a big deal," I told her.

"Me too," she agreed. "I spent most of my youth connected to the family church in one way or another and I loved being a part of it. But when politics got in the way, everything changed. People changed. People who'd been friends for *years turned on one another. It was so very sad to see. It tore the place apart and now all the good memories seem tainted. And the last time I was there – well, they say you can't go home again. It is so true."*

"Well, the little spiritualist church seems to fill the bill for me right now," I said. "I always feel better when it comes time to leave. It certainly isn't the hell-fire and brimstone I remember from when I was a kid, but I feel...more connected somehow. Like I have a place in the universe and it's up to me to try to make my personal journey the best way I possibly can. I'm responsible for my own actions and no one else's. The rest of the folks in the world are on their own journey too and our paths cross with one another from time to time along the way. For better or for worse."

"That's so simple and yet so profound," Grace commented. "The world would be a much better place if everyone looked at life that way."

"Maybe. But sometimes I wonder where the world is headed."

"Guess that's a topic for another day. Do you realize we've been here for three hours? They'll be tossing us out soon. And lunch is on me," said Grace. "I've really enjoyed talking to you."

"I've enjoyed talking to you too, Grace. My treat next time."

A new and deep friendship was forged that day and all because of a chance meeting in a simple, unassuming little church. But had it really been by chance? We'd both come seeking something that day and found ourselves at the same place at the same time. Neither of us had anticipated such a meeting but in years to come, we would surely know why. There'd been no apparent reason for Grace to have chosen the chair next to mine. But she did and in so doing, the two of us set out on a journey together that would continue for many years.

In those years, we would often recall the day of our meeting. And as our friendship grew we fell into a comfortable rhythm with one another. I came to know her family, and she mine. Eventually we began confiding to one another the most intimate details of our lives. She would tell me of her meeting with Keir and how he'd told her their meeting had been ordained, that they'd been destined to marry and build a life together. It was a beautiful story of how Keir had asked his workmate, Jim, about joining a youth group. Keir had been sitting in Jim's car the night they went to fetch Grace for a regular meeting. With the telling of that story she never failed to mention Keir's persistence in pursuing her and the love he'd felt for her from the moment of their first meeting. But throughout the time I spent with Grace, and even while hearing of the profound love she had for Keir, there was still an undertone of unfinished business when she spoke of Lee. Whether

Grace would ever choose to admit it or not, I knew there was still a part of her that would never be able to put her relationship with Lee to rest.

***

We pulled on our coats and left the small lecture room at the local college. We'd just spent a fascinating two hours listening to the words of a local spiritualist.

"That was quite amazing, wasn't it?" Grace asked.

"Yes, it was amazing. I always feel such energy after attending these kinds of events. I like that she said there's really no such thing as coincidence. I've always found that, haven't you? That everything is connected. And there's a reason things happen the way they do."

"Exactly. Just as I've always said, Keir and I were destined to meet. God put us on the same path at the same time so we could marry and share our lives."

"My husband as well, I guess. Though in the end things didn't work out so well for me."

"Oh, I'm sorry, Anna. You must get tired of listening to me go on and on about how Keir and I came to be together."

"That's okay, Grace. I'm happy that you found Keir. But I often ask myself why my life went the way it did. I made a choice. We all have free will to make choices. And there are no choices without consequences. Even choosing not to make a choice has a consequence. I guess I could mull that one over forever and never find the answer."

"Some say we choose our partners because they represent unfinished business from our childhood."

"That's an interesting theory. But I've also heard we choose our mates because they have the qualities we wish we had. I don't like to think about that theory," I said with toss of my head.

"So – how do we really know if we're making the right choices?"

"Sometimes we just know. Our intuition tells us."

"But is it intuition or just wishful thinking?"

I turned to look at my dear friend. "If I had the answer to that question I could control the universe," I said.

Grace laughed and we moved outside. The weather had cooled and the nip of fall was in the air.

"Let's cut through this building back to the parking lot. It's a pretty cool tonight. We all know what's coming, don't we?" She pulled the collar of her coat

up around her colorful scarf and held the door for me. We scurried across the campus, the pathway before us swirling with a little tornado of wrinkled leaves.

"Yep, winter's just around the corner," I remarked opening the next door for her.

"Nice new building, isn't it? Apparently, it houses a 'state-of-the-art' theater. Shall we have a peek?"

"Sure why not. We're here. We should come to a performance here sometime. I've heard the acoustics are world class."

We strolled through the empty corridors, stopping now and again to study some of the art featured. The building reeked of new paint and floor polish. As we approached the doors to the upper level of the theater, I was attracted by a poster in glass display cabinet. I sucked in a startled gasp. Should I alert Grace or say nothing at all and hope she failed to see the poster? But would she ever forgive me if I said nothing and she found out about it later. Grace was on the other side of the hall and had stopped to look at an oddly crafted piece of sculpture near the seating area.

"Uh, Grace," I said breaking the silence of the hallway. "Do you want to come here and look at this?"

"What is it?"

"It's um. I think it's... I think it's Lee."

"What?" she answered absently, still completely absorbed in a study of the artwork.

"Lee. It's Lee. It says he's playing here tomorrow night – and guess what's on the program. Rachmaninov. He's playing Rhapsody on a Theme of Paganini. You've always told me that's your favorite, haven't you?"

"What? What are you saying?" she asked, suddenly tuning into my words. She tripped across the hall, her hasty approach causing her shoes to squeak on the ultra-polished floor. She looked at the poster and gasped, as had I. "Oh, my god, Anna. You're right. It is Lee. And Rachmaninov."

I could see the tears forming in her eyes.

"How many times have you told me how much you love that piece of music?"

"Probably too many," she said softly.

"Isn't that the strangest thing?" I said, my mind returning to the program we'd just attended. "We've just heard the speaker say there's no such thing as coincidence. There is a master plan. Just like with you and Keir. And you and me. Things happen and people cross our paths when they're supposed to. It's all connected. We were meant to walk through this building tonight. To see this poster."

Grace gave me a peculiar look and sniffed. "After all these years, Anna? I don't know."

"I do. It's destiny."

"I put my relationship with Lee to rest many years ago, Anna. It all needs to stay there in the past."

"Are you sure about that, Grace? I always get a feeling hearing you talk about the time you shared with him – a feeling that…"

"Of course I'm sure, Anna. I really don't want to open that wound again."

"Really?"

Grace began to pick nervously at the edge of her scarf and tried to avoid my gaze.

"I hear music – sounds like they may be in rehearsal right now. Why don't you pop your head in and see what's going on – see if he's even down there?" I urged.

"Are you kidding?" she cried. "I can't do that."

"Of course you can. You know you want to. You always said you felt things had been left unfinished between the two of you."

"Well I'm certainly not going to just 'pop my head in' and confront him after all these years about some issues we had when we were kids. He'll think I'm out of my mind. He probably won't even remember who I am."

I looked at Grace and wanted to say, no one forgets the first person they made love to. I was more than aware that Grace had certainly not forgotten that night.

"No. No," she said emphatically. Her mouth said no but her eyes were saying yes.

"Get going."

"Well, if I go in you have to come with me, Anna," she stated flatly.

"No way. This is your gig, Grace. Go on. It might be your last chance. You know. Closure."

"I hate that word – closure. I never had any closure with Keir."

"You'll always regret it if you don't do it, Grace."

She stood for a moment reflecting on my words, willing her feet to move towards the doors to the theater. At last, she moved and I saw her disappear. I wandered over to the bizarre-looking sculpture Grace had been studying earlier and awaited her return.

***

23

Grace had taken a deep breath as she moved through the door. In the beautiful theater, she could see the stage at the bottom of the stairway cutting through rows of tiered seating. The room was the epitome of class and luxury, the product of months of fundraising and philanthropic gifts. It exuded the heady smell of newly varnished woodwork and plush upholstery.

She looked to the stage and saw him there. Lee was seated at the Steinway, playing in concert with the city's philharmonic orchestra. The intense chords of Rachmaninov rose to meet her, and she was instantly transported back to her youth and countless memories of the times she and Lee had spent together, moments entwined in love and music. A tiny tear crept to her eye, and she wiped it away with the edge of her scarf.

She waited for a few minutes then slowly made her way down the stairs to the front of the theater. She wasn't sure she should even be there – once again an uninvited witness to one of Lee's performances. She chose a seat a few rows from the front and sat down. And as she sat there listening to every thrilling chord and haunting theme, the years began to melt away.

Lee, who'd gained some weight over the years, was dressed casually in a plaid shirt, cashmere sweater, and khaki sports pants. That struck Grace as funny given the way his fingers were skimming the piano keys, playing such a classical piece. She'd expected to see him more formally clad in a tuxedo, the tails of the jacket flipped in style over the back of the piano bench.

The music finally came to an end with the dramatic finale, and the conductor put down his wand.

"Good work, ladies and gentlemen. Thanks, Lee. We'll call it a night. See you all tomorrow afternoon for one more run through before the evening's performance."

The members of the orchestra rose and began to pack up their instruments. Grace watched for a moment as Lee picked up a jacket slung over the arm of a nearby chair. She rose from her seat and took the few steps to the front of the stage.

Lee had not seen her and was busy threading his arm through the sleeve of the beige, bomber-style garment.

"That was wonderful, Lee. I never get tired of Rachmaninov," she half-whispered. Her heart was beating furiously.

Lee turned, leaving one jacket sleeve dangling.

"Grace? Wow, Grace, it is you."

"It is."

"Well…and look at you. You look…wonderful."

She felt herself blush at his words and was glad the theater was dimly lit where she stood.

"Thanks. But a good deal older," she said. She laughed nervously. "How are you, Lee? I saw the poster outside." She nodded towards the upper doors. "Thought I'd just…drop in and say hi."

"Well, hi there then," he chuckled. "Yes. It has been a few years, hasn't it?"

"It sure has. I hate to think how many."

"It's good to see you."

"Yes. You too. It's kind of funny, isn't it? That our paths haven't crossed in all these years."

"I haven't been in town a lot – on the road performing quite a bit. I can't believe how long it has been. Too long, that's for sure." He searched her face before adding, "Uh, well after…Paris…and then…well you and Keir got married. I guess we lost touch, eh? We should get together and catch up."

"Yes, we should."

"Are you ready, hon?" came a voice.

"Yes," replied Lee pulling on the rest of his jacket. "Come on over here, there's someone I want you to meet."

Startled, Grace threw a glance to her right and saw a middle-aged man with a violin case approaching.

"Boyd, this is Grace – an old…friend, from back in the days when I was a church organist. Grace was the soprano soloist. Grace, this is my partner, Boyd…"

Grace had stopped listening long before the mention of Boyd's last name. She stood stunned, unable to even wave a hand in acknowledgment. Everything was suspended. She was rooted to the spot, speechless and with a look of total dismay on her face.

"Nice to meet you, Grace," said Boyd.

What was happening? She felt the floor began to move under her feet and reached out to steady herself, grabbing at the edge of the stage. Had she heard that right? Was Lee introducing Boyd as his…life partner? Or was he a musical partner? Nothing was making any sense. But Boyd had called him 'hon.' Lee had a…a male partner. Grace blinked a few times and was finally able to stutter, "Nice to meet you, too, Boyd."

"Sorry to break this up, Lee," said Boyd, "but we'll be late if we don't leave soon."

"Oh, right. Listen, Grace," Lee said turning his attention to her, "I'd like to catch up over a cup of coffee sometime soon. Oh, and will you be coming to the concert tomorrow night?"

"I-I hadn't thought of it," she stammered. "I just found out about it a few minutes ago."

"If you like, I can leave a couple of tickets for you and Keir at the box office."

"Oh. Thanks, Lee. But Keir…" She reconsidered mentioning Keir's death. "Uh, that would be great," she murmured, trying to hold back the tears welling in her eyes. Grace would not recall how long she'd stood there motionless at the edge of the stage. She'd watched as Lee and Boyd disappeared through the side door exit. The rest of the orchestra had also gathered their belongings and retreated, turning off most of the lights in the theater as they left.

ANNA

"Grace? Are you in there?" I called from the top of the stairway.

"Huh? Oh, down here, Anna," she replied, my voice having shaken her from her reverie.

"What are you doing down there in the semi-darkness?" I asked.

Grace had not even noticed most of the lights had been shut off and she was alone in the shadows.

"Shall I come down? Are you all right?"

"No, stay there. I'll be up in a minute."

I saw her take one last look at the concert grand and the rows of chairs surrounding it. Slowly, she turned and took the carpeted stairway up to where I stood waiting.

"Did you see Lee? Where is everyone? I've read every pamphlet about every piece of artwork on display in this building. All I could imagine was that you were in here having a deep and serious conversation after all." I made a dramatic gesture into the surrounding space.

"I'm sorry, Anna. I didn't mean to leave you hanging like that."

Grace took a seat on the top tier and indicated that I should do the same.

"Lee was here. He left with his...partner. Boyd."

"Boyd? Boyd?" I said with a half-laugh. "Are you kidding me? Lee's g...?" I was so dumbfounded I couldn't even finish the word.

"Gay? Yes, it appears that way."

In the darkness, at the top of the theater, Grace could not see my look of dismay, and I imagined it was a look that mirrored her own.

"After all these years," she said. "How do you like that? After all the tears I shed as a girl, after all the waiting for him to make up his mind to talk to me, to tell me why. After all the hours of waiting for him to change his mind. All the conversations I had with myself. All the time I waited for something – anything. Why he broke up with me. He said nothing. We never talked, Anna. Not really. Not about the important things. And when we were in Paris together, when we had

every opportunity to get it out into the open. He seemed to want us to be together, and yet in the end, he just walked away without a word." She slumped down in the seat and drew in a series of long slow breaths.

What could I say? It was almost beyond comprehension.

"Anna, you know that Keir really was the love of my life," she continued finally, "but Lee was my first love. When I fell for him, I never contemplated a life without him in it. I guess you know by now I've never ever been able to put it all to rest for some reason. There's always been something clawing at my soul, a part of me that could never find a resolution. But I guess now I know why things went the way they did. He just couldn't bring himself to say it. It's almost funny when I think about it now, but to a young woman who had her heart broken..."

"I wonder how you'd have taken it back then if he had said something to you," I said. Tears began to escape from my eyes as well, realizing how bewildered Grace was at that moment. "Things weren't as out in the open in those days." I sniffed. "It was something of a quantum leap to be that much out of step with societal norms."

"I guess," she conceded with a sigh. "But we were lovers. I don't get it."

"That's a mystery that might never be solved, Grace. Only Lee knows why he acted the way he did. And this may sound a bit harsh, but this many years later does it really matter? Can you put it all to rest? For once and for all?"

Grace sighed again and ran her hands through her hair. "Yes, I guess what happened tonight puts everything into perspective after all. Anyway, one good thing came of it – we scored tickets for the performance tomorrow night. Maybe it's what I need after all these years. To sit and listen to him play Rachmaninov one last time. Will you come with me?"

"Of course. A final farewell performance?"

"Yes," she sighed. "A final farewell performance."

We stood and moved to the doorway where I gave my friend a sympathetic hug. There had been quite an unexpected turn of events that evening. I held the door for her and we made our way through the building and out into the night towards the parking lot. As much as Grace was trying to keep it together, I knew she'd never completely put the events of that night to rest. Lee would always be her Achilles' heel. Her very body language as we headed to the car and the way she withdrew into silence on the trip home gave her away. She'd ventured into a theater expecting to reconnect with a man she'd once been so in love with and had retreated with an entirely different perspective on her life. I could not help but sympathize with her as she scrunched down in the upholstery, reflecting on it all. And, I wondered, would Grace ever view life quite the same again?

We picked up our tickets from the box office the following evening and took our seats in the front row of the theater.

I watched Grace sitting in rapture, focused on the sight of Lee's fingers dancing across the piano keys, his music-matching pace with that of the orchestra. The feeling in the hall was magical. Even I was mesmerized, drawn in by the beautiful music filling the night.

I saw Grace close her eyes, immersing herself in the moment, recalling memories of her days as a naïve young woman, days when she'd sat in the beautiful old church she so loved. She was enraptured, feeling every note of the music deep within her. And I knew she was recalling the moments so long ago when she'd longed to be alone with Lee, to lay in his arms and feel his breath on her neck, sensing the subtleness of his aftershave. But I wondered. Had Lee ever loved Grace? Her love for him had been so sweet and pure. Watching the woman beside me now and listening to the strains of Rachmaninov, I also found myself wondering if Grace had really ever been in love with Lee. Was it possible that she'd really only been in the love with the music and not the man, the man whose artistry seemed to enchant her so? Could that have been the case? And then I wondered what her reaction to Lee would have been the previous night if his partner, Boyd, had not been there? What would Lee and Grace have said to one another?

So many questions. I would never know the answers. For life is, after all, what it is.

Enveloped in the darkness and my thoughts, I reached for Grace's hand. She opened her eyes, gave my hand a gentle squeeze, and smiled at me.

"Are you all right?" I asked.

"I will be," she answered.

***

Grace would join Keir and her son, Benjamin, a few years later. In her final days of failing health, she would lie on her bed and ask me to put on the recording Lee had made with the London Symphony Orchestra. It was Rachmaninov's Piano Concerto No. 2, the Paganini Rhapsody.

She would close her eyes, sink down in her pillows, and drink in every familiar note and chord. The music soothed and comforted her.

At times, her eyes would flutter open and she would smile at me.

"I was remembering it all, Anna," she'd say softly. "The days when I was young and it felt so wonderful to be in the church, singing songs of praise. Lee was there – he plays so well, you know."

"Yes, I know. I wish I'd been there to hear you. Both of you. To see how you were together."

"They all said we had such talent. That we were perfectly matched."

"You were."

"And I was thinking of Keir and Benjamin and Jane, of course. She's so far away."

"She's on her way, dear. She'll be here soon. And Keir and Benjamin. You'll see them soon too." My words seemed to soothe her and her eyes would close.

But each time the music came to an end, her eyelids would blink open and she would turn to me, raise her hand, and say, *"Put it on again, Anna dear. I never get tired of Rachmaninov."*

No one ever forgets their first love, but it is
the love of one's life that is held long in the heart.
Sometimes the love is the same and sometimes it is not,
and even as we cling to the memories
we are challenged to discern one from the other.

CPSIA information can be obtained
at www.ICGtesting.com
Printed in the USA
LVHW082024031021
699374LV00004BA/118